D0393799

# THE TRUTH SLEUTH

A KIM REYNOLDS MYSTERY

# THE TRUTH SLEUTH

## JACQUELINE SEEWALD

**FIVE STAR**

*A part of Gale, Cengage Learning*

GALE
CENGAGE Learning™

Detroit • New York • San Francisco • New Haven, Conn • Waterville, Maine • London

**GALE**
CENGAGE Learning

**LIBRARY OF CONGRESS CATALOGING-IN-PUBLICATION DATA**

Seewald, Jacqueline.
    The truth sleuth : a Kim Reynolds mystery / Jacqueline Seewald. — 1st ed.
        p. cm.
    ISBN-13: 978-1-59414-963-4 (hardcover)
    ISBN-10: 1-59414-963-1 (hardcover)
    1. Women librarians—Fiction. 2. Murder—Investigation—Fiction. I. Title.
PS3619.E358T78 2011
813'.6—dc22                                          2011004262

First Edition. First Printing: May 2011.
Published in 2011 in conjunction with Tekno Books and Ed Gorman.

Printed in the United States of America
1 2 3 4 5 6 7 15 14 13 12 11

For Monte, who inspires me and is always there for me.
For family and friends, who are my lifeline.
And finally, for librarians everywhere who have not only
ordered my novels but offered encouragement.

# ACKNOWLEDGMENTS

A special note of thanks and gratitude to Andrew Seewald, a New Brunswick, New Jersey, attorney, who generously provided legal information and expertise.

I also want to thank Alice Duncan, who is not only an excellent editor but a very talented writer as well.

"Beauty is truth, truth beauty"—that is all ye know on earth, and all ye need to know.

—John Keats, *Ode on a Grecian Urn* (1820)

# PROLOGUE

They watched Jimmy Sanduski ride to victory at the NHRA SuperNationals, racing a Harley-Davidson V-Rod. He roared through the field, setting the top speed for the event, and the crowd went wild. Sanduski, new kid on the block, had not been expected to win.

Kim Reynolds didn't find the sport particularly fascinating, but she'd gone along with Bert St. Croix and April Nevins, just to see what it was like. She enjoyed the company of both women, and, as they were now into motorcycles, Kim thought she might give it a try. April had generously loaned Kim her bike, riding to the raceway park on the back of Bert's large Harley.

But what had started out as a pleasant afternoon began shifting to something quite different. Kim was developing an uncomfortable feeling of wrongness; a kind of prickling sensation slithered down her spine. She recognized the feeling for what it was but shook her head, trying to dispel the spasm of dread that suddenly gripped her. God, not this again! Would she ever be free of it?

Then Kim gasped, seized by a stab of pain. In her mind, she heard a silent scream, an astonished cry for help. She felt another's panic and terror. She began to shiver and tremble.

"What's the matter?" Bert asked, her dark brows rising then knitting together in concern.

"Someone's been hurt." Those were the only words she managed to choke out.

"Who? Where?" April asked, glancing around in confusion.

"Maybe we better have a look," Bert said. Her height of six feet gave her an advantage over both Kim, who was five foot six inches, and April, who was barely five foot two inches tall.

The crowd was starting to thin out, many bikers revving up their engines in anticipation of leaving now that today's entertainment was over. Kim led, Bert and April following behind her. Although she was not really certain where she was going, Kim plowed blindly through the garbage-strewn grounds. And then she saw him: a very young man sitting in an aluminum beach chair, head slumped forward as if he were in a deep sleep.

"He's dead," Kim heard herself say with certainty. Her voice sounded hollow, expressionless and faraway, as if it belonged to someone else.

"Oh, God, are you sure?" April asked, tossing her gold-tinted curls as if to deny Kim's statement.

"Kim's got this gift of knowing stuff like that," Bert said.

More like a curse, in Kim's opinion.

Bert knelt down, at first not touching the body. "I don't think he's breathing." Bert's voice had taken on a note of professional authority. She looked and sounded like the seasoned police-woman she was. Bert felt for a pulse, then shook her head. "Don't touch anything. I'm calling this in." There was a grim expression on Bert's *café au lait* features. She pulled a small cell phone out from the pocket of her black leather jacket.

Before Bert could make the call, Kim turned and faced her.

"There's something I think you should know."

"I'm listening." Bert stood very still like a figure in a portrait.

Kim let out a ragged breath. "I think that boy was murdered."

# CHAPTER ONE

Mike Gardner was enjoying his Sunday afternoon. He stretched, yawned, and then checked his watch, wondering what was keeping his guests who, he calculated, should have already arrived.

"You think Kim will be here soon?" his daughter Evie asked, voicing his own thoughts.

"Any time now. Maybe I should start preparing the barbecue."

"Kim will want to help us with dinner," Evie said. Gardner thought how mature his fourteen-year-old daughter was becoming, and his chest swelled up with pride.

Just then Gardner heard the sound of motorcycles approaching. "Must be them."

Jean, Gardner's younger daughter, called to them from the front of the house. "Daddy, you have to come and see! They look so cool on their Harleys."

Sure enough, there was Kim, not looking like the Kim he knew, dressed in jeans, t-shirt, and black leather jacket plus helmet. Riding just ahead of her were Bert and April. Three beautiful women, each in her own way. Jean was right: they were cool. The lyrics of "Born to Be Wild" played in his head and he smiled.

The three women divested themselves of helmets and jackets immediately after parking the bikes. It was a warm afternoon in late August; nothing more than t-shirts were required.

"Thanks for letting me try out your Harley," Kim said to April.

"Think you'll buy a hog?"

Gardner noticed a shadow cross Kim's eyes. "Now might not be the best time."

"So, ladies, have a good time today?"

The three exchanged meaningful looks.

"Up to a point," Bert said. Gardner noted her wary look.

"And what point was that?" Gardner asked.

"Oh, about the point Kim found the dead guy," April informed him.

Gardner did a quick turn and saw Kim flush. "You sort of have a talent for doing that."

"It only happened once before," she said defensively.

"It's not a good habit," he said.

"We agree on that," she said.

He turned back to Bert. "Who's investigating?"

"Not us," she assured him. "We're not on duty today, and I intend to keep it that way."

"You can expect to be questioned," Gardner observed.

"We really don't know very much," Kim said.

Gardner gave her a dubious look. Kim always knew more than she let on.

"It's just so sad. The boy was so young." He saw Kim shudder.

"Mortality is a fact of human existence." He hoped that didn't sound too cold.

April shook her head. "Wish I could think that way."

"Mike's a philosopher and a psychologist," Bert said.

"Just a veteran cop. It hardens your psyche."

"Well, I hope you're turning into a great cook. I'm starving," Bert said.

April frowned. "Can't say I feel very hungry after seeing that dead kid."

Jean and Evie's eyes opened wide with keen interest. "What

did he look like?" Evie asked, glancing from April to Kim.

"Yeah, was he covered in blood all gory and disgusting?" Jean added in an excited voice.

Gardner took each girl by the arm. "You're preparing the salads, remember?"

Jean groaned. "Daddy, you never let us hear anything cool."

"You and your sister might be a couple of ghouls, but we're not discussing this now."

"Evie reads vampire stories. I sneaked some peeks at her books. So I know stuff too."

Evie gave her sister a murderous look. "You're such a brat!"

The conversation ended at Gardner's insistence. Gardner knew he couldn't always protect his girls from the ugly side of life, but he intended to do his damned best as long as he was able.

He studied Kim, aware something was troubling her, something more than finding the dead boy this afternoon. He was psychically connected to her and always realized when she was upset, just as she understood his thoughts and feelings.

He finally got his chance to talk to her alone after Bert and April left that evening and the girls were watching television. Kim was helping him stack dishes into the dishwasher. Her expression was vague and distracted. It didn't take a psychologist or a psychic to know that she was trying to cope with a problem she wasn't eager to talk about.

"You might as well tell me," he said, handing her a rinsed dish.

"I guess I'm pretty transparent."

He smiled. "Like a windowpane, but only to me. Let me guess. You think you've lost your chance to hook me because you didn't accept my proposal right away. Well, if you want me to propose again, I'm more than willing. Fortunately for you, I believe in second chances. We can start looking at engagement rings any time you say."

"Soon," she said, smiling for the first time that evening.

"How about tomorrow evening?"

She touched his cheek. "Not quite that soon."

"So what's really troubling you if it's not our relationship?"

Kim let out a deep sigh. "Part of it is about that boy we found dead today. Mike, I felt him die! I've been trying to block this sensitivity I have. I thought I'd been more successful lately, not so aware of ghosts, of sensing the dead who aren't at peace. But it hit me really hard today. It was awful!" Kim shivered.

Gardner held her tight in his arms, comforting her as best he could. He had his own sensitivity, which caused him often to be aware of what people were thinking and feeling, but his psychic ability was limited to the living. In comparison to Kim, his awareness was easy to cope with, and he was glad of it. His ability only made him a better cop, someone who could see into rather than merely look at people. It was Kim who was the real truth sleuth. She sometimes had paranormal visions. But he knew that she ruthlessly suppressed her ability as much as possible. Her awareness seemed to bring her too much misery and emotional suffering, as it was doing tonight.

"You'll handle it, honey. You're strong."

"I guess I'll have to. What's the alternative?"

He saw the shadows in her eyes. She had such warm, expressive eyes. Such a beautiful woman. What made her especially attractive to him was how unspoiled she was, unaware of her loveliness, artless and natural. Kim dressed plainly and rarely used much in the way of cosmetics. But it made no difference. Her inner radiance shined through.

"Is there something else?" He'd never seen her looking so down.

"I wasn't going to tell you tonight, but you are so much a part of my life. You have a right to know. The university held off on renewing my contract in the spring. They said there might be cuts. Well, the new semester begins very soon. I found out on Friday that I'm not being rehired. I was told it has to do with cuts in state aid." Kim's large dark brown eyes, usually so bright, appeared dull.

Gardner felt terrible for her. "It's the economy," he said. "Everywhere you look, they're cutting jobs, slashing budgets."

"Last hired, first fired I suppose. Pity I'm not a football coach instead of a librarian."

"I'm glad you're not a football coach," he said with an insinuating smile.

"Academics are less important than sports to the university in the scheme of things. Besides, I think I might have embarrassed the university when I uncovered that inferno collection at the library last fall. Maybe offended some people in authority, and stepped on a few toes. I'm certain it didn't help matters. They were probably delighted to have an excuse to let me go."

"Actually, the university administration should have been very impressed that you managed to bring a killer to justice."

"Somehow, I don't think it works that way. Kind of like with whistle-blowers. Those in charge tend to view us as traitors of sorts."

"Maybe they'll hire you back when the economy rallies," Gardner said. "You can't tell."

Kim bit down on her lower lip, looking miserable. "Possibly, but right now I feel lost."

Gardner held Kim in his arms and gave her a reassuring hug, then kissed the tip of her nose. "Honey, I'd love you to marry me and move into this house. Personally, I don't care whether you work or not."

Kim caressed his cheek. "That's what I love about you. You're so generous and kind. I can always rely on you. But Mike, that isn't the answer for me. I need to be independent. I need to work. When I marry you, it has to be a marriage of equals. Kind of like a partnership. Do you understand?"

"I guess." He took her hand, leading her out of the kitchen and into the living room. Then he sat down on his comfortable old recliner and pulled her onto his lap. "I remember you telling me that you used to teach high school English before you got your master's degree in English and your MLS degree. Do I have that right?"

Kim gave him a puzzled look. "That's correct. It wasn't for very long, just two years when I was straight out of college."

"Dr. Bell, the school superintendent here in town, owes me a favor. I could find out if he can give you a job at the high school. I think I heard that they were short a couple of positions at the last minute. Happens all the time with people jockeying around for better jobs. I'll find out if he's got something for you."

Kim flushed slightly. "Mike, I don't want you asking for favors from people on my behalf. I'll find something myself."

"Hey, if I can't help the lady I love, what good am I?" Gardner planted a smacking kiss on Kim's lips. He had every intention of getting her a job. And they'd be married soon. He was certain of it. Things were definitely looking up!

# CHAPTER TWO

Bert St. Croix, on her way to her own job, had come over before Kim left for work. Bert wished her good luck on her first day back as a high school English teacher.

"You look great," Bert assured her, giving Kim a cheerful smile. "Serious suit. Chic chignon. Very professional."

"I haven't worked in a high school in a lot of years. I'm really nervous."

"It's like riding a bicycle. Once you learn the skills, you never forget."

"Did I ever tell you how I fell off my bike and split open my lip? My mother took the bicycle away and wouldn't return it. And so ended my bike-riding experience."

"Kim, you've been teaching for a good number of years."

"Teaching high school isn't like being an instructor at the university. It's totally different in regard to discipline."

"Don't go psyching yourself out, sister."

"Are you sure I look all right?"

"None of my teachers back in Brooklyn ever looked as good," Bert observed. "Of course, some of them were really old—with warts on their faces and hair growing out of the warts."

Kim knew Bert was exaggerating to lighten her stress. "Two-eighty-eight," Kim said, rolling her eyes.

"Are you speaking in logarithms?" Bert offered a puzzled frown.

"I just meant that was too gross."

"Okay, whatever."

Kim handed Bert a cup of black coffee.

"Thanks. You remembered how I like it."

"With just a touch of sugar to sweeten your day," Kim said.

"None for you?"

"I had tea this morning. It has a more calming effect."

"Have a good day."

"Before you go, anything new about the dead boy we found at Raceway Park?"

"A little," Bert said. "Looks like you were right. The M.E. found a puncture wound in his neck. According to the angle, someone must have come up from behind him and stabbed him with a hypodermic syringe injected with propofol."

"Propofol? Was that the stuff that killed Michael Jackson?"

"It can be a toxic substance. His blood level of propofol was really high. He had no history of drug abuse according to his grandmother, and the M.E. found no evidence of drug use at the autopsy. He died from probable homicide just like you said." Bert's expression was grim.

"This drug. How would someone acquire propofol?" Kim frowned thoughtfully.

Bert took a sip of coffee. "Well, that's the weird thing. It's the type of drug you might find in a hospital, the kind doctors or nurses might have access to in the course of regular duties in a surgical intensive care unit. It's used as an anesthetic for operations."

"A peculiar choice for a murder weapon," Kim observed.

"It sure is," Bert agreed.

"And you now know who the young man was?"

"Yeah, name was Sammy Granger. There was I.D. on the body. He was going into his senior year at the high school. You'll probably hear more about him at the school. Since I pulled the case, you might even see me over there. I'll be talking to people. This'll be the first homicide case the captain's let me handle on my own without Mike." Bert raised her chin. "I want to do a kick-ass investigation. Show everyone I know my stuff. I intend to find the boy's killer."

Kim nodded her head. "Then I guess we'd both better get to work. I'll do whatever I can to help you with the case. If I hear anything of interest at the school, I'll let you know."

"Yeah, you do that. Just be careful. Remember when you turn over a rock, you could find a killer snake lurking, ready to strike."

Kim didn't reply, but she felt a chill slither down her back.

"Thanks for the coffee. It beats the nail polish remover they serve at headquarters. See you."

She and Bert left the apartment together. Kim was feeling a bit more confident. It was good to have friends. Most of her life she'd been a loner. That wasn't healthy. Friendships were important. She and Bert came from very different backgrounds, but they both had troubled pasts and it served as a bond of understanding between them.

Kim's hand trembled slightly as she unlocked her car. Firsts were never good for her. Last night, she handled the butterflies screaming in her stomach by dosing on chamomile tea and rereading *Crime and Punishment* until sleep finally obliterated the torture. Today, she'd woken up with the alarm blasting off at six. She managed to nibble a slice of dry toast and chase it down with a cup of green tea, but even that small amount of breakfast was too much. She groaned inwardly, imagining how embarrassing it would be to throw up all over her new colleagues. Now that really would be too gross! Somehow that scenario lacked dignity and might leave them just a tad unimpressed with the new English teacher.

The normal twenty-minute drive to the other end of the forty-square-mile township turned out to be more like an hour in the morning traffic, and she grew anxious. She hadn't expected the traffic to be quite this heavy heading southeast. She didn't want to be late and make a bad impression, not on her very first day. She needed this job, needed the money to support herself. It was not just herself but her family that had to be considered. Ma might not want Kim to send money to her in Florida, but Kim knew how much her financial contributions were needed.

The road leading directly to the school was being re-paved. Should she make a right and try to go around it? As she slowed hesitantly, a horn blared behind her.

Startled, she glanced in her rearview mirror and saw a handsome blond man scowling his annoyance. Which way to go? She hated making quick decisions; she who could debate an hour on which brand of coffee to buy. Oh, well, she'd have to guess; it was a lot like trying to hit a piñata blindfolded.

Mr. Impatient was hanging right in there with her. When she took the next left, her old car suddenly stalled out. Mr. Impatient honked again, nearly rear-ending her. Kim was so infuriated that she shook her fist at him. She saw the angry expression on his face. She was not in the mood to put up with arrogance, tempted to give him a middle-finger Jersey salute, but it was not her style. He gunned the engine of his fancy sports car and roared by her, gilt hair taken by the wind.

Her car finally started up again. There was little in the way of traffic, and she was able to turn back to Vail Road where Lake Shore Regional High School was situated. The teacher's parking lot was nearly full. As she brought her car to a halt, her eyes caught sight of a tall, broad-shouldered man standing by a powder blue Corvette. Oh, God, no! Not him! But it was him all right, talking pleasantly to one of the other teachers, his jacket slung over his shoulder, a striped red and navy tie loosened to display a thick neck of corded muscle. So Mr.

Impatient was a teacher here. Well, she didn't have to be friendly with everyone on the staff, now did she?

As Kim walked past him, head held high, his cold blue eyes narrowed, indicating he recognized her. A thunder cloud expression crossed his face. Probably a hired assassin wouldn't look nastier. Was he considering garrote or gun as weapon of choice? She had the feeling he was decidedly not the sort of person one wanted for an enemy.

Kim walked quickly ahead, passing the steady stream of arriving students, keeping her eyes fixed on the American flag billowing from a metal flagpole in the late summer breeze of hazy morning.

Inside the sprawling brick building, the newly waxed corridors assaulted her nostrils with their antiseptic odor. Her stomach, already out of sorts, lurched, and she experienced a vortex of visceral gyration. Someone banged into her just as she located the main office, and she had to stop to pick up her briefcase from the floor. She had a sudden intuition that this might not be one of her best days.

This hypothesis was born out later. For one thing, the students were not exactly what she'd anticipated. Besides spending four periods teaching English to seniors, she spent the rest of her assigned day in the library assisting the educational media specialist, who viewed her as slave labor. However, that was actually the best part of her work day.

One elective poetry class of seniors seemed completely indifferent. A few students yawned in her face as she explained the course requirements. The other class, composed mainly of football players, came as a decided shock. They were huge boys, and the room positively shrank with them sitting in front of her. They were also rowdy. The excited comments about her looks could hardly be ignored.

"Wow, Coach Tremain, have you ever changed!"

"Teacher, teach me anything and everything!"

That drew raucous laughter, hoots, and a few whistles. Kim put up her hands to indicate silence. Since that didn't work, she called out for them to quiet down and was totally ignored. In the university classes where she'd worked as a teaching assistant, discipline had never been a problem. *Well, Dorothy, you're not in Kansas anymore.*

Kim was flustered as she considered what her next action should be. Then a very tall blond man stepped through the door of the classroom. He leaned negligently against the doorjamb, arms folded over his broad chest. His sleeves were rolled up so that the golden hair on his muscular forearms was visible. His frown was intense as he glared at first one student and then the next until every boy in the classroom fell silent. He looked formidable and dangerous. As she recognized him, her stomach did a flip-flop. It was all she could do to hold the bile down in her throat. Her heart was pounding with a heavy thud.

He began speaking in a soft, silky voice that managed to carry a clear note of menace. "I want to introduce your new English teacher to you. I'm sure you've already heard Mr. Tremain has left us. Mr. Oberly will be taking over as head coach of the football team. This is Ms. Reynolds. I expect that you will show her the same courtesy and respect you gave Mr. Tremain. If you don't, I'll hear about it and I'll be very unhappy." There was no mistaking the threat in his voice. His eyes were dark thunder clouds; he looked like a fierce Nordic god ready to hurl lightning bolts. "Does everybody understand? Good. Please continue, Ms. Reynolds."

Kim felt a hot flush of mortification rush up her body and prayed her face wasn't scarlet. She started speaking immediately, hoping she sounded coherent.

The intruder remained for about ten minutes, until things had gotten underway, then quietly left the room. Kim knew she ought to feel grateful, but in reality she felt angry. *Who was that masked man?* She couldn't reveal her ignorance to the students, who obviously recognized him.

If he'd just allowed her more time with the students before getting involved, she could have gotten them under control herself, she decided indignantly. He should have given her enough space to find her own way. She ignored the traitorous small voice in the back of her mind that said without his intervention, the class would likely have been a total disaster.

The following day Kim sat down wearily in the teacher's cafeteria at lunchtime. The blond man was sitting at a table across the room from her. On impulse, she decided to have a word with him.

"Excuse me. I want to thank you for helping me with my class yesterday, but I think in the future, it might be best to let me fight my own battles."

He viewed her through narrowed eyes. "Is that right? You think I was interfering?"

"As a matter of fact, I do."

"And you weren't at all intimidated by the class?" He spoke softly but his expression was intense.

"You shouldn't have gotten involved. It undercut my authority." With that, she walked hurriedly back across the room. When Kim turned and found him still looking at her, she felt disconcerted. She clutched at her midsection in a nervous gesture.

"Tummy not feeling very well?" A thin, balding man eyed her with amused speculation as he picked up his lunch tray and prepared to leave.

"A little queasy," she admitted.

"A touch of malaise?" He gave her a knowing look and nodded. "We've all been there, my dear. I cursed like a sailor yesterday morning. Twenty-five years of teaching, and I still hate coming back to teaching classes after summer vacation. I'm William Norgood, by the way. I teach English here. And you are?"

"Kim Reynolds. I'm in your department."

"So you're the new one." He smiled as if pleased. "You weren't here for our first faculty meeting before the students returned."

"I was hired late and couldn't come in earlier. I had a few things to take care of at the university." She was grateful to have picked up an expository writing course, which would meet twice a week in the evenings. The class would help offset what she was losing in income.

"Have no fear. I'll shepherd you to our flock at the faculty meeting this afternoon."

She appreciated his friendly overture. The sarcastic, theatrical voice did not put her off in the least. Many of her English professors had spoken in a similar pretentious manner.

At the rear of the cafeteria that afternoon, the faculty congregated. Kim took a cup of tea, bypassed the Danish pastry, and sat down beside her newly acquired colleague.

A pleasantly plump woman not too much older than herself greeted William Norgood in a friendly manner. "Hey, Will, how's it going?"

"As well as can be expected." He let out a deep, lugubrious sigh.

The doe-eyed woman laughed softly, reacting to his sour tone. "You sound like you're at a funeral—your own. Lighten up, man."

"We are back here again, and as far as I'm concerned that

marks the death of summer."

"You are worse than the students." Her cheerful smile displayed even white teeth.

"My dearest one, I don't merely teach Greek tragedy, I live it." He held his hands over his heart and sighed again.

"Just be grateful ham is not on the endangered species list."

"That would be pig, my darling."

"You got that right." She gave him a meaningful, saccharine-sweet smile.

Will laughed and then proceeded to formally introduce Kim to Shandra Wallace, who, it seemed, was a math teacher at the school.

"You'll probably have some questions, so feel free to ask me about anything." Shandra's warmth relaxed Kim. There were no airs or pretensions about her. Shandra had short brown hair and a freckled pug nose. She wore dark-framed glasses, no makeup, and was dressed in a boxy linen suit.

The faculty meeting started promptly. Shandra sat on one side of her and William Norgood on the other. At the podium stood a short, stocky man with sparse white hair. Kim recognized Dr. Bell, the superintendent of schools who had hired her. But she did not see Mr. Sorensen, the high school principal with whom she'd taken an interview.

Dr. Bell cleared his throat and began to speak. After welcoming remarks, he announced that Mr. Sorensen had suffered a heart attack and there was no telling when he'd be well enough to return. A buzz went up in the audience of teachers, and Dr. Bell raised his hands in a quieting gesture, much as the teachers did with their students. "In the meantime, it's been decided that Henry Anderson will be acting principal. You all know what a terrific job Hank has done for us these past three years as vice principal. He's seen to it that discipline's been improved one hundred percent throughout the school. So let's welcome Hank into his new position."

"The school law enforcer is climbing the ladder of success," Will quipped dryly.

Much to Kim's chagrin, the man who came to stand next to the superintendent was none other than the fierce Viking who had interfered in her poetry class the previous day. Kim felt a sinking sensation in the pit of her stomach. Oh, God, no!

Shandra caught her expression of surprise and misinterpreted the reaction. "Quite a hunk, isn't he?" Shandra whispered as enthusiastic applause broke out among those assembled. "You wouldn't think a guy just over thirty-five would move ahead so quickly, but he's really good at his job. The kids respect him as much as the faculty."

"Please, don't make me ill," William Norgood said. "You know the real reason they're moving him ahead so quickly. Don't let those good looks blind you to the truth."

"Will's a cynic," Shandra said with a good-natured smile. "Don't let him prejudice or influence you unduly. Make up your own mind about our acting principal."

Unfortunately, Kim already had.

The applause and expressions of congratulations finally died away. Henry Anderson stepped to the podium. He looked imposingly tall and exuded strong masculine appeal. Lean and muscular, he appeared formidable and confident, as if he could accomplish anything. Kim tried to tell herself that she was not impressed; it was all a facade. *Right, and birds didn't fly in the sky!*

"Ben Franklin said fish and visitors stink after three days. That's pretty much true of speeches that exceed three minutes. So I won't bore you to death by talking longer than that." As promised, his remarks were succinct, and the audience was mesmerized by his charismatic presence. He spoke with compelling enthusiasm and vitality about the job ahead of them in the coming year, his well-modulated baritone voice at times as smooth as rich chocolate. His energy, idealism, and commitment were contagious.

By the time he finished speaking, a large round of applause was again emanating from the staff, most likely because he'd kept it short as promised.

Henry Anderson flashed a dynamic smile as he glanced around the room, but when his quicksilver eyes settled on Kim, he seemed to bore right into her. Now she knew what the desert felt like when it was being scorched by the hot, unforgiving summer sun. Her hands pressed tightly together in an effort to maintain control; she dug her nails into her palms. Here was the one person she would have to avoid at all costs. Right, and how was that going to be possible?

Will Norgood leaned close and whispered, "Hank Anderson was our football coach at one time. It shows, doesn't it? He still loves to give those rousing rah-rah pep talks. I rather expect the cheerleaders to come out shaking their pom-poms."

The snide remark was something of a comfort to Kim; it seemed to cut the big man down to size.

Dr. Bell, who only came up to Mr. Anderson's shoulder, resumed his position at the podium and introduced the new faculty. Except for herself, there were just two others, a vocal instructor and a French teacher. Great, that meant she would probably be watched very carefully, especially by the acting principal.

Morgana Douglas, the English chairperson, also referred to as supervisor, zeroed in on Kim as the faculty meeting broke up. "Come, dear, you and I must become acquainted. Although we haven't met, I've been looking forward to working with you. Mr. Sorensen and Dr. Bell told me about your splendid academic background. I'm quite impressed."

Ms. Douglas gave her a sharp, condescending smile. "I too

have a diverse background. I was a museum curator at one time. After I married my late husband, he insisted that I retire from that profession. Too demanding of my time. When we weren't blessed with children, I decided to attend classes and try my hand at teaching English. It has proven a rewarding second career."

Kim studied the English chair. Ms. Douglas was an imposing woman, nearly six feet tall in her four-inch stiletto heels that clicked against the glistening floor in precision as they walked along the corridor. Her blue-gray hair was cut short and attractively permed. In spite of a youthfully trim figure, she was easily in her late fifties. Kim was aware of a certain vague sense of insecurity that the woman tried to cover up with an air of sophistication.

"Have you ever considered a career in the theatre, Ms. Reynolds? Your looks are really quite striking."

Kim was surprised by the comment. "No, I can't say I've ever thought about acting as a profession for myself."

"It certainly helps one in teaching to have a touch of the actor. We must keep our students entertained and amused or risk losing their attention."

"One of my undergrad professors observed if a teacher really loves the subject and knows it thoroughly, good teaching will follow."

Ms. Douglas's laugh had a fluted, fluttery quality. "The naive idealistic notions of ivy tower people. They don't teach out here in the real world. You will quickly discover children these days have rather a short attention span. They expect the instant gratification and entertainment that they receive from television viewing and video games from us as well. We have to know how to compete. If you don't recognize that, you won't be here very long."

Kim decided the last remark sounded more like a threat than

an observation. It made her distinctly uncomfortable and wary. She had no intention of putting on a clown suit, wearing a red nose, and honking a horn.

"Incidentally, don't take anything William Norgood says too seriously. I noticed him talking to you. He strikes a discordant note around here. He's an overage rebel without a cause. Definitely not the sort of person a teacher just starting out here should choose as a friend or mentor. If I were you, I would discourage his overtures." Ms. Douglas gave Kim another frosty smile that had her envisioning fudge pops. Then the supervisor clicked away.

When Kim looked up again, she found Mr. Anderson staring directly at her. His face was devoid of all expression, but the hard ridges and stark planes of that handsome face underlined a strength and power that made her feel more than a tad uneasy and vulnerable.

Will rejoined her, glancing after Morgana Douglas with a sniff of disdain. "Keep a brave heart, dear one," Will said in a stagy whisper. "You must learn never to empower your enemies."

She'd never thought of those in authority as *the enemy*. The idea disturbed her. Will gave her a mock salute and sauntered away. Kim, lost in thought, hardly heard the footsteps behind her.

"I think you and I will have to talk, Ms. Reynolds. My office, right now." The voice was dangerously soft.

Kim looked up into riveting blue eyes and tried not to tremble. But her heart began to hammer. God, what next?

# CHAPTER THREE

Henry Anderson seemed to tower over her. She refused to let herself feel intimidated. Kim faced him directly and prayed that he could not tell how rapidly her heart was beating.

"What did you want to discuss with me, Mr. Anderson?" Her voice sounded much too breathy.

"First, I think we ought to clear the air between us. I believe in talking straight. I think your behavior in the classroom was more indicative of an ill-prepared student than a mature teacher." His gaze met hers with a cold, metallic gleam. He'd gone straight for the jugular!

She felt heat rush to her cheeks, angry at his condemnation. "It might also be said that educators, administrators in particular, are supposed to set a model of patience for others."

He squared his broad shoulders and fisted his hands against lean hips. "Look, I know you were hired only a week ago to fill the position that developed after Mr. Tremain's sudden departure. It was an emergency situation and I think a mistake might have been made, both for you and the school."

So now he was questioning her ability to teach, before she'd even had a fair tryout. Kim felt herself fill with indignation. What right did this man have to stand in judgment? Why, he didn't even know her!

"Excuse me," she said as coolly as she could manage, "how can you be so certain that I won't do a good job?"

"From what I understand, your teaching experience is as a

college instructor. You're coming into a high school situation cold turkey. Sure, it might work out if you were taking on purely academic classes, but you're not. Mr. Tremain was our previous football coach. He was a good disciplinarian. He could control students. He did an especially good job with the special learning disabilities that make up our basic skills classes, including those students who are emotionally disturbed and sometimes act out. Frankly, I don't think you can handle it. You're taking on two of those senior classes as well as the poetry elective. You may be okay in the library, but that's only part of your program here."

She faced him directly, her spine straight as a broomstick. "You don't know me at all, Mr. Anderson. You have no idea of my capabilities, and what I can do or what I can't."

"Very true, but I do know our students, and there isn't a cream puff in the lot."

"Are you suggesting that I am one?"

One golden brow lifted in a patronizing manner. "Complete with whipped topping."

"I find your arrogance infuriating." She stood on tip-toes, her head elevated.

"Ever taken a special education course, Ms. Reynolds? No, of course not. That would be beneath a scholar, an intellectual who aspires to teach literature at the university level." Now he was openly hostile and sarcastic.

"I am not an intellectual snob, Mr. Anderson. Far from it!" She could hardly contain the tremor in her body. The anger she felt reduced her voice to little better than a hiss.

"Level with me. How long do you intend to stay here? You have no commitment to high school teaching. What happens when one of your students refuses to obey or threatens you? And it will happen, Ms. Reynolds, I can assure you of that."

Kim felt her stomach muscles clench. "I will learn to cope

with those students. I'm a quick study." Her mouth tightened mutinously. "Contrary to what you think, I have taught high school English classes before. I admit it was only for a short time, but I do have some classroom experience. And I'm not easily intimidated—by anyone."

"You'll come to me for help when you need it. Is that clear? No false pride."

"I will do whatever is necessary. Don't forget, I'll also be teaching a senior poetry elective. I'm eminently qualified for that responsibility." She raised her chin in a gesture of defiance.

"About that." He cleared his throat. "You should know Mr. Tremain promised the football players an easy elective if they chose his class."

She controlled her anger. "That doesn't change a thing. I will do a competent job," she said.

He ran his fingers through cropped gilt hair that was sand-colored beneath. "You're a stubborn woman. I'm trying to give you an out."

"I don't need one. What I need is a job for the coming year. Why are you so determined to get me to resign? Do you have a brother or sister standing in the wings?"

"I'm an only child."

She was tempted to retort that it was fortunate for his parents but thought better of antagonizing him further.

"Look," he said with a deep sigh, as if he were showing saintly patience to someone of inferior mental comprehension, "I'm only trying to do what's best for you as well as the students and the school. They're going to make mincemeat out of you."

"I rather doubt that. If you're as fair-minded as you purport to be, Mr. Anderson, then you'll have to give me a chance. Even if you decide to fire me, I believe I'm entitled to sixty days' notice. I did sign a contract."

He frowned and Kim knew she had him there. Now it was

her turn to feel smug and superior—if only she could.

"It would be better for all concerned if you handed in your resignation today."

"Somehow, I rather doubt that." Kim raised her chin in a combative manner.

He was prejudiced against her and was rationalizing his behavior. She fisted her hand in an effort for control. "I have no intention of quitting. So if you'll excuse me for now, Mr. Anderson, I believe I had better work on my lesson plans for tomorrow."

"I'll be keeping an eye on you."

"You just do that," she said with a challenging smile.

He gave her one dark look that made her tremble inwardly. But she would rather be struck dead by lightning than admit the effect he had on her. The man was obviously too full of his own self-importance. He was probably used to women falling all over themselves to please him just because he was dynamic and strong-minded, not to mention physically attractive. Well, she wasn't going to let him push her around! Confrontation with Mr. Anderson was something she hadn't wanted or expected, but she couldn't forget how much she needed this job. There wasn't a snowball's chance in hell that she was going to just walk away without giving it her best. She would not let the man deprive her of what she needed.

Kim went back to her classroom and forced herself to return to her preparations. The trouble was, she acknowledged ruefully, she was indeed ignorant of the special techniques needed for teaching the intellectually and emotionally challenged. Her experience in that area was at best limited.

A knock at the door made her look up.

"Am I disturbing you?" Will Norgood proffered a lopsided smile.

"Not at all. I'm just wrestling with the materials."

He pulled up a chair and sat down beside her. "Well, don't let it take you down for the count. I too have been given difficult classes. It should come as no surprise that our illustrious chairperson lustily hates me. She never was a museum curator, you know, although I'm certain she wanted to be. Actually, she was a dancer on the stage, a chorus girl. I believe there was even some talk of stripping in Vegas. Then she managed to tap-dance herself into marriage with a rich widower."

Kim thought that if this teaching position didn't pan out, she might very well find herself considering a job pole-dancing in Manhattan like certain former female stockbrokers. At the moment, she had no idea what to say, but Will did not seem to require a response. Whatever his faults, he was not a man easily at a loss for words.

"In any case, I am probably more able to help you than most." He handed her several books. "These are good choices for working with your special education classes. The books are interesting, have suitable questions for each unit, articles and stories along with appropriate vocabulary. You'll find sufficient copies for your classes in the book room. Just be firm with your students."

"Thank you." She smiled at him in gratitude.

"For God's sake, don't smile at your students at least until Christmas!"

"Right."

"Occasionally, my dear, I'm capable of an act of kindness. And you're going to need that. I'll help if I can. Shandra will also. She shares the same sort of pupils as you and I. You'll find her advice is quite sensible and sound. Probably better than my own, if the truth be told." He gave her a rueful smile. "But pray do not tell anyone I've offered to help you. It would ruin my reputation as an evil curmudgeon."

"I have taught before," she said. "I don't know why everyone assumes I haven't."

"Really? You look too young and innocent."

"I'm pushing thirty."

He opened his eyes wide in surprise. "It must be that wholesome image of yours, those large, cow brown eyes, toasty warm, making you look young and inexperienced. Definitely, you must wear more makeup, my dear. A harder look is required for this job. Otherwise, the piranhas will feast on your flesh." With that, he stood up, ready to leave.

"Will, what do you think of Mr. Anderson?"

"The golden boy wonder? They adore the fair-haired lad around here. They believe he can walk on water. But I remain something of a dubious skeptic, a heretic they'd like to burn at the stake. Here's a thought. How far would wonder boy have gotten if his father weren't filthy rich and a pillar of the community? For that matter, would a certain hoofer have become English department chairperson on her own merits if her deceased husband hadn't at one time been a member of the board of education and loaded besides? Don't be fooled or misled. She and Anderson are both ruthlessly ambitious people. They'll do whatever it takes to get ahead. They love exerting power over others. Wealth has made that possible. Money doesn't talk, my dear, it shouts out loud. Food for thought, perhaps?"

It was indeed. She'd have to masticate what he'd told her like a cow chewing cud. She'd ignore and avoid Mr. Anderson. And she vowed to do a good job teaching this year, if for no other reason than to make that arrogant man choke on his words.

"So Hank, what do you think of our new teachers?" James Bell entered the vice principal's office without bothering to check with his secretary. The superintendent of schools believed in the informal approach, Anderson observed coolly.

"They seem like good choices, all except for the English teacher."

Dr. Bell shot him a look of surprise. "Why, Hank? What don't you like about her?"

Hank paced in the confining space beside his desk. "She's attractive, but that's hardly any reason to give her Tremain's job. Do you know what kinds of classes she'll have to contend with?"

"I'm not worried," the superintendent said, bestowing his best beatific politician's smile. "You'll give her a hand. Guide her along with the techniques of discipline. She already knows subject matter."

"Really? Does she know how to make English interesting for students who are physically adults but can't read past third-grade level? Did you bother to explain what she'd be dealing with when you interviewed her?"

"So we'll have her take a few courses."

"Yeah, right." Hank Anderson shook his head. "I don't think we're being realistic here."

"Give it a chance, son. Lighten up." Dr. Bell gave him a friendly slap on the back. "Your dad would tell you the same thing."

Hank hated it when people brought up his father. It was like emotional blackmail. Besides, if he'd listened to his father, he'd never have gone into education in the first place.

After Dr. Bell left, he tried to concentrate on the many details that needed his attention. The devil was in the details. He'd be carrying the burden of two jobs this year. Only a few people knew how seriously ill Dave Sorensen was. In all likelihood, the principal would retire. But until that happened, there would be no other administrator, and no one knew better than he did how demanding the job could be.

Still, he'd always wanted the opportunity to do things his way, to improve public education. He hadn't forgotten the countless heated arguments between Dad and himself concerning why it was important for him to become a math teacher instead of a business executive. Todd Anderson could not understand why his only child would not work for him in the multimillion-dollar business that was a family heritage and, to his father's way of thinking, a privilege.

Dad called him a misguided idealist. "You'll never change the system. I sent you to private schools for a reason. Now you want to throw your life away on the undeserving?"

"If you recall, I transferred over to Lake Shore from prep school for my junior and senior years of high school and I never regretted it. I think teaching is one of the most important jobs there is, when it's done right."

"You're spitting on the opportunities I'm offering you, and for what? To serve the great unwashed?"

"Dad, if your nose was lifted any higher, you'd get a nosebleed. You're such a snob!"

"If I'm snooty, you're snotty. Just remember this conversation when your sainthood is tarnished and the rabble proceed to bite you in the ass."

Hank hadn't listened, and he hadn't looked back. He loved his father; he just didn't agree with him. As far as he was concerned, a better country and ergo a better world meant a commitment to public education. He'd do whatever he felt was necessary to make that happen. He vowed nothing would stand in his way. He wouldn't shrink away from taking ruthless action when it was necessary.

Hank also knew he was right about Kim Reynolds. She would fail miserably. Lake Shore Regional High School, something of a social experiment so typical of New Jersey, wasn't an easy place to work. This was a school of extreme contrasts: the wealthy and privileged community of Lake Shore, some of whom sent their children here to show their liberal views on education; the poverty-stricken area, Wicker Hollow, which sent minority students; and the working-class enclave of Mooresville, all part of Webster Township. These children mixed for the first time in the freshman year of high school. The results were sometimes violently combustible. That was one reason he walked the halls every day and checked out each area of the building personally.

He thought again about Kim Reynolds. She'd actually been angry at him, accused him of interfering. He shook his head in disgust. Did the woman have no common sense whatever? She should have felt grateful for his intervention on the previous afternoon.

Well, he wouldn't accomplish much if he kept thinking about Kim Reynolds. She was going to be nothing but trouble; he felt it deep in his bones.

Kim Reynolds wasn't teacher material and everyone would see that soon enough, including her. Unfortunately, it would be left for him to pick up the pieces. He was not looking forward to that.

# CHAPTER FOUR

"So why are we out for drinks this evening?" Kim asked.

Mike gave her his most seductive and mysterious smile. "I thought we'd celebrate your new job. We didn't get to talk about it yesterday. I ended up pulling a double shift because Mitch was out sick. Thought I'd make up for it tonight."

Kim shrugged. "I don't think there's much to celebrate at the moment."

Mike gave her a sharp look. "And why's that?"

"For one thing, the principal doesn't like me."

"Sorenson?"

"No, he had a heart attack. Henry Anderson's the acting principal. Do you know him?"

"Not personally. What doesn't he like about you?"

"He thinks I'm a cream puff."

Mike looked genuinely surprised. "He actually said that?"

"Those were his words, not mine. He doesn't believe I'll be able to handle Coach Tremain's classes."

"Well, you'll prove him wrong."

"That's what I told him," Kim said.

Mike reached over and took her hand. "That's my girl."

Kim lowered her gaze. "The thing is, I'm not all that sure I can do a good job."

She looked up again and saw Mike's fierce scowl.

"I oughta punch his lights out. He's new to his job too, or he wouldn't talk that way to you, make you lose confidence in yourself." Mike's features, all angles and planes, took on a determined expression. "There's nobody around more qualified than you. Don't doubt yourself, and don't let this guy undermine you."

"You always know the right thing to say." She squeezed his fingers.

"Damn right, I do! And you're the best. Don't let anyone make you doubt that."

She had to smile at his fierce expression. Being with Mike was always good for her self-esteem. He was generous in every way possible.

April Nevins arrived to take their drink order, interrupting their conversation. The Galaxy Lounge, where April worked as a cocktail waitress, was a relatively new establishment in Webster Township. The locals, or *townies,* never went there—too new and fancy for their tastes. The townies liked their watering holes old and disreputable-looking. The Galaxy was a hangout for the emigrant New Yorkers who inhabited the luxury condos, garden apartments, and housing development complexes, and as such, the place boasted a classy veneer. It wasn't the kind of place where Mike Gardner usually hung out, which made Kim curious. She sensed that he was in an odd mood this evening, tenser than usual.

"So what would you like to order?" April asked, giving them each a friendly smile.

April's blond highlighted hair was pulled back from her face and neatly parted down the middle. However, her costume was anything but prim. A black velvet micro skirt barely brushed the tops of her thighs. Her white satin blouse, cut very low, loosely covered her well-endowed breasts and emphasized her bronzed cleavage. Kim observed that Mike was staring appreciatively. He'd have to be made of stone not to notice, she conceded.

"Beer for me," Mike said.

"I'll just have a cranberry juice," Kim said.

"How about a glass of wine? You like merlot, don't you? Kick back and relax."

Kim nodded and let Mike change the order. She wasn't much for alcohol, but she also wasn't in the mood to argue about anything this evening. She was feeling plain exhausted from the stress of the day. She hoped to get in the groove eventually.

Kim studied the inside of the cocktail lounge, which was very dark, walls black and tablecloths blood red. Tapered red candles were at each table, but only the bar itself was crowded. Soft music was piped in from somewhere. The only unusual thing was the ceiling: some aspiring Michelangelo had painted the universe there. It was hardly the Sistine Chapel, but Kim thought the artwork made the place stand out. She observed a number of men and women socializing at the bar. The atmosphere was pleasant and Kim wasn't sorry Mike had chosen to bring her here this evening.

After April deposited their drinks and some pretzels and mixed nuts to go with them, Mike raised his glass. "I want to offer a toast to the woman I love." He took a sip of his beer. "I have something for you." Mike reached into his jacket pocket and pulled out a small black velvet box.

Kim stared at him. She should have expected this but hadn't been tuned into Mike the past few days. She'd been concentrating too hard on dealing with mental preparation for her new job.

Mike slipped the box into her hand. "Please open it," he said. "I know this has been the last thing on your mind of late, but I think it's time we made things official."

She opened the box. The multifaceted diamond ring could not have been more perfect. Kim viewed it through a shimmering mist of tears.

"If it's not what you want, we can return it and you can pick out something else. I know it probably has to be sized too. I wasn't certain of the fit."

"It's lovely, so very beautiful."

"The jeweler said it's a perfect blue-white stone. I don't know much about jewelry but I thought you'd like it."

The solitaire winked at her. "I do, very much."

"So can we make it official? Will you marry me?"

She swallowed hard. What was wrong with her? Why was she hesitating? How could she still be uncertain? There would never be a man more perfect for her than Mike Gardner. They were so right for each other. He loved her and she loved him. She should simply accept that. Think less. Act more. Be normal for once!

"Yes, Mike. I'll marry you."

His smile was as dazzling as the diamond ring he'd given her. He kissed her hand, palm up. "Let's go to dinner," he said.

"Are we picking up the girls?"

"If you don't mind," Mike said. "They're supposed to be doing homework, but there's no keeping anything from them. They're pretty excited."

"I do want to share this evening with them," Kim said.

Mike left a large tip for April, who came over before they left the lounge and exclaimed over the ring, then hugged Kim and wished them both every happiness.

"Want me to tell Bert?" April asked.

"No, I'll tell her at work tomorrow," Mike said.

"She'll be very happy for you. Bert thinks you're both terrific people."

When they got to Mike's car, he turned to Kim. "Stay over tonight?"

She shook her head. "I'd like to but I need to prepare for tomorrow. This first week of school sets the program for the year. I've got some things I need to go over. Can I take a raincheck for the weekend?"

"Sweetheart, whatever's best for you, though I have to say, I think you worry too much and you're overly conscientious."

"You're probably right," she conceded. "But it's part of who and what I am."

"Well I'm not trying to change you," he said with a warm smile. "I happen to love who and what you are."

Then Mike gave her a kiss that Kim felt right down to her toes and wouldn't soon forget.

Kim had left for work the following morning knowing she'd prepared herself as thoroughly as possible. She'd been about to put on her new engagement ring, then thought better of it and placed it back in the box. She realized that she didn't want to share her new status as an engaged woman with anyone at the high school. For the time being, she wanted to keep it a private matter.

Dinner with Mike's two daughters had been especially pleasant. She was left with a good feeling. So why did she feel like a prisoner walking the green mile on death row at this moment? Could it be because her classes were turning out to be everything Mr. Anderson warned about? Each of her two basic skills English classes had only fifteen students. Most of them were also on some form of supplemental instruction. All of them had learning or emotional difficulties.

The easier class was the one with the highest number of truancies. Out of fifteen, only seven students showed up. She soon ascertained that many of her pupils were dyslexic, withdrawn, or disinterested. But at least they were not overtly rude. Mainly, the attitude was one of boredom. When she asked questions, Kim was greeted with stony, apathetic silence.

She determined that the students were not going to be allowed to merely ignore her. She intended to get in their faces—in a positive manner, if there was such a thing.

Nick James and his friend Billy Kramer had not come to class for the first two days of school. This turned out to be a blessing. When they did arrive, it was long after the bell, and both boys reeked, smelling like human ashtrays. The odor was stronger and more pungent than ordinary tobacco and Kim suspected they'd been smoking weed.

"Why are you late for English class?" When Kim questioned them, she quickly realized they were hostile and a threat to her authority. Nick, the bigger and more aggressive of the two, stepped forward in an intimidating stance.

"I lost my way," he said. He lifted his fists, taking a pugilist's stance.

The other students snickered.

"Don't be late again." Her manner was firm. She crossed her arms and stood her ground, even while attempting to be non-confrontational. She realized that with student discipline, teachers had to choose their battles with care.

As the class progressed, Kim learned that Nick was not mentally challenged like Billy, whose pasty, pock-marked face made him the butt of some cruel jokes. Nick was a natural leader, defiant and confident. And because he didn't want to learn, he determined to make it difficult for others to do so as well.

Kim stood beside Emory Dunne, a boy with serious health problems who was also dyslexic. Emory and his motorized wheelchair, according to some of the other teachers, were the scourge of the hallways. Emory refused to answer questions either in oral or written form. Kim had the inspiration of giving him a notebook.

"Maybe you would like to write down some of your thoughts and feelings? They don't have to be in any special form or order.

This is for you to keep. You won't have to show it to anyone. Just try to write a few words in it each day." She handed Emory the notebook.

He pushed her hand away. "I'm no writer."

"Everyone has something to say."

"Not me." The boy's manner was sullen, and Kim wondered if she would be able to reach him.

"Leave him alone, lady," Nick James said. "Stop bothering the sorry runt. How'd you like it if I bothered you?" His look was long on mean.

"Is that a threat, Nick? Because, if it is, I would have to report you."

She set her steady gaze on him. He was tall and burly, obviously used to bullying others with his superior size. It was very important the boy did not think she was afraid of him—even if she really was.

The bell rang at that moment and she dismissed the class. What she could not dismiss was the rude smirk on Nick's face. Kim knew she would eventually have to do something about his behavior or lose the respect of the class.

At lunchtime, when Will joined her in the faculty room, she asked if he happened to know Nick James.

"I had that Neanderthal throwback as a freshman, a nasty piece of work if ever there was one. I failed him. You should do the same. Of course, the powers that be wouldn't be happy. They'd love to unload him. He's been here so long, he'll soon be ready to collect Social Security."

"Should I contact his parents?"

"If you can get hold of them. Try in the evening."

Across the room, Mr. Anderson was sitting with several other supervisors. He caught her eye and she quickly looked away. She did not want him to think that she was staring at him. The room suddenly felt hot and crowded.

"I see you brought your own lunch," Will observed, drawing her attention back to him. "Very clever. I've heard a rumor that the board of health plans to condemn our kitchen."

She smiled at his witticism. "I bring lunch as an economy measure."

"You new teachers aren't very well paid." His brow furrowed sympathetically.

To her surprise, Will who was so often sarcastic, was sensitive to her feelings and changed the subject as if to forestall any embarrassment on her part.

"I hear Sorensen won't be coming back."

Kim glanced up from her tuna sandwich in surprise. "Is he that ill?"

"The word is his doctor ordered him to retire. The job is too stressful for a man in his condition. Besides, he's as old as Methuselah. Don't feel too sorry for the buzzard. He has a very nice pension coming to him."

"Does that mean Mr. Anderson will be the new principal?" She felt a sudden sense of foreboding. She had a vision of black vultures picking her bones.

Will shrugged. "One never knows, does one? The board usually advertises. I believe by law they must. But don't be surprised, barring any unexpected complications, if the golden anointed one gets the job. His father can buy and sell the whole lot of school board members."

"Shandra is right about your cynicism."

"Right as rain. I'm suspicious of all in authority and proud of it."

Morgana Douglas joined the other supervisors for lunch. She glanced over at Will and Kim with a disapproving frown.

"Perhaps I'll sharpen my tongue in case she pirouettes past our table later."

"I really wish you wouldn't."

"Nonsense. That's half the fun in my life. There's very little she can do to me that she hasn't already done. However, perhaps you ought to keep your distance. I don't want you caught in the crossfire. The untenured are always vulnerable."

"I believe I have a right to choose my own friends."

"Foolish but well said, fair maiden." He patted her hand. Will did have a way of making her feel better.

That afternoon, Kim stayed late to work on her lessons for the rest of the week. Her cramped apartment was too small for proper concentration. Besides, all her books and materials were here in school. She even made a trip to the guidance office to obtain the phone number of Nick James.

She was feeling pretty satisfied with herself until she got to the parking lot and found that her car had been keyed and the front tires flattened. Standing there in the hot sun, she wondered what to do. She'd never changed a tire herself, never had to do it. With a heavy heart, she started back to the school.

Clearly, this had to be done by a student. Had it been done purposefully? Had the student selected her automobile, knowing it was hers? If so, it was done by someone who bore her animosity. Someone like Nick James? Wearily, she wondered if Mr. Anderson hadn't been right after all. Maybe she wasn't cut out to be a public school teacher. She hadn't really loved it the first time around either. Had she made a serious mistake accepting the job?

At that moment, a jogger nearly collided with her.

"You all right?"

Large, strong arms reached out to steady her. She looked up into the steady gaze of Hank Anderson.

# CHAPTER FIVE

"I'm fine," she said and tried to look as if she meant it. The truth was, she felt like crying, but she'd never give him the satisfaction of seeing her fall apart in front of him.

"Aren't you going in the wrong direction?"

There seemed no help for it; she had to tell him about the flat tires. He listened courteously without interrupting her. His face betrayed no emotion whatsoever. She had to admit, even if he didn't like her, he wasn't showing any sign of satisfaction at her expense.

"I'll take care of it for you." He had a reassuring voice, deep and soothing to the ear.

"No, that's all right. I'll call a service station." She felt the color rise to her cheeks in embarrassment.

"I won't hear of it." In the end, there was nothing to do but let him change the tires for her. It was a good thing she had two spare tires in the trunk. Maybe the flat ones could be repaired.

She watched Hank Anderson as he worked. He had the grace and coordination of a natural athlete. The cut-off shorts he wore and sweat-soaked t-shirt contoured a flawless masculine body, wide shoulders, hard, lean muscles. The hair on his sinewy, tanned arms and legs was golden; he reminded her of a tawny lion, all power and grace.

He looked up and saw her studying him. "I guess you were wondering about the informal attire," he said. "I like to work out at the end of the day. Takes the edge off the stress."

She nodded her head. Actually, she hadn't thought about why he was dressed that way at all.

"Thank you," she said awkwardly as he finished. "You've saved me a good deal of time and trouble, not to mention money."

"Hey, administrators ought to do something useful for their teachers now and then." His self-deprecating smile betrayed perfect white teeth. He was full of surprises. "Care to join me for a soda before you go?"

It would have been rude to refuse, wouldn't it? "Sure, but I'm buying. It's the very least I can do to show my appreciation."

"Since I'm not carrying any change, that sounds good." His tone of voice was cheerful. If she didn't know better, she'd think he was actually being friendly.

He wiped the perspiration from his face as they walked back into the school, heading down the deserted corridor to the faculty room. "You stayed very late." He gave her a questioning look, one golden brow rising.

"I'm getting into the habit. I like to get all my work done for the next day before I leave. That way, I'm set to begin in the morning."

"Watch out or I'll start thinking you're dedicated to your job."

She didn't like the tone of that last comment, although she decided to reserve judgment. Gingerly, she placed coins in the soda machine. "What would you like?"

He pressed the button for iced tea and she took a diet cola. Then he surprised her by sitting down on the more comfortable of the two available couches and indicating the spot beside him. Reluctantly, she sat but kept her posture stiffly erect. Strange how the room began to close in on her, shrinking in size.

"I really ought to be going," she said.

"Could we talk for a few minutes first?"

What would he want to talk to her about? Since he thought so little of her, it couldn't be anything good. But he had very generously fixed her tires. She couldn't very well refuse.

"I just wanted to tell you that I'm aware you've been putting a lot of effort into teaching your classes."

"How would you know that?" She was more than a little surprised by his remark.

"Oh, let's just say I have my sources."

"You have spies you mean." She wasn't going to let him get off that easily.

He eyed her thoughtfully. "Not exactly. I work out with the football team. I talk to the boys about things."

"And let me guess. I was on the list of topics. Before or after a discussion on the need to wear jock straps?"

Astute eyes searched her face. "Don't get bent out of shape. I just want to make sure everything goes all right for you and your students."

"What you really mean is you don't trust me." She was finding it hard to hold on to her temper.

"Don't tell me what I mean." His expression became severe as he gritted his teeth. They were practically nose to nose, and his nostrils were flaring like a bull seeing a red cape.

Good, let him get angry too; she didn't really care.

"Look, I'm not the kind of person who sneaks around. I'm looking out for everybody's welfare. That's an important part of my job. Can't you understand that?"

She moved as far away from him as she could without appearing rude.

"I'm not trying to intimidate or harass you. I want to help you in any way I can. Will you please believe that? I know we haven't gotten off to a good start. Maybe that's partly my fault. I'm brand new at being an acting principal. But I do know about being a teacher. I think I could help you if you let me."

She recognized that he was being conciliatory. Probably she should meet him halfway. "I promise if I need help, I'll ask for it."

"Will you?"

She felt her cheeks heat with color. "What's that supposed to mean?"

He turned and gave her a hard look. "Your tires had some help today. Someone slashed them. Someone keyed your car. You must have some idea who did it. You want to tell me about it?"

She shook her head again. He looked frustrated and ran his hand roughly through the gilt-edged hair that was now untidy.

"Why protect a vandal? Whoever this kid is, he ought to be punished."

"I have to think about what I should do."

"What you should do is turn the incident over to me. I'll handle it. It's a disciplinary matter."

She hesitated. "The thing is, there are probably two boys from my class involved. But I can't be certain. I didn't see them do it."

"Still, you have a suspicion. Did they threaten you?"

His riveting blue eyes were fixed on her now. She sensed his strength, his power. She wanted nothing more than to turn to him for help, to lean on his strength, yet she held back.

"In a manner of speaking one of them implied a threat. I think I ought to talk to the parents of the one boy. I planned to do that even before this happened."

"Look, why don't you just tell me the boy's name? I've had contact with every student in the school who's been in any kind of trouble. Maybe I can give you some insight. I won't lay my hands on the situation any further if that's what you want. Deal?"

He rose as if preparing for action.

"I'll have to think about it."

He squared his jaw. "We need to talk about this right now." His gaze impaled rather than implored. "Who is the boy you think did it?"

She let out a deep sigh. "All right, I'm having some problems with a student named Nick James. He and his friend Billy Kramer are very hostile toward me. I thought I'd call Nick's parents."

Mr. Anderson was thoughtful. "Sometimes a word from a parent works, sometimes not."

"You don't think I should phone them?"

He seemed hesitant. "Nick's father has a bad temper. Real bad. The boy's a lot like him. It's been noted that the two have had some ugly fights. We're talking physical confrontation. One time Nick's arm was broken, and another time it was his collarbone. Nick was removed from his family on several occasions. Family counseling was required. Unfortunately, the situation remains volatile. I think it would probably be best if I took charge."

"What will you do?" She still had her doubts.

"For starters, have a talk with him. Destroying property is vandalism. It's a police matter. We can't let him get away with it. Do you want to file a police report?"

She shook her head. "I don't think it would do any good. As I told you, I didn't actually see who did the damage."

"Well, you'd get the incident on record at least. Just let me know what you decide to do."

She rose unsteadily to her feet. She felt hot and dizzy, yet chilled at the same time. He took her arm as if to assist her, but that only made her feel all the more unsteady. Dear God, if she weren't more in control, he was sure to be convinced that she was the pathetic wimp he'd pegged her!

"I'll back you in every way possible."

She turned and met his gaze squarely. "As long as I act in a manner you consider suitable, you mean." She was issuing him a challenge. No way of misinterpreting that.

"Don't underestimate me," he told her. "I'll be fair with you if you'll do the same for me." He held her gaze for another moment. She was the first to turn away.

He escorted her to the side door and out of the building. In her rearview mirror, Kim saw that he was watching as she drove off, and then he resumed his jogging.

The phone was ringing when Kim returned to her apartment that afternoon. She caught it on the third ring. It was Mike and he sounded cheerful.

"I was hoping I'd catch you," he said. "I just talked to the girls. They're both home from school."

"Where are you?" she asked.

"Back at headquarters. Got a small mountain of paperwork to catch up on. Evie insists she's cooking dinner tonight. Wants to make certain you'll be at our place around six. She's going to bake a special cake for us."

"I didn't know she could bake."

"Neither did I. Guess we'll find out together. Jean's going to help her. So no matter what the meal tastes like, be sure to tell them how great it is."

Kim smiled at the phone. "You know I will."

"Actually, Evie happens to be handy in the kitchen. She had to learn, what with my crazy hours. I couldn't always manage a sitter either."

Kim realized that being a single parent wasn't an easy job for a man or woman. Usually, it was the husband who took off, but in this case, Mike's wife Evelyn had ditched her family, gone off with a boyfriend, and started a new life on the West Coast.

Mike didn't talk about it much; still, Kim knew it had hurt him and the girls badly.

"I'll change and get over to your house. I'm sure the girls won't mind if I help."

"Take your time. I think this is something they want to do for us themselves. Part of our family celebration."

"Sounds great," Kim said and meant it.

After their conversation ended, she removed her shoes and pantyhose, then lay down on the sofa, which, when opened, acted as her bed. The next thing she knew, it had grown dark. Instead of feeling refreshed by her nap, Kim felt groggy and just a bit disoriented.

There had been a dream, she realized, and not a good one. Something vague, a warning of sorts—what had it been about? A blond woman was threatening her, not physically but with words. Kim shook her head. She often had weird dreams and hated them. Her dreams tended to be prophetic, maybe because she so strongly attempted to suppress her psychic sensibility, avoiding and ignoring her special intuition as much as possible. She shook her head again as if to clear all the nasty cobwebs that had gathered there.

It was time to change into casual clothes to get ready to visit Mike and his children. She combed her hair, brushed her teeth, and tried again to lose the sense of feeling fuzzy around the edges.

She got a later start than she'd intended. It was past six-thirty P.M. when Kim pulled up to Mike's house. The fact that it was all lit up seemed kind of unusual. There was an unfamiliar car in the driveway. Kim parked behind Mike's Ford in front of the house. She heard loud voices inside raised as if there was an argument going on. She knocked, but no one responded. Finally, Kim opened the screen door and walked into the foyer. An ominous sense of something being wrong hit her hard.

In the living room, Mike, Evie, and Jean were in deep conversation with a blond-haired woman. Oh, God! It was the woman she'd seen in her dream. Kim pressed her palm to her head, desperately trying to dislodge the sick sensation, telling herself it was just something she was imagining.

"Looks like you have a guest this evening," Kim said in a quiet voice. "Mike, are you going to introduce us?"

Mike was pale. He looked almost ill. Because he didn't speak, the woman appeared to feel it necessary to fill the awkward silence.

"Mike, you're being rude."

Jean came toward Kim with a big smile and took her hand. "Oh, Kim, isn't it great? My mom came home." Jean spoke in the innocent, enthusiastic way of a child of nine.

"That's right, darling. Mommy's back. And I'm so glad to see my two special girls." The woman held out her arms and Jean ran to hug her mother. Kim watched as Evelyn Gardner embraced her younger daughter.

Evie shook her head and went to stand beside her father. "Dad, tell her to get lost. Tell her we don't want or need her anymore." Evie's manner was angry, belligerent.

"Mike," Kim said in a small voice, "what's going on?" But really, she knew.

Evelyn turned to Kim. "Mike told me about your plans. I think there's something you should know. As I just explained to Mike, I never did get around to filing the paperwork for the divorce decree. He can't marry you or anyone else because he's still legally married to me." Evelyn turned a high-voltage smile on Kim, her expression one of triumph. "So sorry for you, dear." But, of course, she wasn't really sorry at all. Everything about Evelyn Gardner appeared phony, from her big boobs and bee-stung, collagen-injected lips to her bleached blond hair.

No wonder Mike was unresponsive. He was still in a state of shock.

Kim somehow found her voice while still searching for composure. "You haven't been in contact with Mike or your children in years. What made you show up here now?"

Evelyn's bright smile disappeared. "My reasons don't concern you. This is my family and my home. I think maybe you should go. This really just concerns family. We need time to bond."

Kim said nothing. She turned on her heels and rushed out the front door. As she walked to her car, feeling totally numb, she heard Mike coming up behind her, calling her name.

"Kim, wait! Don't go."

She turned and faced him. "I think your wife is right. I'm not part of this. You have to work this out as a family one way or the other. But I can't be involved."

Mike ran his hand through his dark brown hair, his gray eyes troubled. "Of course, you're involved. I love you and you love me. I signed the papers Evelyn sent me and thought she filed them. My mistake was trusting her to handle it. But it's just a temporary setback. Nothing you have to worry about."

Kim touched his cheek. "Mike, I have a feeling it's not going to be as easy as you think. And with me being around . . . well, it will just make everything more difficult. Until this business is resolved one way or the other, I can't see you."

She saw the color rise to his cheeks. "That's just plain crazy. We're engaged to be married."

"I've made it a point of honor never to date a married man."

Mike shook his head. "But I'm not really married."

"Legally, you are." She took the diamond ring off her finger and pressed it into his hand.

Mike vibrated with agitation, his face a blood sun. She'd never seen him like this. Mike was so easygoing, a cop with a sense of humor, a man normally in control of every situation.

"Sweetheart, don't do this to us. Have some faith in me. Trust me."

This was the hardest thing she'd ever had to do in her entire life. "I do trust you. It's her I don't trust. I have to walk away from this situation. I know you can handle it. But I can't be part of it. Don't you see? That would be ethically and morally wrong, and it's against my personal code of honor. You're a man of integrity. I know you understand how I feel."

With that, Kim turned and walked away from the only man she ever expected to love. She was shaking, but she would not allow herself the luxury of tears until she was curled up on the sofa in her apartment. She held back her emotions, coiling them tight within her. But God, the pain!

# CHAPTER SIX

Kim saw Hank Anderson again at the high school sooner than she anticipated. She had hoped to avoid him but evidently that was not possible. Well, what did she expect after all? She'd admitted to having a problem with a student. Major mistake? Of course, he knew the tires were slashed so there really wasn't any other way to go. Besides, she was a terrible liar. He'd have seen through her in a Jersey second if she'd gone that route. Those penetrating eyes spoke of insight into people, of a man who was not easily fooled. In that respect, he reminded her of Mike.

The first time she saw Mr. Anderson this particular day was in the cafeteria while on lunchroom duty. Kim didn't find cafeteria patrol quite as demeaning an assignment as she'd expected, mostly because Shandra Wallace was assigned to it with her. Shandra was interesting, perceptive, and had a sense of humor, which made the time pass more quickly.

Kim was walking up and down the aisles when Hank Anderson strode into the cafeteria and surveyed the students. Then he spoke to three boys who were throwing food around, and eventually he proceeded toward her. There was no mistaking his sense of authority. Although he walked through the area in shirtsleeves, his imposing height and commanding posture left no doubt that he was someone to be reckoned with. His expression was cool and controlled as he approached her. "I just want to inform you that I spoke with Nick James this morning. He shouldn't be a problem anymore, but if he is, let me know."

She didn't answer right away. Malevolent obsidian eyes were fixed on her. They belonged to Nick, who ate lunch this period and would have class with Kim two periods from now. She'd find out firsthand if Mr. Anderson had actually succeeded.

"How did you deal with him?"

Hank Anderson shrugged. "Let's just say we came to an understanding, a meeting of the minds. At least, I like to think so. But you're the only one who'll know for certain. Keep me informed. Okay? Don't let anyone in this place intimidate you, including me."

She decided to ignore that last comment. "So you made Nick an offer he couldn't refuse?"

"In a manner of speaking." One golden brow lifted. "How's it going? Gaining on it?"

Kim realized he was trying to lighten things up. Too bad she couldn't seem to reciprocate. When she didn't answer, he drew closer.

"I'm around if you need me."

She nodded her head, not trusting herself to answer him. His eyes stayed fixed on hers just a little too long. He turned away and quickly left the cafeteria. The noise level rose again. Shandra walked toward her with an expression of concern in evidence on her face.

"That seemed kind of intense. Everything all right?"

Kim cleared her throat. "I know you like Mr. Anderson, but is he really good at his job?"

Shandra gave her a thoughtful look. "Let me put it to you this way: Some people talk the talk, others walk the walk. Hank Anderson walks the talk. I've been in this school almost as long as he has. Same department. I came the year before they moved him up to math supervisor. He was a terrific teacher. The kids loved him. It's tough to make both algebra and basic math exciting, but he did it. Never saw anyone as dynamic in a classroom. When old Mr. Spencer retired, it wasn't surprising that they chose Hank as his replacement. I mean, he had his supervisory certificate and a master's in math. And he was good. No one ever worked harder. He went to college nights every spring semester and summer, taking the extra courses for his certification, coached football every fall semester and still found time to give extra help to every kid who needed it. Think that would be enough? Not for him. He even got another master's degree in guidance and counseling. Eventually, he became the head of that department as well. He could have had things easy, everything handed to him on gold plates, but he didn't want it that way. His old man's rich, just like Will told you. But take the easy way? Not him. He has ideas about improving public education, and he's trying to make them work."

"Wow, so now tell me what you really think of the man?"

Shandra flashed a bright smile. "Okay, maybe I do get a little carried away on the subject of Hank Anderson."

"You think?"

Shandra offered an embarrassed little smile, but she wasn't quite ready to drop the topic. "He does go all the way helping other people. He offers demonstration lessons because he believes that administrators should never lose sight of what really matters, namely, teaching children. Want to hear more? I could continue but I don't want to bore your ears off."

"Okay, I surrender. I'm convinced."

"No, you're not, but you will be if you stick it out," Shandra said in a firm voice.

Their conversation came to an abrupt conclusion as two burly boys began shoving each other. Shandra immediately moved off to break them up. Kim watched the smooth way Shandra handled the students, all business and competence. Maybe someday she would attain that level of self-assurance in handling the pupils. She could only hope.

Kim felt a presence beside her before she turned and saw him. Nick James frowned at her unpleasantly, inky eyes inscrutable.

"Something you wanted, Mr. James?"

"Yeah, why did you sic the Gestapo on me, lady? That was real nasty."

"What happened to my car was real nasty too."

"So what? Keep your insurance paid up."

"More threats?" Kim kept her voice calm but inwardly, she was furious.

"Me? No way! I got a week's central detention and a promise of suspension if I get in trouble again. You and the big kahuna will both get yours, but I won't have a thing to do with it."

She had begun to shake with anger. The youth glowered at her in return but walked away without further comment. It was then that Kim realized she'd stepped back against the cinder block wall of the cafeteria when she involuntarily retreated from Nick James. She felt something sticky on the back of her suit jacket, brought her hand around and took away some rancid-smelling butter. Oh, yuck! The jacket would need to be dry-cleaned before it could be worn again. Between the tires and the clothing, Nick James was getting to be an expensive problem, one she could ill afford.

She watched Nick walk over to a girl from his English class. He and Anita Cummings engaged in conversation. Then he sat down beside Anita and put his arm around her. Pale and mousy, Anita looked pleased and grateful for his attention. Too bad. She was really a very nice girl and reasonably intelligent. In fact, she was only in basic skills English because of truancy; Anita was way behind simply because she was absent so often.

Getting involved with Nick James could only lead to added problems for her.

The fact that Anita entered her class holding hands with Nick James that afternoon did little to relieve Kim's mind of concern for the girl. However, this was soon replaced with another kind of anxiety when just a few minutes into her lesson, Hank Anderson entered her classroom and took a seat at the rear. In his hand was a pen and notebook. She realized he'd come to observe her lesson, to sit in judgment on her teaching performance. She immediately felt a sense of resentment.

She told herself to forget his presence and shut out everything but teaching the lesson itself. "Since today is October first, I thought we'd begin with a unit on mystery and horror fiction. These books I've given out have famous stories in them. Many of you are familiar with Edgar Allan Poe. I decided we'll begin by reading part of *The Telltale Heart* aloud together. I'll start while you follow along in your books." Will had told her how much her students would love a good horror story. "The more gruesome, the better. Stephen King rules with these young vampires." Will might be cynical, but she'd found his teaching advice to be sound.

Kim began to read dramatically. Just as the class was settling in, a crashing sound came at the door. In rode Emory Dunne whirling around in his wheelchair, scattering furniture noisily as he smashed into unoccupied as well as occupied desks.

"Hey, man, watch it," Billy Kramer warned. He might have said much worse, but a glance at the acting principal sitting in the rear of the room subdued further comment.

Kim handed Emory a book and pointed to the page number written on the blackboard. "You're very late to class. We'll discuss the matter at the end of the period." She went back to reading the story without further comment, determined that

Emory was not going to get the excuse he wanted to disrupt her class further. She focused on the reading.

In general, the class was cooperative and quiet. Nick James was surly and refused to read aloud but he caused no real problem, merely putting his head down on the desktop. When Kim ended the oral part of the lesson, she asked the students to finish reading the story silently on their own. Then she passed out copies of story guide questions they would be required to answer, all the time aware of Hank Anderson sitting there at the back of the classroom judging her ability to teach. Occasionally, he would be jotting notes for a formal report.

When the bell finally ended the period and the other students left, Emory Dunne went charging toward the door. Kim moved directly in his path, blocking his exit.

"Hey, what are you doing?" Emory obviously wasn't used to anyone standing in his way.

"I said you'd have to explain why you were so late."

"Look at me? Did you think I could sprint to your class?" The tone of voice was more self-pitying then hostile.

"You were ten minutes late." Kim had her hands on her hips and wasn't about to back down.

"I had to use the bathroom. I need help even in the handicapped one, and there wasn't nobody around. Satisfied?"

"Just don't make a habit of being late to class, Mr. Dunne."

"What difference does it make anyway?" He glowered at her.

"It matters to me. And no more knocking into furniture or other people."

"It's the only fun I get. You should see them all fly when I get really moving. I bet this baby could win me a prize at the Indi Five Hundred." He patted his motorized wheelchair affectionately.

"Please show more consideration for others."

"Like they do for me?" Emory didn't say another word but

shot through the open door.

She decided the boy had a cruel, possibly homicidal streak. However, she had other things to worry about at the moment. Mr. Anderson was approaching her.

"I suppose you're going to accuse me of picking on a handicapped child?" Kim hurled an accusing look in Hank Anderson's direction.

He threw up his hands. "Hey, I'm not on the attack here. Got a few minutes?"

She nodded. "This is my prep period."

"Anyone else using this classroom now?"

"No. I usually stay in here and work until my next class arrives."

"Okay, so that means we can have a private conversation. I thought you read well. They enjoyed that part of the lesson. The students were totally with you."

Her body began to relax a little. "They were really into the part about the heart being cut out. Doesn't say much for humanity, does it? Like the way people stop to watch an accident? Morbid curiosity I guess. Probably the top-rated TV show would be an execution. Forgive me. I seem to be babbling."

"Why don't you sit down?"

She hesitated, so he pulled out a chair for her.

"That was a good choice. Students enjoy gory stories. In fact, that book of mystery and supernatural tales seems to work very well."

"I can't take credit for the choice," she said. "Will Norgood suggested it. He thought it might break the ice, get unwilling readers interested. The stories are simplified in vocabulary so there won't be much frustration when the students read them."

Mr. Anderson frowned. "Just how good a friend is Norgood?"

Kim stared at him in surprise. The tone was clearly disapproving.

"He's been very helpful to me. Why don't you like Will? He's a good teacher, isn't he?"

Hank Anderson looked uncomfortable and didn't appear willing to answer her question. "About Emory Dunne . . ."

"I knew you'd come back to that." She eyed him warily.

"He is physically challenged, as the politically correct jargon goes. Emory suffers from a degenerative neuromuscular disease. But it's more than that. Like Nick and Billy, he has a bad home life. There's only a mother, no father. She works, but I understand there's a drug problem. A younger brother is supposed to see to Emory's needs. Unfortunately, like a lot of kids, he's often unreliable. There are nights when Emory doesn't leave his wheelchair because no one helps him into bed." He saw her expression and hastened to continue. "I'm not telling you this so you'll make special allowances for the boy. In all honesty, I think you handled him just right. Emory has all kinds of psychological as well as physical problems. Letting him run wild and take advantage won't help him or the other students. He needs a firm hand. You've got some very difficult students to contend with, and no one knows that better than me. I really mean it when I say I want to help you."

She gave an imperceptible nod.

"What about Nick?" he asked. "Any further trouble today?"

There was the slightest hesitation on her part. "Not directly, but I have a feeling that he might try something sneaky."

Hank Anderson frowned again. "Keep me posted."

She gave him a small smile. "I will. Thank you."

"By the way, Mrs. Pierson told me what a great job you're doing in the library. She said you've done wonderful preparation and teaching of library orientation for the freshmen."

"She does most of it. I've just done a few of the classes."

"Well, apparently you've made a very positive impression there. Leona wishes you were with her all day long."

"I have to admit I wish the same thing. I'm a lot more comfortable in a library than in a classroom. Well, thank you again." She felt embarrassed. Sometimes it was easier to accept criticism than praise.

For a moment, there was an awkward silence between them.

"I thank you, Ms. Reynolds," he said with pronounced formality. "You'll have a written copy of this observation in your mailbox in two days." His manner was austere and stiff, but courteous.

Kim stood up with well-mannered politeness, just as tense and uncomfortable as he was. He looked as if he wanted to say something more but instead left quickly without uttering another word. Maybe the ice was breaking and they would manage to get along. She could only hope so.

# CHAPTER SEVEN

"Are your ears burning, my dear?"

Kim studied Will Norgood's long, bony face. His sardonic smile piqued her curiosity.

"Am I missing something?"

"Our fearless leader is watching you attentively. Haven't you noticed?" Will's smile was decidedly crooked. "You'd be easy prey for a stalker. You must sharpen your powers of perception." If Will only knew! She spent half of her life toning down her awareness.

Kim looked up and saw that Will was correct; Hank Anderson was staring directly at her. Heat rushed to her cheeks. Quickly, she looked down at her sandwich.

"Have we done something naughty?" Will clucked his tongue.

She could understand why his type of humor irritated others. Kim studied her hands.

"Eat your lunch, dear heart. It wasn't my intention to upset you." He pursed his thin lips. "However, a word of advice. As a new teacher here it is much to your benefit to keep a decidedly low profile. That is my lesson for today in survival one-oh-one."

She studied Will's sharp, alert features. "Mr. Anderson offered to help me with Nick James. There was a problem."

"The lad is a piece of work all right. But you should ask me what to do if he continues to be a problem. The best thing is to call the father immediately. The man has even a meaner disposition than the son and will beat the young hooligan into a blob of protoplasm if school behavior is unacceptable. James will always test a teacher to the limits, especially a younger one who happens to be new. As for our noble new principal, it is best that the golden boy not know you ever have discipline problems."

Her peanut butter sandwich stuck in her throat. "Why shouldn't I take him up on his offer to help?"

"Because my naive, innocent girl, all administrators write off as weak and incompetent any inexperienced teacher who comes to them for help with discipline. As Jack London maintained, only the strong survive."

"Mr. Anderson was very supportive after observing my class the other day."

"Ha! Already observing you? And this early in the year? Now I understand why he's keeping a careful watch on you. He thinks you're the weakest link. You must disappoint him. Have as little to do with him as possible. If he should ask you how things are going, respond with a cheerful smile and say that everything is just fine. It's the only way. Otherwise, the local gunslinger will add a notch, namely your hide."

"All right," she agreed but wasn't convinced that Will was right.

"Trust me, sweet girl, Will knows best." He patted her hand the way some people petted their dogs. "Now let's practice a bit. A psychotic terrorist, ergo Nick James, enters your classroom with machine gun and grenades ready. What action do you take?"

"Get on the intercom and call for help?"

"No, dear one, you handle the problem as best you can yourself. You push Emory at him."

"Now I can't take you seriously."

"Actually, what I'm saying is serious. Take care of your own problems whenever possible. I'll suggest some innovative methods, perhaps a bit unorthodox but guaranteed to work."

Kim bit down thoughtfully on her lower lip. Was he right? Will did know quite a lot about teaching and the school pecking order. And she was at the bottom of the food chain. Maybe her initial decision to avoid the principal had been the correct one. She did need to hold on to her job and avoid trouble.

"Thank you for your guidance," she said.

"Come to me if you have any problems in the future."

"I'll do that."

Will looked very pleased. "We shall be the best of friends," he said.

That afternoon as Kim worked on her lessons for the following day, Evie Gardner walked into the empty classroom.

"Kim, is it all right if I come in?"

"Of course. I'm always happy to see you. Did you want to talk to me about something in particular?"

Evie hesitated, licking dry lips. "The thing is, well, I wanted to talk to you about my dad."

Kim tensed. "Evie, I don't think that's such a good idea under the circumstances."

"Why not? I mean he's really miserable. Don't you care?" Evie glared at her, pointing an accusing finger.

Kim swallowed hard. "Of course, I care. I care a lot. I've been feeling pretty unhappy myself. But your father is a mature, intelligent man. He'll handle the situation."

Evie shook her head, and her honey-colored hair swirled around her heart-shaped face. "My mother manipulates people. She's not like you, Kim. She's very self-centered and self-absorbed. You know, like the wicked stepmother in Snow White. She's always looking at herself in a mirror, admiring herself. She and my dad were high school sweethearts. He was totally loyal to her all those years. But she cheated on him. Now she's back because her boyfriend dumped her. She's got no job, no money, no other place to go. I overheard her tell Dad. She tried to make him feel sorry for her. So he let her stay at the house. He's got such a big heart. I'd have kicked her out."

Kim looked up, wanting to ask the question yet unable. But Evie was perceptive, like her father. She seemed to know. "He's not sleeping with her. He won't. He loves you. She's got the guest room. Kim, please call my dad. Talk to him."

"Evie, your mother does want your father back. She wants her old life. It was obvious to me. If they were really divorced, then it would be different. As matters stand, I would be the other woman."

"It wouldn't be like that."

"Yes, it would. Your mother obviously has decided that she wants to reconcile with your dad. That's something they have to work out between them. No third parties should be involved."

Tears formed like mist in the young girl's gray eyes, so like those of her father. "Kim, you've got to stop her. You're the only one who can. She's a bad person. She's evil, right down to the dark roots of her blond hair. She'll only make our lives awful again. She'll lie and tell us how much she cares about us. Then we'll let our guard down and trust her again. But she'll leave us first chance she gets. I haven't forgotten how awful it was when she left us before. I never will."

Kim ached for Evie's suffering, for Jeanie as well, and most of all, for Mike. "I really do want to help, but I can't. It's not up to me to interfere. It would be wrong." She reached out to Evie, but the girl pulled angrily away.

"You say the words, but you don't really care or you'd do something. You'd stop her. You say you love my dad, but you don't really. It's just empty words. If you cared, you'd find a way to get rid of her." Evie ran from the classroom sobbing.

Kim felt an agonizing pain shoot through the vicinity of her heart. Her personal life was in shambles and she didn't have a clue what to do about it. She felt completely lost. Taking the high road could be awfully lonely.

Back to School Night the second week in October was not something Kim looked forward to with any kind of anticipation. Parents had a right to expect to meet their children's teachers. Still, it was unfortunate that she had to cancel the evening school class she taught at the university. Her expository writing course, although only a freshman requirement, was composed of adults who were conscientious about learning. She felt as if she were cheating them, letting them down.

Since it would have been a waste of time to drive back and forth to her apartment again, she stayed in her classroom and graded papers for several hours. The time passed slowly and she began to feel drained of energy. She'd left an extra sandwich in the faculty room refrigerator and decided to take a break at five-thirty. Schoolwork put away, she headed downstairs stifling a heavy yawn.

The deserted school seemed eerie. Lights had been turned off as an energy-saving measure. In the corridor, she heard footsteps moving in her direction. For a moment, grim fantasies of Nick James with a gleaming switchblade in his hand ready to pounce on her bolted through Kim's brain. So much for Mother Courage. She saw no one. Too much Edgar Allan Poe, she supposed, but then her mind was always filled with grim notions.

As the sounds grew closer, Kim let out an involuntary gasp. Suddenly, someone was upon her and she turned, blinking rapidly.

"Sorry, I didn't mean to frighten you." The dim overhead lights caught the glint of golden hair.

"You didn't. I was just a little startled. I didn't think anyone else would be here at this hour."

He flashed a smile that made him look almost boyish. "I was just walking around inspecting the place to make sure we're ready for the hordes of parents tonight. What about you? Why are you still here? Just can't get enough of the place?"

She cast her eyes downward. "I decided to just hang around until Back to School Night is over."

"What about dinner?" Was his look one of actual concern, or was her imagination playing tricks again?

When she mentioned her waiting sandwich, frown lines appeared around his mouth. "I think we can do a little better than that. There are some very nice restaurants nearby."

She shook her head. "I really don't know this part of town."

"I'd be happy to escort you."

She felt totally embarrassed. "I didn't mean, that is to say, I wasn't hinting . . ."

"I have to eat too and I get tired of eating dinner alone."

She really didn't think for one minute he was the type of man who had to eat alone unless it was what he wanted.

"The truth is, I'm on a tight budget. I can't afford to eat out very often." The admission was humiliating but necessary.

"I intend this to be my treat. Lake Shore hospitality should extend to new staff."

She knew charity when she saw it or heard it. One had to maintain some sense of pride. "No, Mr. Anderson. I appreciate your offer but I couldn't possibly accept."

She could see that he wanted to question her regarding what she'd told him, but much to her relief, he seemed to think better of it. He viewed her thoughtfully.

"Please be frank with me, Ms. Reynolds. Is it that you really don't want my company? I make you uncomfortable, don't I?"

She found her face flushing. "No, Mr. Anderson, that isn't the case at all." God, she really was a rotten liar!

He smiled again. "Glad to hear it. Then there's only one possible solution to our little problem. Don't worry. I won't insist on dinner at a restaurant. I respect your decision. But you deserve better than a cold sandwich for dinner. Meet me in my office in ten minutes."

He walked away, not allowing any further comment or any chance for her to refuse. There was nothing to do but make a quick stop in the ladies' room to repair her appearance and then go downstairs to his office.

As she expected, his secretary was gone for the day. With some trepidation, she knocked at the door to his private office and was told to come in. He was just getting off the telephone.

He stood, no longer in shirtsleeves but dressed in a tailored navy blue suit jacket, his white shirt accessorized by a bold print tie. He looked every inch the successful administrator, confident, self-assured. She could easily picture him as a top-level executive at some vast corporate conglomerate.

"Ready?" he asked. His eyes swept over her.

When she assented, he took her arm in a supportive, solicitous gesture. The car he led her to was not the blue Corvette she'd seen him drive before; instead, a shiny silver Mercedes awaited. She looked at him questioningly.

"Belongs to my father," he explained with a smile that displayed his dimpled cheek and strong white teeth. "Dad's out of the country right now so I alternate vehicles. Cars are like people, if they don't get their exercise, they lose their ability to perform."

He opened the passenger side of the automobile for her. Kim could not recall ever being in such an elegant vehicle.

"Have you seen much of this side of the township?" He started the engine.

She shook her head again, not trusting herself to speak and hoping he was unaware of how awkward and out of place she felt.

"I'll take you on the scenic route then," he said.

She wanted to ask where they were going but it seemed easier not to do so. Instead, she sat back, enjoying the drive as best she could.

"This is Sunrise Lake in all its glory. This road follows the lake all around."

They snaked along the serpentine road and headed up a steep incline. At the highest point overlooking the lake, he drove onto a shoulder, a lookout point, where they could pull over and admire the view.

"Breathtaking," she managed to say.

He seemed pleased with her response. Back in the Mercedes, he continued to drive until they passed through a gated drive. She had the sense of being on a private estate. The house at the end of the tree-lined road was a huge white colonial with an impressive circular driveway where Hank Anderson parked the car. Kim was reminded of pictures she'd seen of antebellum southern mansions. Then again, this was the wealthy part of the township.

"There's someone I'd like you to meet."

He helped her out of the car and guided her through the large vestibule of the house. Her impression was one of size and space and shiny marble flooring. A large, crystal chandelier hung overhead.

"Dory," he called out, "we're here."

A plump, middle-aged woman with wispy gray hair approached them. She was drying her hands on an apron as she turned to Kim. "It's nice to meet you. When Hank called to say he was bringing home company for dinner, I was so pleased. He's alone too much." The woman extended her hand.

"Ms. Reynolds, this is Dory Tracey, my father's housekeeper, but really more a member of the family, as you can probably tell by her comments."

Dory gave her a welcoming smile.

"Please call me Kim," she said, responding to the warmth in the older woman's hazel eyes.

"Well, now, aren't you pretty! Just what this young fellow needs in his life."

He gave the housekeeper a quelling look. "Why don't you just say whatever pops into your mind?"

Dory smiled, clearly unfazed by the putdown. "Thanks, I do believe I will. I've always spoken freely and don't think I'm about to change at my age."

They chatted for a few minutes, making polite small talk. Kim gathered that Dory had worked for the family for many years. She seemed devoted to Hank Anderson and his father. There was no mention of Hank's mother, however, and Kim wondered about that.

Dinner was served in a large, formal dining room, although only she and Hank were present. Kim was seated across from Hank and found herself studying him without meaning to do so. She looked away in discomfort when his eyes fixed on her own.

The meal was simple but superb and caused Kim to relax a bit. Fresh fruit cup, marinated chicken breasts in wine sauce, wild rice, and a large vegetable salad. Kim complimented Dory, who flushed with pleasure as she began clearing the table. Kim offered to help with the dishes but Dory wouldn't hear of it.

When the housekeeper served them coffee, Hank refused any dessert. "Unless you'd like something?" He turned to Kim.

She shook her head. "Thank you. That was a very satisfying meal. I'm quite full."

"You didn't eat much," Dory said.

"I don't usually," she said, starting to feel uncomfortable again.

For a moment, she caught Hank Anderson looking at her, assessing her. Then his expression shuttered. She supposed that he too felt uneasy.

"Would you like to take a walk around the grounds?"

He led her through the back hall and out to the patio. She let out a small gasp of surprise.

"It's drop-dead gorgeous! So I guess teaching pays better than I realized."

"Not exactly."

"Let me guess: you make *mucho dinero* selling bootleg term papers over the Internet."

He smiled. "Nope, not that either."

"I can't imagine anyone not being happy living in such a beautiful place. I should pinch myself just to make certain I'm not dreaming."

Living here most of his life had obviously left Hank Anderson unaffected by the beauty of the place. She supposed he took it all for granted. Kim, on the other hand, was taking it all in, including the manicured landscape of the gardens, which was overshadowed by the view of the lake below from their vantage on top of the hill. She commented on the in-ground pool, the tennis court, even the marble statuary and benches.

"I've never seen anything like this," she said. "I'm really impressed. You're very fortunate to live this way."

He shuffled awkwardly. "None of it is mine," he hastened to explain. "It all belongs to my father. I don't even live in the house. I rent the guest cottage from him. I won't take anything from him. I pay my own way."

"I admire you for that." She gave him a reassuring smile.

"What's your home like?"

A wave of sadness swept over her. "I don't have a home anymore." She hoped she didn't sound pathetic. She fixed her eyes on the view and avoided looking at him. "Our old house is in the process of being sold. My mother now lives in Florida."

"I'm sorry." He seemed genuinely sympathetic.

"It doesn't matter really. My childhood wasn't a particularly pleasant one. I wouldn't go back to the house unless I had to."

She turned back and looked at him, then fixed a determined smile on her face, deciding a change in subject was called for. "I was told that you were a wonderful teacher. Do you miss that now?"

"I like being in the classroom working directly with students. I felt that I could make a difference. But as an administrator I can make an even bigger difference. That is, if I do the job right."

"I have a feeling you'll do just that." Their eyes met and held.

"I'd like to spend less of my time dealing with discipline. It's the part I enjoy least."

"I can understand that. Did you have much contact with Sam Granger, the boy who died recently? Was he a discipline problem?"

He threw a started glance in her direction. "Sammy had some issues, but I thought he was working them out. Why do you ask?"

"Just wondering."

"What did you hear?" He suddenly looked tense.

She had the distinct impression that Hank Anderson was sensitive on the subject. The boy's death had obviously disturbed him. Well, they had that in common. She shook her head, not wanting to comment further.

Hank Anderson looked relieved. "How about you?" he asked, changing the topic of conversation. "Did you really want to be a teacher?"

"I loved school and admired most of my teachers. I think I could have been a very good university professor. I do enjoy British and American literature. But I didn't get accepted into the Ph.D. program. So I opted for a graduate degree in Library

Science. I really enjoy working in a library. I like working with students and teachers, helping them. Reference work is exciting and challenging. The quest for knowledge, well, it's very satisfying."

"Then why are you now working among us mere plebeians instead of in the lofty towers of academia?"

His question hit a sensitive nerve. "In a word, layoffs. We all have to eat."

"Are you hung up on money?"

She gave a small laugh. "No more than most people. When you have money, you don't worry about it. When you need it to survive, then it becomes important."

"Why teach at all if money is a major priority?"

Her eyes searched his face. "I'm not greedy. Besides, I always did want to teach."

"Just not in a high school?"

She bit down on her lower lip and paused, considering her words carefully. "I'm not certain I'm cut out for it."

"Give yourself a chance. You're showing real potential."

"You'll give me the year, won't you?"

"At least." His look lingered.

She studied the view before them from the hilltop. "Look at that beautiful sunset over the lake. It's a blood sun. What an incredible sight. I don't think I've ever seen anything so magnificent before."

He studied her face. "Neither have I."

She felt her face become hot. "Thank you for the wonderful dinner and for sharing all this with me."

"Oh, it's been my pleasure."

She couldn't help but wonder what he was thinking. No doubt that Hank Anderson was a complex man. She sensed he too had many secrets.

# CHAPTER EIGHT

The school was still deserted when they pulled into the parking lot. Kim was actually relieved to return to the peaceful sanctuary of her own classroom. Her emotions were in a chaotic state. She'd been warned to keep her distance from Hank Anderson, yet she'd just had dinner with him at his house. She could just imagine how Will would react if he knew. No point thinking about it. She needed time to get herself together for the coming ordeal.

However, not many parents actually came to see her. She discovered that few parents of basic skills students wanted to meet their children's teachers, particularly since she taught seniors whose parents had heard it all said before. As for her poetry classes, this was an elective subject for seniors and didn't seem to generate much parental interest either. On the whole, the children of the parents she did meet were those who never presented problems and always put forth some sort of effort. She could honestly say positive things and be encouraging. The evening passed more quickly then she'd anticipated.

Coffee was being served in the cafeteria. With her classroom empty, Kim decided to have some caffeine so she wouldn't be too tired to drive back to her apartment. She didn't see anyone she knew, which was just as well. She planned to leave as soon as possible. There wasn't enough coffee in the universe to fend off her killer exhaustion.

"I thought you'd be here tonight." The plastic cup slipped

from her hand, splattering coffee on her shoes and the floor. "Sorry, I didn't mean to startle you," Mike said.

He grabbed some napkins, just as she did. Their hands touched for a brief moment as he helped her clean up. She felt a shock of heightened awareness, but did her best to ignore it.

"Where's Evelyn?"

"She didn't come. Evie didn't want her here tonight."

"I see." But she didn't really. Mike's relationship with his wife was all so confusing and disturbing.

"I was hoping we could talk." His eyes snagged hers.

She tried to look away, not to look at him at all. She didn't want to see the strong features of the man she'd made love with, who she'd thought she just might be able to share the rest of her life with.

"I don't think it's a good idea for us to talk, Mike. You're still a married man. Unless Evelyn signed the papers?"

Mike frowned and shook his head. "Not yet."

"Then we really shouldn't be talking."

"Not even as friends? Weren't you the lady who once told me that a person could never have too many friends?"

She ignored the killer smile and met his steady gray gaze. "You think we can honestly be just friends? Don't try to fool yourself or me."

"Lt. Gardner?" A woman with frizzy salt and pepper hair moved between them.

"That's right," Mike responded politely.

"I'm Miranda's grandmother. You might not remember me. Your daughter Evie and Randi shared a history class together in middle school, and you were kind enough to bring Randi home when the girls studied at your house."

"Of course, I remember," he said. "How have you been?"

"Well, to tell the truth, not so good lately. My grandson, Sammy, he died not too long ago. There's been a police detective investigating, a black lady. She thinks he was murdered."

Kim noted the troubled expression on the woman's face, the shadows under her eyes.

"I'm sorry to hear that," Mike said. He briefly touched her hand in a gesture of sympathy.

"The thing is, I think maybe I didn't do right by the boy. My daughter and her husband got a divorce some years back. Truth be told, he left her when he found out she had cancer. Just took off. Then my daughter died and I was left to take care of the kids. Well, I work at a department store. You know how that is: long hours, low pay. The kids were on their own a lot. Randi's a good girl. But Sammy, he was kind of lost. No male role model to look up to. He refused to use his father's last name, used his mother's maiden name instead. He was bitter about his father leaving the way he did. Sammy even started hanging with some rough characters. Wouldn't listen to me when I said they were no good."

"Did you tell all this to Detective St. Croix?" Mike asked.

"Well, sure I did. She went and wrote everything down in a neat little black notebook. I thought maybe you could talk about it with her."

"I'll confer with Detective St. Croix and get back to you, Mrs. Granger."

"Thank you. I'd feel better if you looked into things."

"No problem," Mike assured her. "I'll do whatever I can to help find out what happened to your grandson."

"Sammy was once a very good boy and a good student. All that changed after his mother died. I wish I could have done more for him."

Kim saw the woman's lower lip tremble and thought she might be close to tears.

"Detective St. Croix and Lieutenant Gardner are the best at

finding things out," Kim said, her manner reassuring and compassionate.

Mike said good night as the bell rang and then he left to meet another of Evie's teachers.

Mrs. Granger smiled at her. "Are you a teacher here?" she asked.

Kim introduced herself. "Your grandson died at Raceway Park. I'm the person who found his body. I am very sorry for your loss."

Mrs. Granger accepted Kim's expression of condolence with a slight nod of her head.

"Did Sammy go to the raceway alone?"

Mrs. Granger was thoughtful. "He might have. I'm not sure. He had an old motorcycle he'd fixed up and was proud of. We fought about that. I thought it was too dangerous to go riding around on. He wouldn't listen to me. Called me a frightened old lady. But he had those nasty friends, and I couldn't help worrying about him."

"Who were these friends?" Kim asked.

"Two boys mainly. They were in his classes. One was named Nick James. The other boy was Billy Kramer. I didn't like either of them. They were disrespectful. Troublemakers, both of them."

Kim almost agreed out loud with Mrs. Granger but caught herself. She realized that would have been very unprofessional on her part. Yet she must say something. Kim glanced around. No one was watching or listening to their conversation. She reasoned she could speak openly.

"You should tell the police about that. I'm certain Detective St. Croix will be interested."

"Well, if you think so."

"I do," Kim said emphatically. "And again, I'm really sorry for the loss of your grandson."

"Thank you," Mrs. Granger said in a choked voice.

Kim had found that poor boy's body. She'd felt him die. They were connected. Kim very much wanted to help find his killer. However, she would leave the investigation in Bert's hands. Bert was a good policewoman, a professional law enforcement agent, unlike herself. Bert would take care of it. But that didn't mean she couldn't help when and if it became necessary.

She saw Mike again shortly before leaving that evening. He stopped her in the hall.

"Evie's teachers claim she's been withdrawn in class. I think our home situation is having a really negative effect on her."

"I'm so sorry to hear that."

"What about you? How's the job going?"

She thought about her problems with Nick James and shrugged. "All right, I guess, a few problems here and there."

Mike's forehead wrinkled as he studied her. "It appears I didn't do you any favors helping you get the job here."

"It's just a couple of students out to test the new teacher. It'll be okay."

"Maybe. Maybe not. Come to me if I can make things easier in any way. Don't stand on ceremony. I know how independent you are, but I am your friend."

Could ex-lovers simply be friends? Kim wasn't convinced of that. She decided not to tell Mike about Nick's threats or the slashed tires. Mike would insist on doing something about it and she didn't want him involved. She didn't need any further complications in her life.

During the next few weeks, Kim's classes became easier to handle. Nick James never worked in class, but if he showed up at all, he generally put his head down on the desk and went to sleep. When Nick was present, Billy Kramer followed his example. Of course, she allowed a really professional teacher would not have permitted this behavior, but her own feeling was as long as she could teach those who were actually willing to learn, the situation was tolerable.

She did have to draw the line, however, when Nick showed up one day flashing an iPod.

"Man, that is so cool," Billy said admiringly. He reached out his hand, but Nick pulled it away.

"Nobody touches this but me."

"Then put it away, Nick. It doesn't belong in this classroom."

He didn't argue with her, but he gave her a killing look. Kim did her best not to shudder.

Emory Dunne was often absent; however, that was due to illness. When he came to class, he did try to listen and participate. Her control of the basic skills classes had improved.

As to her poetry classes, her own enthusiasm for the subject matter had proved infectious—that is, for all except one student. Betsy Peters wore a sour expression to class when she came at all. Unlike Kim's basic skills English students who either cut class or were often absent from school, Betsy was a yearbook editor and always presented a pass from the faculty advisor. But regardless, she missed so much work that when the time came to take a major test on poetic terminology and do a poetry analysis, the girl failed. For the first marking period interim report, Betsy Peters was the only poetry student to earn a grade of F.

One day, Morgana Douglas came in to observe the poetry class that Betsy attended. Kim looked up in mild surprise.

"I'm giving a test today, Ms. Douglas. Maybe you'd like to come back tomorrow when I'll actually be teaching?"

The English supervisor gave her a tight little smile. "No, I saw that you were giving a test today from your lesson plans. Give me a test copy, please, so I can sit here and review it."

Kim thought the request was odd but she wasn't about to

argue with the supervisor. Morgana Douglas sat down in the rear of the classroom and began studying the test with a deep frown. When she wrote, there was a ferocious look on her face, like a lion gnawing on an antelope. Kim wasn't the only one to notice it. Betsy Peters was watching and smiled broadly. Kim could not help but note the look of smug self-satisfaction that crossed the girl's normally dour face. It troubled her.

The following morning, Kim learned that she was right to be concerned. A scourging observation appeared in her mailbox. She read the words with a rising sense of indignation and then anger. She'd been accused of grading unfairly, of giving tests too difficult for comprehension and not commensurate with the ability level of senior high school students. Ironically, this was the one area where she'd felt some sense of confidence and expertise.

At lunch that day, she told Will Norgood what had happened. He listened in silence and then proceeded to offer his usual high level of insight.

"Off hand, I'd say that our illustrious chairperson is tap-dancing on your reputation for a reason. Have you offended any students with important parents?"

"I failed a girl named Betsy Peters in the class Morgana observed."

"Ah, now that explains it. Betsy Peters's father just happens to be on the school board. Our former dancer turned educator sucks up to board members. That's what got her into her position of power in the first place. I see one of two alternatives. You can crawl to Morgana dearest and apologize abjectly, telling her you will mend your evil ways. Then proceed to give the Peters brat all A's."

"I have to say that doesn't hold much appeal. What's the alternative?"

He gave her a wry smile. "I thought not. Then again, you can always tell Morgana where to go and dramatically quit your job."

"I'm definitely not an extremist. Committing career suicide is not my thing. Isn't there some sensible middle ground that won't force me to slit my wrists?"

"Certainly," he took her hand in his. "You can always let me handle the matter for you."

"I couldn't allow you to do that."

He smiled lopsidedly through narrowed lips. "Of course, you could. I know where the bodies are buried, figuratively speaking, naturally. I can bring a bit of pressure to bear on her ladyship."

"But then she'll be angry at you."

"Dear heart, she already despises me. As I told you, I have the worst program in the department. There isn't much she can do to me that she hasn't already done. Never fear. She and I have done battle before and we will again. I consider this a worthy cause. Just call me Sir William, knight of the lunch table." He patted her hand and then withdrew as the passing bell sounded. "And unlike the godfather, I don't ask for favors in return." His nostrils flared. He was steeled, ready for battle.

Kim found herself relieved that he added the last remark. William as a friend was just fine, but he could never mean more to her than that. Clever man that he was, he seemed to understand and sought to reassure her.

During her prep period, Kim passed the English supervisor's office. She happened to overhear part of a heated argument.

"Well, I never!"

"Oh, please, Morgana, you certainly have, and often. And a lot of people will find out if you don't leave Ms. Reynolds alone."

"That's blackmail!"

"Really? I consider it delicious gossip."

"You mean malicious gossip, you bastard."

Embarrassed, Kim hurried by quickly so neither Will nor Morgana Douglas would know she'd been listening.

As Kim had learned back in high school physics, for every action there was an equal and opposite reaction. Will's threats got Morgana off her back, but the supervisor remained an implacable adversary. That was soon manifest in the next conversation Kim had with her. Ms. Douglas insisted upon discussing the observation.

"Ms. Reynolds, I have reviewed your testing procedures, as you know, and decided not to make an issue of the matter. Nevertheless, I suggest that you make an effort to choose your friends more wisely, nor should you be complaining of unfair treatment. You are a new teacher here and therefore in need of improvement. Don't consider my observation as critical. View it as constructive advice."

"I'm quite willing to explain to you or Betsy Peters's parents why she's failing my course so far for the marking period, Ms. Douglas. The fact is, if she doesn't come to class or put in any effort, she'll probably fail for the entire semester." Kim was satisfied that she'd kept her tone of voice coolly polite.

She hoped the matter was at an end but somehow had a visceral feeling that it wasn't. Ms. Douglas sat poker straight in her chair, her face a mottled purple. Kim quickly excused herself and left.

On cafeteria duty that afternoon, Hank Anderson approached her, a worried expression on his face. She sensed that this had something to do with Morgana Douglas's observation.

Shandra waved to the acting principal from across the large open area and he waved back. Then his eyes turned back to

Kim and he was frowning. She braced herself. Administrators stuck together and supported each other, didn't they? What could she expect?

"How have you been?"

"I'm fine." Terrific! She sounded as upset as she felt. She avoided meeting his gaze.

"I heard something that disturbed me."

"What was it?"

"Morgana Douglas tells me that when you received a critical observation, you complained to Will Norgood who interceded on your behalf. Did you instigate a confrontation between them?"

She felt the anger rise up in her. "I suppose you have to accept and believe whatever your supervisor tells you. So what would be the purpose in my offering an explanation?"

"You could assume that I am a reasonable person and would listen with an open, objective mind." He folded his arms over his chest.

"And pigs fly." Of course, he immediately assumed her to be in the wrong before finding out what had actually happened. "I don't think I care to discuss the matter further."

His dark blue eyes were sharp as the metal edge of a knife. "So you're saying you don't trust me to be fair. Have I got that right?"

"I'm saying before you accuse me of wrongdoing, you should discover the facts."

"That's exactly what I'm trying to do."

The very air seemed to vibrate. She pressed her hands down on one of the metal tables to steady herself. "I am not some inferior, foolish creature that needs to be humored. I understand that you're obligated to support Ms. Douglas. However, I don't believe I did anything wrong."

"Then tell me your side of it."

She was unable to turn away from him. And so, she succinctly told him what had happened. God help her, she did care what he thought of her, although she knew very well that it shouldn't matter.

"I'll talk to Morgana," he said. "It doesn't make a difference which student makes a complaint. Everyone has to be addressed impartially and without bias. As to your association with Will Norgood, I'd watch that if I were you. Morgana isn't that far off when she says he's a troublemaker. He feeds off incidents like this like a vampire sucking blood. I believe there's some sick thrill in it for him."

She raised her chin mutinously. "Will has only shown me friendship. He was trying to help me handle a difficult situation. Please don't think the worse of him for it."

"You should have come to me." His steady stare held her to him.

"Could I have?" She felt like a fly caught in a spider's silken web.

"Always."

"I'm not so sure."

"Then you're wrong." A muscle in his jaw was working.

"Mr. Anderson," she said, finally managing to break the fixed gaze between them, "I better pay attention to my duty."

"I wouldn't have it any other way." His chin jutted forward.

After he stalked out of the cafeteria, it took several minutes and more than a few deep breaths for her to stop trembling.

Shandra joined her. "You okay?"

"I've been better." Kim hadn't meant to do it, but somehow she ended up blurting out the entire story to Shandra. Her friend's intelligent eyes were reflective.

"I think Hank was right. You probably ought to have gone to him in the first place. You shouldn't get yourself caught between Will and Morgana Douglas. Believe me, those two are well matched and have been going at it for years." Shandra glanced around as if to make certain that no student was overhearing their conversation. Then she continued to talk in a low voice. "Will and Morgana had a thing going for a while."

"You mean they were romantically involved?"

Shandra nodded her head. Kim didn't know why it surprised her as much as it did to hear that.

"Isn't she a little old for him?"

"Sure, but that doesn't have much to do with anything. She's a cougar, I guess. It was going on when I started working here. Morgana hadn't been a widow for very long. I suppose she wanted some comforting. How do you think Will got to know so much personal stuff about her? Anyhow, they fell out in a big way. You know how they are, both very opinionated and acerbic. They've been at each other's throats ever since."

There was so much Kim didn't know about the people she was working with. "I feel like someone who's stepped into quicksand."

"The thing is, you have to do your own thinking. Don't allow yourself to fall completely under anybody's influence, even me. As for Hank, he doesn't take sides until he's got the facts straight. Anyway, I think he likes you." Shandra smiled at her.

"I doubt that." It wouldn't matter, regardless. She was definitely not looking for a new relationship. Her life was messed up enough.

"It's okay if you like Hank. You wouldn't be human if you didn't find the man attractive. Good luck. He needs a woman in his life. That man works much too hard and takes life too seriously. Nothing like a good relationship between a man and a woman to add perspective to a person's life."

"You sound like you're speaking from personal experience."

"Not as much experience as I'd like," Shandra said with a wry smile. "I'm still looking for Mr. Right. Not that I wouldn't have snatched Hank up in a minute if he'd noticed me, but we're just friends." Shandra let out a deep sigh.

"Well, as someone recently reminded me, a person can never have too many friends."

"Or be too thin," Shandra agreed. She sighed again. "I'll have to work on both of those."

"I hope you'll consider me a friend," Kim said.

"Oh, I plan on it. And maybe you can give me a few pointers on how you manage to keep your weight down."

"That's easy—aggravation. But you're not fat."

"My mother calls it pleasantly plump. Unfortunately, there's nothing pleasant about it. If I don't watch what I eat, I'll be confused for the Goodyear Blimp."

After their talk, Kim felt better. Shandra obviously had her own insecurities, but she was a good teacher and would be a good friend. Yet Kim couldn't help thinking there probably would never be anything resembling a polite relationship between Hank Anderson and herself. The emotions he aroused in her were turbulent and contradictory. She promised herself not to think of him further. She again promised herself she'd do her best to avoid him.

That afternoon after working until five at her desk, Kim got into her car and tried to start the engine. It wouldn't turn over. The old car had been stalling out regularly but this was the last straw. However, she could not afford a new car. And even repairs would be terribly expensive. Who was she to call? No way she was going to phone Mike. Those ties had to be severed, at least for the time being; probably for good, she conceded.

She walked back purposefully into the school and headed for the main office. The secretaries were gone for the day, but she managed to locate a phone book. Then Kim realized that she'd left her cell phone in the charger back at the apartment. Of all the days to be without it! She was angry with herself. But anger wasn't helping, was it?

She needed to use a school phone. The problem was, all calls went through the switchboard. She looked at the door to Hank Anderson's office. He would have a phone with an outside line. But she did not want to ask him for favors. Then she remembered the pay phone in the commons area and breathed a sigh of relief. As she quickly turned to leave, Kim accidentally knocked a ceramic pen and pencil holder off the secretary's desk. The crashing sound mortified her and she bent to pick up the pieces. This was definitely not turning out to be one of her better days. Lately, there'd been too many bad days.

"What's going on?" Hank Anderson came hurriedly out of his office. Then he caught sight of her. "I thought you might be a vandal."

"Almost right. I did destroy something." Her cheeks burned in embarrassment.

"It doesn't matter."

"Tell your secretary that tomorrow. I'll certainly pay for it."

"It was nothing special. Don't worry about it."

"She just might feel differently."

Hank Anderson gave her a careful look. This was going badly. Kim could hardly breathe.

# CHAPTER NINE

Kim noticed that Hank Anderson had changed to gray sweats, cut off at the sleeves and knees; he looked very much the athlete.

Abashed, she told him what had happened. "I'm on my way to the commons to phone around and see if I can get someone from a service station out here."

"I'll take a quick look at the car for you," he offered.

"No, that's not necessary."

"Sure it is. Can't have my teachers stuck without transportation, can I?"

When he put it on businesslike terms, she felt less awkward and thanked him politely.

He tried starting the car with no more success than she'd entertained; then he went under the hood and poked around for a while.

"I'm no expert but I think someone fooled around with your wiring system."

Kim thought immediately of her most difficult student, but considered that it was unfair to accuse Nick James when she hadn't seen him do anything to her car.

"Look, one of our graduates is a terrific mechanic. He works close by. Suppose I have him tow the car over there?" Hank's steady eyes focused on hers.

"I guess that would be all right."

"But?" He obviously sensed her hesitation.

"Well, if he can't fix it right away, is there any bus transporta-

95

tion nearby?"

"I'll give you a lift." His voice was calm and reassuring.

"I appreciate the offer, but it's out of the question."

"Is there someone you could call to pick you up?"

She shook her head. "There really isn't anyone."

"Then it's settled." His voice was firm. He squared his jaw. "I'm taking you." His response was somewhat overbearing, and coming from another man she probably would have resented it.

"I don't want you to take charge of me. That is, I don't want to take advantage of you."

"You're not." His reply was brusque and curt yet somehow kind.

And that was the end of it. He just wasn't the sort of man people could refuse for very long; at least, she couldn't.

Lake Shore Auto Repair was a friendly enough place. Jeff Miller seemed to have nothing but respect and admiration for his former math teacher. The young man checked out Kim's car while Hank asked questions and watched him work.

When Jeff finished looking over the car, he came toward her wiping away the perspiration that rolled down his forehead and through the mop of curly copper hair. His hands were covered with grime. "That ol' car of yours isn't in such good shape. Buy it secondhand?"

She indicated she had.

"No offense, but it's a junker."

"It was working fine this morning," Kim said, somehow feeling it necessary to defend her vehicle.

"Yeah, well, like Mr. Anderson thought, someone's been at it."

"So you think my car was vandalized?" Kim asked the mechanic bluntly.

"No question about it."

She and Hank Anderson exchanged looks. It was clear to her that he was thinking the same thing she was. Nick James had likely been at her car. But with his sneaky way of doing things, she had no proof—again.

"You can work your magic on it, can't you?" Hank Anderson was definitely a hard man to refuse.

"I won't have time to start work on it until tomorrow afternoon. Give me a call the day after, and I might have it ready in the morning."

Kim felt panic fill her stomach. "That's impossible. I have no other way to travel."

"Sorry, it's the best I can do."

Hank turned to her. "I'm driving you home."

"No, there must be a bus or train. I could call a cab. I really can't impose on you further."

"This isn't an imposition. I want to help you."

"You shouldn't feel obligated."

"Stop arguing." He gave her a look that would have shut up Oprah.

Still, she'd have stood her ground, but then she looked into his face and saw genuine concern there. Her resolve melted like chocolate on a July afternoon.

On the drive to her apartment, they spoke very little. She considered offering to prepare him dinner but could not imagine serving him a meal in the tiny, cramped alcove that passed for the dining area of her apartment.

"I have no way of properly thanking you," she said, aware that her words sounded very much like an apology. She felt guilty for putting him to so much trouble on her behalf.

His eyes left the road and momentarily flickered to her face. "Wasn't it Emerson who said that the expectation of gratitude is mean?"

"Yes, and he also said we bite the hand that feeds us, but I promise to leave your digits intact."

He threw her a smile. She spoke again only to offer directions from the highway. He played easy listening music on CD, which she suspected was for her benefit. He was clearly sensitive to her feelings and knew she was anything but relaxed.

When they finally pulled up into a parking space close to her building, Hank Anderson turned in her direction. "This is a nice location."

He parked and then stepped around to help her out of the car. The gesture surprised her because she'd expected him to drive away as soon as she got out. But he followed her into the building, and she realized he had every intention of seeing her to the door of the apartment. Kim was about to remark on his courtesy but before she could say a word, he took the key from her hand. It was obvious that he intended to be invited in, and for her to do less would be tantamount to total lack of manners, considering how far out of his way Hank Anderson had gone for her.

It turned out that her upstairs neighbors were home. The two roommates were sitting on garden chairs at the front of the building. She was not at all pleased. Their proximity just increased her embarrassment.

Jessica, ever outspoken, took one look at Hank and put on her most flirtatious smile. "Introduce us, Kim. Does this incredible hunk belong to you exclusively or can he be shared?"

Kim groaned inwardly. But Hank merely smiled at Jessica's aggressive manner, stepped forward, and clasped her hand.

"I work with Kim. Nice to meet both of you." His clear, steady gaze took in both Jessica and Su, who stood back shyly. He told them about the car trouble.

"Tough luck," Jessica said in a sympathetic manner. "What are you going to do?"

Hank Anderson answered before Kim did. "I can't see Ms.

Reynolds commuting from here. There's a place she could stay not far from the school for the next few days. Maybe you could help her pack some things? I think she's a little dazed right now."

Kim stared at him incredulously. How could he just take over her life that way? Why, they hadn't even discussed what she might do. On the drive, she'd been considering taking several personal days off until the car was ready. She trembled with outrage. How dare he make such a decision for her! Yet infuriated as she was with his arbitrary behavior, she wasn't going to discuss the matter in front of her nosy neighbors.

Kim strived for self-control. "I'd like a word with you in private." She wanted to denounce him for the arrogant male chauvinist he'd shown himself to be but knew that would simply create more problems for her.

"There's no need for further discussion," Hank asserted. "I've got the problem all worked out. I'll wait out here while you get your things together."

Jessica's hazel eyes narrowed with interest. Su was also watching intently, her dark, almond-shaped eyes as alert as those of Jessica.

"Why don't we just come in and help you?"

Before Kim knew what was happening, her young neighbors had followed her into the apartment and closed the door.

As soon as the girls were alone, the questions began just as she feared they would.

"So are you going to bed with him?"

"Jes, have you no courtesy?" Su spoke with disapproval.

Jessica's blunt California demeanor was in complete contrast to Su's polite Chinese manners, smacking of traditional propriety and formal upbringing.

"Sorry to disappoint you, but Mr. Anderson is what he said, a co-worker, who also happens to be a Good Samaritan. He's been kind enough to chauffeur me."

Jessica eyed her suspiciously. "I wouldn't blame you if you shacked up with him. He's a total babe, a really hot dude. If you don't want him, then talk me up to him. And keep us informed."

"I'm not shacking up with anyone. I'll be back as soon as my car's out of the shop."

"Can we help you get your stuff together?"

"Not necessary." She hoped they would take the hint and leave but they stayed, watching Kim throw some clothing, underwear, and toiletries together and slip them into her carryall.

There was a rap at the door that startled her.

"Can I suggest taking a bathing suit? The place where you'll be staying has a heated pool."

Jessica's eyes screwed into bullets. Even Su looked downright accusing.

"Hey, I'm not going off on a vacation, but if I were, I'd expect that you'd be happy for me." She was disappointed in their attitude. They were obviously thinking the worst of her, and she resented it. She'd practically been a nun during her time at the university, until she met Mike. Even then, their relationship had been discreet. And here her neighbors were looking at her as though she were selling herself on street corners. Without another word, Kim finished packing her carryall and hurried out of the bedroom, followed closely by Jessica and Su.

Hank insisted on carrying the bag for her, although she told him it wasn't necessary. She was still angry with him.

"Okay, what's wrong?" He tossed her bag in the trunk as soon as they reached his car.

"Thanks to you, my neighbors are thinking all sorts of terrible things about me."

He lifted his gilt brows as he started the engine of the Mercedes and glanced over at her. "Does it matter all that much? I mean, isn't that really their problem? Why should you care?"

"Where are you taking me?"

"To the nicest place in town."

"Then I can't afford it."

"Believe me, you can." He gave her a mysterious look.

They pulled up in front of Hank Anderson's palatial home in slightly under half an hour.

"Not bad," he said, "considering rush-hour traffic."

"You have a lead foot."

"Hardly. I go with the flow." He offered a disarming smile.

It wasn't easy to remain angry with the man—although she'd probably be better off if she could.

"I really can't stay in your home. That would be totally improper."

"Sure you can stay here. I'll make it easy and proper. I'm giving you the guest cottage."

"But isn't that your place?"

"I can stay at the main house for the time being. It's no big deal. No one's there right now. My father's off on his honeymoon with wife number three. When they return, most likely she'll want to live in the Manhattan townhouse. His new lady thinks we're out in the boonies around here. Regular hayseed hicks. She's a city slicker."

Kim wondered about Hank's family but thought it an inappropriate time to ask.

"I just don't feel right about this," she said.

His eyes took on the hard penetration of steel. "Look, there are no motels in town. And Webster Township is spread out. The Lake Shore area is strictly residential. You said something about being on a budget as I recall. Well, hiring cabs to take you from your apartment to school might not be the swiftest move."

She cast her eyes down and confessed. "I was thinking of lying low at the apartment and taking off some personal days until the car is fixed."

"Playing hookey? Sets a bad example for your students. I'm surprised at you, Ms. Reynolds, and a tad disappointed. You wouldn't really want to do that, now would you?" His tone was lightly mocking. "And you never know when you might need those days for something really important."

"I consider this important." She swallowed hard.

"It doesn't look good for a new teacher to take off days in the beginning. Makes people think she's not serious about the job. You did assure me you were a conscientious teacher, didn't you?"

"It doesn't look right for me to be staying at your home. People are bound to get the wrong idea."

"Only if they find out, which they won't. I'm not going to tell them, are you?" His golden brows rose.

"There's another saying of Ben Franklin you may recall: Three can keep a secret if two of them are dead."

"Well, our housekeeper isn't going to tell tales. She doesn't gossip. She's very discreet. So stop worrying. Your reputation is safe."

"Actually," she said, biting down on her lower lip. "I'm thinking you have more to be concerned about in that respect than me."

"I think I'm safe enough, unless you're a convicted felon or a serial killer, which I doubt. You don't have a jealous husband lurking somewhere, do you?"

She shook her head.

"Good. Just decide you're going to be the lady of the manor for a few days. You seem to have the right manners for it, now that I think about it."

"Why are you doing this for me?" She looked up at him, her

eyes wide and searching.

"I'm the acting principal, remember? It's my responsibility to keep my staff in school and keep morale up."

*Morale maybe, but what about morals?* Yet even as she considered that, Kim knew she was safe with him. Her sensitivity told her that this man was someone she could trust, a man of integrity, of honor. The only other man she knew with similar attributes was Mike Gardner. But she really didn't want to let herself think about Mike. It hurt too much.

Hank Anderson lifted her bag and carried it to the guest cottage, which she soon discovered was a charming, miniature house. The interior was decorated in a masculine manner. She could even smell his woodsy after-shave wafting in the air. Brown leather chairs, a beige sofa, and chocolate carpeting comfortably furnished the small living room.

"The kitchen's tiny but decently stocked. Dory sees to that. As to the bedroom . . ." His voice trailed off.

She felt her heart beat more rapidly and her cheeks start to burn.

"Ms. Reynolds? Are you all right?"

"What? Sorry, were you saying something?"

"I was just mentioning that I'll remove some of my things, so that you'll have room for yours."

"No, please don't bother. I don't want to disturb or inconvenience you. Since I won't be here very long, why not take just what you need for the time being? I don't need very much space."

Hank Anderson's bedroom was very much like him: neat, organized, conservative. But there was a manly quality about the room that was appealing. He went to a closet, removed a few suits, emptied out some shirts and underwear from dresser drawers, and then turned to her.

"Dory goes home by five unless I ask her to stay. She always leaves something ready in the refrigerator. Why don't you unpack while I put some supper out for us on the patio?"

Hank Anderson set out cold pheasant and a pasta salad as he considered what he'd done. God, he'd practically kidnapped Kim Reynolds, and after promising himself that he'd stay away from her. What was wrong with him? If there was anything he prided himself on, it was his common sense. Unfortunately, where Kim Reynolds was concerned, his smarts were lacking. Face it, the part of him doing the thinking was definitely not his brain.

He sensed her presence before seeing her. She'd changed from her neat, boxy work clothes into jeans that hugged her bottom and a Shakespeare t-shirt that outlined her slender curves. Her hair was pulled back into a pony tail with auburn tendrils hanging over each fine-boned cheek. She hardly looked much older than the teenagers she taught.

Kim insisted on helping him set the food onto the plates. He watched her, fascinated by the supple, graceful movements of her hands and body. He liked her natural, unaffected manner, not at all what he expected from the university crowd.

They ate for a while in companionable silence until she looked up and their eyes met.

"You didn't have to do all this for me."

"I want to help you."

He touched her hand. Their eyes held for a moment until she looked away. He felt her hand tremble under his. It seemed important to put her at ease, although the tension between them could hardly be ignored.

"Tell me about yourself. I don't know anything about you. Where do you come from?"

She shrugged. "No place very impressive. I'm a small-town Jersey girl."

"Were you happy as a child?"

"Not really. There was a lot of tension in my family. You could say we had a failure to communicate. My mother kept certain things from me." She pushed an errant strand of hair back from her forehead. "I can't talk about it. Let's just say New Jersey will always be home to me, if not a happy one."

He could hear the loneliness in her voice; a wistful sadness was in her dark brown eyes.

"What about your family? Do they still live around here?"

She lowered those remarkable eyes of hers as if there were something very painful about the topic. "I don't have much of a family. I do keep in touch with my mother though. I call her every Sunday morning."

Talk about mothers never failed to disturb him. "Finish up. We've got frozen yogurt for dessert."

"Just some fruit would be fine."

"Okay, come along with me and we'll select something together."

They raided the refrigerator like children. His rummaging made her laugh. "You look like a pirate going through a treasure chest. All you need is a patch over one eye."

He thought how attractive Kim looked when she relaxed and let down her guard. They were talking more easily now; conversation had begun to flow naturally between them. She no longer seemed strained or tense. He liked being this way with her.

They ended up settling for oranges for dessert. He watched the way she sectioned each part of her orange and the delight she took in sliding individual portions between her lips. As his hands reached forward to pull her into his arms, he fought for control of himself and won. What the hell was he doing? Somehow, he managed to ball his hands into fists and thrust them into his pants pockets. He let out an uneven breath. For the moment, he'd won the battle. But when she insisted on helping him clean up and he watched her bend over in those snug jeans, his eyes followed the lines of her hips, the curve of her nicely rounded derriere with fascination, and he knew his hard-won control was just a temporary reprieve. He'd never been a religious man before but it was enough to make him pray for help.

# CHAPTER TEN

Kim tossed and turned for several hours unable to sleep, which sometimes happened when she was overtired or overstimulated. The scent of Hank Anderson permeated the still air in spite of the fact she'd put fresh linens on the bed. She punched the pillow down and called herself every kind of a fool. Finally, she wrapped her robe tightly around her nightgown and walked outside. She knew the worst thing was just to lie there in bed wondering if sleep would ever come. A little fresh air might free her from the restlessness she felt.

The evening was unusually mild for October. It was as if summer didn't know yet that its time was at an end and had decided to remain. Summer simply refused to die. She could respect that. The grounds looked mysterious shrouded in darkness. The sky above was black velvet sewn with glittering diamond stars.

Kim was walking across the dark landscape in the direction of the well-lit pool when she saw a figure kneeling, a hand circling in the water. The pure perfection of his male form in bathing trunks made her stop in her tracks, catch her breath, and stare in admiration. The night lights of the pool caught the glow of the golden hair that covered his broad expanse of chest. His arms and legs were powerfully muscled, the waist tapered, hips narrow. As she watched, his tall, lean frame came to life and she saw him gracefully dive into the pool.

She drew closer. "Nice dive," Kim called out.

He swam to where she stood and looked up. "I thought you were asleep."

"I couldn't."

"Neither could I. Want to come in for a swim?"

"I'm not much of a swimmer, which is ironic considering that I grew up near the ocean."

"Pool's heated and I give free lessons."

"Very tempting."

A boyish grin appeared along with a dimple in his left cheek.

"Good, then I've convinced you. Water therapy is a cure for insomnia."

"I'm not certain. What's another cure?"

"Best not to talk about that."

"Warm milk," she said quickly.

"Coward!"

There seemed nothing for her to do but go back to the cottage and change into her bathing suit. Maybe he was right; some exercise would help her get a few hours of sleep.

He was clearly waiting for her to return. She was glad her suit was a modest one-piece garment; he was making her feel self-conscious.

"Join me," he said. He held his arms out to her.

She hesitated. "I usually inch into the water."

"That's because the water's usually cold. This water is just right. Trust me," he said and held his arms out to her again.

She moved into the water, slipping over the side of the pool. Strong arms gently took possession of her.

"Feel all right?"

"Just fine." That was a lie. She usually didn't lie, but this was an unusual situation.

"Swimming is therapeutic. I especially enjoy it when I have things on my mind or feel physically tense." He released her. "I better swim a few laps."

She watched his smooth, graceful movements as he glided through the water. He might have been a large fish or even a merman. Finally, he returned to where she floated. He hardly seemed real.

"Want to relax in the hot tub for a few minutes? I heated it up. It should be just about right."

When she acquiesced, he helped her out of the pool. His hand lingered. But all too soon the chill of the night air on their skin caused them to rush toward the hot tub, whose waters immersed and cocooned them in bubbling warmth. Only then did Hank release her.

"How does it feel?"

"Wonderful."

"You'll be able to relax now."

She closed her eyes and tried to make her mind go blank, but that was impossible since he was so close. When she opened her eyes again, it was only to find Hank looking at her intently.

"A dollar for your thoughts."

She smiled. "Pretty steep price."

"Your thoughts are worth it. Besides, I'm allowing for inflation."

"I was thinking how beautiful it is here."

"I was thinking about beauty too." His eyes were on her lips.

She sensed that he wanted to kiss her, but he hesitated and didn't move toward her. She almost closed her mind to the insistent warning of what hazards it could cause if either of them acted on the feelings that were starting to develop between them.

"It's late. We both better try and get some sleep."

He responded to her words by hurriedly hauling himself out of the hot tub. He got the towel he'd brought for himself and handed it to her, then took off for the main house as if a demon were chasing after him. Clearly, common sense had prevailed in the nick of time. How would she have reacted if he'd acted on impulse and actually kissed her? It was best not to think about that.

Kim breathed a sigh of relief. Much more slowly, she walked back to the guest cottage. But it was a long time before she could manage to sleep.

That night she dreamt of Sammy Granger. In the dream, he wasn't dead. They were walking together through the woods, dead brown leaves crunching beneath their feet.

"I need your help," he said.

"I like to help people. It's what I do," she said.

"Then please help me. Find out who killed me so I can be at peace."

And then he began to fade away, until finally he disappeared entirely. Kim woke with a start. The dream had been so real. Try as hard as she might, Kim couldn't shake the feeling that she'd been talking to a ghost. She didn't sleep again.

The following morning, Kim was working in the school library, helping out with the early-morning rush of students and teachers who came in before classes looking for a variety of materials and A.V. equipment.

A girl of about fourteen approached her. There was something familiar about the teenager, although Kim realized she didn't actually know the girl.

"How can I help you?" Kim asked.

"I'm looking for a biography. It's for a book report. We're doing *The Miracle Worker* in class. Our teacher says we need to find a biography of a famous American. Evie said you'd be the one to ask."

"Evie Gardner?"

"That's right."

"You're a friend of Evie's?"

"We used to be friends. Now we are again because we're in some of the same classes, like English and Social Studies." The girl stared at Kim intently. "Evie told me you were the one who found my brother's body."

The book Kim was holding dropped from her hand. "You're Miranda Granger." She looked at the girl more carefully now, remembering the dream of the night before, and shuddered involuntarily. Brother and sister shared the same haunting eyes.

"I'm so sorry about your brother," Kim said, aware that the words were inadequate.

The girl's lower lip trembled. "Me too. The police haven't found out who killed him or why. It's just so unfair." Her face crumbled, and her eyes filled with misery.

Kim nodded her head. She'd been so involved in her own problems lately that she hadn't given much thought to those of other people. She was falling short of her librarian's credo of helping others find information. When was the last time she'd spoken to Bert? It had been a while. She vowed to make time to discuss Sammy Granger's death with her friend. First Sammy, now his sister; both were requesting her help. She must provide it if she was able. The expression in those haunted eyes remained with her the rest of the day.

"You look the way I feel."

"Thanks a lot," Kim said. She was exhausted. Still, she wasn't about to admit that to Hank Anderson.

"Pack up your things, I'm driving you straight back to the house so you can get some rest."

"You'll quit working now? I know you don't normally go home at four."

"School's deserted. TGIF. That's the motto around here."

"Mine too," she responded with a sigh. "I'm really glad it's Friday."

"So then you agree with my plan?" He began gathering her books and papers.

Hank was taking charge of her again. At one level, she resented it. After all, she was an adult woman perfectly willing and able to take care of herself. She'd been on her own since she was eighteen and didn't need a man to tell her what to do.

There was no one around when they walked out to a virtually empty parking lot. Only the cars belonging to detention teachers and coaches remained.

"Dory's cooking for us tonight," he told her as he opened the passenger side of his blue Corvette for her.

"I hope you're not making her stay late on my account."

He glanced over at her. "Nope, it's for both of us. I called Dory early today so she could plan on coming to work later. She's a widow with no children living at home so it's not an inconvenience for her."

"You're very organized."

"Goes with the territory." He concentrated on his driving.

For a time, she forced herself not to look at him, not to speak. She was afraid of what she might say. However, the atmosphere grew palpably tense. It was Hank who spoke first.

"How's Nick James doing?"

She was relieved that he was keeping the conversation impersonal.

"Things are going better with the class."

"Which isn't saying much. Nick's still causing trouble, isn't he?"

She recalled Will Norgood's advice. "I didn't imply that. By the way, Nick is involved with a girl who's in his class. Her name's Anita Cummings. She's really a sweet kid. I can't imagine what she sees in him. I suppose it's the lure of the bad boy."

Hank glanced over at her thoughtfully. "New girl, isn't she?"

"Yes, a polite, quiet teenager. She has such big, sad eyes. Always hunched over, as if trying to make herself fit into the least possible amount of space, afraid to be noticed or called on."

"I met the girl and read her records." He was pensive for a moment. "I think there's something you should know about her, although I'd appreciate it if you keep what I tell you in the strictest confidence. Anita doesn't live with her mother. It appears there's no father in the picture. I gather the mother was less than a model parent. In any case, Anita was living in foster care for quite a few years. She's now in a group home."

"Poor child! I suppose that explains a great deal."

The adolescent psychology course Kim had taken as an undergrad to help her prepare for high school teaching had dealt with this subject. Maybe Anita found an aggressive bully like Nick James appealing because she had such a poor self-image. Her insecurity might lead her to admire someone like Nick who acted out his anger and frustration, while she could only turn hers inward.

"Thank you for telling me. I don't know that I can help her. I'm certainly not trained for it, but at least I can understand her with greater insight."

"If it makes you feel any better, Anita's being seen by both our psychologist and a social worker regularly. We're not ignoring her problems. There just aren't any easy solutions for kids like her. People seem to think schools should be able to solve all the ills of society. It doesn't work that way." Apparently thinking he was getting too serious, Hank cracked a smile and loosened his tie. "So how's the teaching business going for you?"

"Some days better than others. I'm still pretty much of a

newbie at the high school and I know it. Let's just say the students have a way of reminding me of that. Yet it's amazing how much I learn as I teach, probably more than the pupils."

"Teachers are usually the best students," he said.

Hank drove along silently for a time. Above them, the day was warm and sunny. Cotton candy clouds hung heavily in a cerulean sky. Her eyelids drooped.

"We're here," Hank said.

Kim stirred, realizing with some embarrassment that she must have dozed off.

"You need to catch a nap."

"I'm fine. It's such a lovely day, I want to sit by your swimming pool and bask in the sunlight for a while."

She didn't even bother changing her clothes, instead making herself comfortable on a chaise lounge. The sun arabesqued on the rippling waters while overhead Yankee clipper ships glided at half-sail across an azure sky. She drowsed pleasantly.

Kim awoke to the sound of someone jumping off a diving board. She opened one eye and peeked. Hank hit the water with vigor. It was hard not to admire the grace of his form, the sureness of his movement. She forced herself to shut her eyes again as he swam laps. It wouldn't do to have him think that she was watching him, staring at him, although that was really what she wanted to do.

"Kim?"

Dory was standing there looking down at her. "I hope I'm not disturbing you, but Hank asked me to bring out something cold to drink. He thought you might want it."

"Thank you," Kim said politely, and helped herself to a glass. "I didn't realize how thirsty I was. Wonderful lemonade. It tastes freshly squeezed."

"Oh, it is. I can't see serving anything else."

"The Andersons are fortunate to have you."

Dory looked pleased by the compliment. "Believe me, it's mutual."

"How long have you worked for Mr. Anderson?"

Dory smoothed the apron she wore over her ample hips. "Let's see. It was more than twenty years ago, right after Mrs. Anderson . . ."

"Dory," Hank interrupted, "can I have a glass too?"

"Sure thing, I didn't notice you'd come out of the water."

Hank stood beside Kim, shook himself like a wet puppy, and managed to soak her. Kim let out a gasp.

He smiled. "Thought you looked like you needed to be cooled off a little."

"I prefer the lemonade," she said in mock annoyance. Kim turned back to Dory. "Can I help you with dinner preparations?"

"No, dear. Everything's set and will be ready whenever the two of you like."

"Then maybe I'll change now," Kim said.

Inside the cottage, Kim removed her conservative gray linen business suit and changed into comfortable jeans and an oversized sweatshirt. She took down her long, glossy hair, combed it, and then twisted it into a casual knot, which she pinned on top of her head.

Kim went directly to the kitchen of the main house where she found Dory hard at work. "Where's Hank?" Kim seated herself casually on a stool by the counter at which Dory was chopping lettuce, tomato, and carrots. "Is he still swimming?"

"No, he changed too. But he got a call. His father phoned."

Kim admired the cheerful, modern kitchen with its sunny yellow wallpaper and lacy, scalloped curtains. "Did you decorate this room?" It seemed to reflect Dory's personality.

"Yes, I did, as a matter of fact. Mr. Anderson asked me to tell the decorator what I liked since I spend so much time here. He's a very considerate boss."

"What's the family like?"

"There isn't much family really, just Hank and Mr. Anderson." Was Dory suddenly guarded or did she just imagine it?

Kim helped put the colorful array of raw veggies into the salad bowl. "What about Hank's mother?"

"Dory, what are we having for dinner?"

"Poached salmon."

Hank's sudden appearance startled Kim. From the expression on his face, he'd obviously overheard part of the conversation and hadn't been pleased. Color crawled into Kim's cheeks; she felt like a pupil caught cheating on an exam. Then her temper flared. Why should she be embarrassed? She hadn't done anything wrong. Wasn't it perfectly natural for her to be curious about his family?

After Dory served dinner, Hank told the housekeeper that she could go home. "We'll clean up ourselves."

"See you Monday then," she said with a broad smile.

There was a certain uneasiness between them after Dory left. Nevertheless, Hank said nothing about her questioning of the housekeeper.

"I hope you like fish," he said. "My father has high cholesterol, so Dory's in the habit of making low-fat meals even when he's not around."

"It's fine. Good to eat healthy."

He gave her a wry smile and then spoke in a conspiratorial whisper. "If you don't tell Dory, tomorrow I'll take you out for the best cheeseburgers and fries in the entire state of New Jersey." His eyes twinkled mischievously.

"Sounds terrific to me."

He reached across the table and turned her palm up, holding her slender hand in his large one. "You've got long, artistic fingers. Do you play a musical instrument?"

"No, but I paint a little, although I'm not very good at it. I also write bad poetry."

"That's okay. Frankly, I'm not sure I can tell the difference."

They shared a laugh; then his hand tightened on hers. He immediately let her go as if burned. They concentrated on eating their dinner and didn't talk again until after rinsing and stacking the dishes in the dishwasher.

"Want to watch a movie? I asked Dory to pick up some DVDs on her way over today. We have a choice."

When she agreed, he led her into a spacious recreation room, which possessed, among other things, a large-screen television, a mirrored bar, and an elegant billiard table. Everything about the house spoke of wealth and privilege, directly opposite to the manner in which she'd been raised. The carpeting and drapes in vibrant tones of orange added cheer to the austere, dark colonial pine furniture. Hank handed her three DVDs, from which she selected a suspense thriller with the thought it might especially appeal to him. Still, she was pleased that he'd offered her the choice without summarily deciding on his own. He'd behaved in a considerate manner rather than being dictatorial, a decided improvement.

They settled back cozily on a comfortable sofa in front of the large-screen television. As the plot of the movie unfolded, a beautiful, mysterious woman was entering the witness protection program after testifying against a gangster don. When attempts were made on her life, a wise-cracking private investigator was hired to keep her safe.

"Not a particularly original plot," Hank observed.

"As the Book of Ecclesiastes says, there is nothing new under the sun."

"True, and I suppose the acting is pretty good," he agreed.

"Now you're being charitable," Kim said as the mysterious lady and the private investigator embraced.

It was all he could do to keep from kissing her. He prided himself on his abundant self-control in any situation. And he'd promised himself he wouldn't take advantage of the situation; it wasn't right. For God's sake, she was a guest in his house. But just looking at her beautiful face brought on a rush of lust. So intense were his feelings that he didn't hear the phone ringing immediately. Its persistence brought him back to his senses with a jolt. He moved quickly to the table that held the telephone.

"Mr. Anderson?"

He responded in the affirmative, his voice barely more than a grunt.

"This is Jeff Miller. Could you please let Miss Reynolds know that I'm still at the shop working on her car? I know I promised to have it ready tomorrow, but the old gal needs another part, and I can't get it before Monday morning. So I'll have the car ready Monday afternoon at the latest. I'm real sorry."

"Okay, Jeff, I'll tell her."

Not until Monday. He conveyed the bad news to Kim, who took the information with stoic calm.

"Would you take me back to my apartment tonight? I'll find some means of transportation to school Monday morning, and then you can drop me off at the garage on your way home Monday afternoon."

That sounded very sensible, so why should he feel a terrible sense of wrenching loss at the contemplation of her plan? "I've got a counter offer: stay here for the weekend." The words just seemed to burst from him, tumble out as if they had a will of their own.

"I'd be imposing. You have a life to live, and it doesn't include me. I wouldn't feel right. I've already put you to a great deal of trouble."

"Did you ever consider that I enjoy your company?" He hadn't meant to say that either. He never told women things like that, let alone a woman who worked with him.

"It wouldn't be right for me to camp out here for the entire weekend."

"Sure it would. Look, why don't we both get some sleep. We can discuss it again in the morning."

As he walked her to the guest cottage, it was all he could do not to put his hands on her. "Lock your door," he said tersely. Then he turned on his heels and forced himself to stalk back to the house, his hands clenched into tight fists.

# CHAPTER ELEVEN

On Saturday morning, with no alarm clock to wake her, Kim slept deep and late. The dream she vaguely recalled on rising was erotic, and Hank Anderson was at the core of it. She pushed it out of her mind, willing herself to forget the provocative details. She wasn't going to get involved with him or any other man again for a long time. Her life was in enough of a flux as it was without adding emotional entanglement to the mix. That was a formula for disaster. She wasn't even over her feelings for Mike—maybe she never would be. She liked Hank Anderson and was physically attracted to him, but in no way did she want a relationship with her school principal.

After dressing casually, she discovered that the morning was brilliant and sunny, another perfect day. She knocked at the front door of the main house but no one answered. She discovered that the door wasn't locked, walked inside, but found no sign of Hank. His Corvette was still in the driveway. She expected that he was around somewhere. With that thought in mind, she began to explore cautiously.

Should she see if he was still asleep? There was a sense of awkwardness; she felt like an intruder, an interloper. She had to ask herself what she was doing in this house. This was Mr. Anderson's home and she did not belong here. Yet she ventured upstairs as if drawn by some powerful unseen magnetic force.

Kim found Hank in a well-appointed bedroom, eyes closed, breathing softly, looking handsome and virile in repose. She thought wildly for one brief moment how wonderful it would be to climb into bed with him and snuggle her back against his bare golden-haired chest.

Instead, she did the proper, sensible thing and slowly retraced her footsteps. After all, he probably wouldn't appreciate her pouncing on him. He would get the impression she was easy and immoral. That was the last thing she wanted or needed.

Better to throw her energy into some practical outlet. Why not demonstrate to Hank that she was appreciative of his hospitality? She began to look through the kitchen cabinets and the refrigerator. In less than half an hour, Kim had a respectable breakfast put together.

When Hank ambled down the stairs to join her in the kitchen, she was ready to serve up scrambled eggs, bacon, and toast. Hank let out a sleepy yawn and ran his hand through tousled golden hair.

"Quite a feast you've put together."

"You sound surprised."

"I didn't know you could cook."

"Proves you don't know me very well."

"That's true." He took on a more wide-awake look. "But I'd certainly like to know you better."

The insinuation in his voice, whether intentional or otherwise, made gooseflesh rise on her arms. With the pretext of pouring orange juice, Kim turned her back to him so he wouldn't notice how she was reacting to his proximity.

"Great eggs. What did you do to make them so delicious?"

She shrugged. Compliments always made her uncomfortable. "A touch of cottage cheese for lightness, American cheese for taste, tomato, onion, and pepper for flavor."

He let out a soft whistle. "A creative cook."

"My mother taught me to make use of whatever happened to be on hand. Ma's the kind of person who can adjust in any emergency. Not that I had to do it here. Dory really does keep this place well stocked."

At the mention of the word *mother,* a pained expression had come over Hank's face; then the look just as quickly disappeared and he was shuttered again. It made her wonder, but Kim knew she had no right to ask him personal questions. Hank was a very private man. Since Kim kept her own council as well, she respected that.

"What? No fresh-squeezed o.j.?" he teased. The smile was strained.

"Nope, just what was in the container, but I did brew coffee instead of giving you the instant stuff."

"Then I definitely want some."

She poured them each a cup of coffee and discovered he drank his black. She took a generous measure of milk for herself but skipped the sugar.

"Now I remember what drew me down here in the first place. That aromatic fragrance shot me so full of caffeine, I practically hurdled over the bed and jogged down the stairs to get at it. I see I managed to coax a smile out of you. Guess you don't believe me? Think I might be exaggerating?" His eyes were bright with amusement. He was clearly a man of changeable moods.

"You're quite a talker, Mr. Anderson, when you want to be."

"And you, Ms. Reynolds, are a gifted chef. What other talents do you possess?" He raised his coffee cup in a mock salute.

Why did it seem that so much of what he said was charged with sexual overtones? Was her imagination working in overdrive? For a few minutes, they sat quietly sipping their coffee. He was studying her face and his scrutiny made Kim uneasy.

"More coffee?"

His hand touched hers as if to stop her from pouring. She felt an odd electrical tingle where their fingers joined. When she looked into his eyes, she saw a recognition, an awareness he felt it too.

"Let's go for a ride," he said. "What about Atlantic City?"

"It's awfully far from here. Anyway, I don't think much of gambling. It's something for idle minds. Plus I don't have the money to waste on it."

"It's not so far. Only a little over an hour's drive from here. There are other things to do there besides gamble. It's a resort area. We can walk by the ocean, have dinner, and see a show at one of the big hotels."

"I would only consider doing it if I could pay my own way, and I can't afford the luxury."

"Okay, let's go somewhere else then." He looked annoyed that she'd shot down his suggestion.

"You shouldn't feel obliged to entertain me."

"I don't."

"I really would appreciate it if you drove me back to my apartment."

He frowned at her. "It makes more sense for you to stay here."

It made no sense at all. Why was he insisting?

"How about a walk by the lake and maybe a picnic outdoors? And we'll discuss this further."

She hesitated. He was being kind and generous. She didn't want to insult him. "Sounds good," she said.

"The catch is you have to help fix the basket. I have a confession. I've never been on a picnic."

She smiled. "Why, you poor deprived man."

At the moment, he did feel deprived sexually but also depraved for wanting to keep this woman with him as long as possible. "You've decided to take pity on me?" He felt the warmth of her sunny smile right down to his toes.

"Just call me soft-hearted because I intend to honor you with the picnic lunch to end all picnic lunches. So why don't you catch up on your reading while I plan what we'll be taking?"

"I'm no fool. I'm out of here. I like a woman who takes charge."

Kim blushed. He couldn't help but smile at the innocent look of her face. Thoughts of that face and willowy body had kept him tossing and turning most of the night. His own body was acutely uncomfortable. The fact was, he ached with physical need for her; it was pure torture to want her yet feel honor-bound to deny himself.

He tried to go over some paperwork he'd brought home from school, but his thoughts kept straying. A half hour later, he left the study and found himself back in the kitchen. She'd located a hamper he'd never seen before. He was about to look inside when she gently smacked his hand away.

"No peeking until lunchtime."

"Yes, ma'am."

She handed him the picnic hamper.

"God, this is heavy. We're not eating bowling balls for lunch I hope?"

"Wait and see." She gave him a Mata Hari smile and walked on with the regal hauteur of a princess.

Hank drove the Corvette around the lake at a leisurely speed. Then they left the car and walked along a hiking trail through the woods and back around the lake.

"This is such a lovely day and a beautiful park," she said. "We won't have many more days like this before the cold weather sets in."

She favored him with a warm smile. He felt like kissing her. That was when he decided to pick up the pace. Kim kept up, matching his long strides.

Kim was interesting, intelligent, and easy to talk with. He realized how much he enjoyed being with her. It was a revelation for him. His inclination was to avoid closeness with other people, especially women. Outside of school, he was something of a loner, friendly toward everyone, but with no close friends. Generally, he enjoyed his privacy and liked being alone to indulge his interest in computers when he was at home. Kim's company pleased him more than he was willing to admit.

After a time, they returned to the Corvette and Hank removed the picnic hamper, carrying it to a secluded location where a picnic bench was shaded by large pine trees and overlooked the tranquility of the lake. They ate in companionable silence.

Kim had put together potato salad, turkey and roast beef sandwiches, and juice to drink. It was a very satisfying meal. He watched her savor a wedge of sour pickle and decided it was time to indulge in dessert. Maybe that would sate his appetite for other things. He rummaged around in the basket.

"How did you know I love chocolate cake?"

"A sure bet. Most people do." She favored him with another warm smile.

"Then again, some people are allergic."

"Are you?" Her voice revealed concern.

"No, but just like you said, we don't know much about each other." He took a large bite of cake and chewed thoughtfully. "Tell me more about you."

"I don't think there's very much to say."

"You grew up in a poor but honest family?"

Her dark auburn lashes fluttered. "Not exactly."

"You've got dark family secrets?" His tone was light, but his expression was serious.

"Like finding out the man you were told was your father wasn't? Or that he went crazy and killed innocent people?" Her gaze no longer met his.

"You're not joking, are you?"

"Afraid not. Carl Reyner was in the military and was badly wounded. Unfortunately, his wounds weren't just physical. He didn't behave rationally."

"Serious injury does strange things to people."

Kim studied her fingernails. "In Carl's case, it drove him to crime. He killed several people at a V.A. hospital. He blamed innocent people, the wrong people."

Hank realized this was not easy for her, yet she was forcing herself to be open and forthright with him. "I value your candor," he said.

At that point, Kim looked up. "You should also know that I decided to change my name, to reinvent myself. I didn't like who I was. The fact is, I'm still evolving as a person, changing all the time, searching for a true identity."

"All right, I guess I understand. Did Carl Reyner die?"

She nodded her head solemnly; her eyes had lost their bright luster. "The only good thing he did was kill himself. Unfortunately, my mother and I had to deal with the aftermath. It was hell."

Overhead, clouds suddenly obscured the sun. A crow cawed as if in warning. Time to think of the living, and bury the dead.

Hank tossed Kim a golden delicious apple and took one for himself. "Dory's idea of a good dessert."

"Mine too," she said, brightening again.

Kim did not like talking about the man she'd once believed was her father. But in spite of that, the day was proving to be special. The park seemed like an enchanted forest. A nice romantic illusion, Kim told herself, and nothing more. Still, Hank hadn't been turned off by the admission regarding Carl; she considered that a good sign. It was not something she would readily confide to just anyone.

Hank was quiet on the return to his home; he seemed lost in thought and just a tad distant. Of course, she might just be imagining it.

Hank left her and went for a swim. He invited her to join him but she begged off. Weekends were the time to catch up on her work. It was very comfortable on the patio: shaded yet not too cool, a perfect place to grade papers. He kept his distance again for several hours. Kim told herself that was perfectly all right with her; she had work to do after all. There were lessons to plan and papers to grade for her expository writing students at the university as well as for the high school.

Around six, Kim started to get hungry and noticed it had grown very chilly. With a sigh, she put away her work. She'd caught up on her lesson plans and graded all her essays. Maybe she'd see if Hank was inside the house. She thought of telling him she would spend the evening alone in the cottage to continue her studies. Being at his estate would be less awkward that way.

She found him in the kitchen standing over the stove and stirring spaghetti sauce. The kitchen table was set, and there were fresh autumn flowers in a crystal bowl as a centerpiece.

"What's all this?" She was surprised, if not a little over-whelmed.

"I can only cook one real meal and this is it. So just sit down and enjoy."

She did exactly that. It was actually relaxing to watch him work. Someone had taught him well. His mother? She thought it unlikely. Probably Dory.

"Do you like doing domestic things?"

"I like working with my hands, gardening, making basic home repairs. There's a certain satisfaction in it." With a smooth motion, he poured the spaghetti into a metal colander and strained the water from it.

"Did your father teach you?"

"No, he considers menial work beneath him. And he'd never take the time from his business anyway. I learned from watching, reading, and experimenting. I made my share of mistakes, but you might say I also learned from them." There was a strength and maturity in his manner she found reassuring.

"I suppose that's what's happening to me—in teaching, I mean. I learn from my mistakes."

"Everybody makes mistakes. That's how you learn what not to do. As long as you try to get the students involved and interested, you can't go very wrong."

They talked their way through dinner, so involved in the easy flow of conversation that neither of them really wanted it to end.

"Want to try another of Dory's video picks?"

"Sure, but first I'll help clean up."

"No, you just go in the family room and decide. This dinner's completely on me."

Sometimes, his generosity of spirit blew her away. When he joined her, she was still holding the two DVDs in her hand, trying to make a choice.

"Would you rather go out to see a new movie?"

"No, these are fine, but I'd like you to choose this time. It would make me feel better."

His choice turned out to be a romantic comedy rather than the action adventure she was certain he would prefer. She realized Hank chose what he thought she'd like.

He made an effort to be courteous but remained somewhat distracted. She wanted him to sit close to her the way he had the evening before. Of course, she understood he was just trying to be sensible, to behave in an appropriately professional manner. She realized that it wouldn't do for them to become involved. Clearly, he was just as aware of it. Hank wanted to move slowly. He was cautious, careful. That was the way she must be as well.

As they watched the film, the romance on the screen began heating up. There seemed a natural chemistry between the leading man and his lady. Maybe it was just good acting; she didn't know.

"Listen, I don't think I can watch any more of this. Would you be offended if I went out for a walk?" he asked.

"Of course not. Why don't I come with you?"

"No, you see the rest of the movie. You can tell me what happens when I get back. I'm feeling restless right now, but I won't be long."

She realized he didn't want to be with her and so she did not persist. He was not easy to understand. One moment he appeared attracted to her, the next he was eager to be free of her company. She would not even try to guess the thoughts that ran through his mind. All she knew was after he left, the movie suddenly lost most of its appeal.

Hank returned an hour later and handed her a white paper bag. She opened it to discover a frozen yogurt sundae.

"I walked by this yogurt store. Thought you might enjoy some."

"Would you share with me?"

He grinned. "I gave into temptation and already ate mine."

He watched her eat with interest, which only served to make her feel self-conscious. As she licked the hot fudge off her fingers, Kim considered whether chocolate was erotic. Hadn't she read that it was something of an aphrodisiac? She remembered Hank telling her that it was his favorite too. Looking over at the brooding expression on Hank's face made her appetite falter. She pushed the sundae away.

"Don't you like it?"

"Love it, but I don't want to get fat."

"I don't think you have to worry about that."

"Did you have a nice walk?"

"I kept thinking about you." His eyes were very dark, his expression intent. "I've been trying very hard not to come on to you. I have no intention of seducing you."

"Who says I'd let you?" She looked away from him. "Do you think you're so irresistible to women that if you decide to hit on one, the lucky female would fall at your feet feeling privileged because you chose her?"

"Do I come off as that arrogant?"

"You can answer your own question."

"I seem to insult you without even trying."

"I like to think I take responsibility for my own actions and decisions." She took a deep breath and let it out shakily. "Have you ever been involved in a meaningful relationship?"

"Meaningful relationship? Kind of a jargon term, isn't it?" His tone of voice struck her as patronizing.

"I think you know what I mean."

He pushed back the shock of golden hair that dropped across his elongated forehead. "I've dated a number of women but things never got serious."

"You mean to say you had sex with women but you never loved any of them?"

He let out a soft whistle. "You certainly know how to be blunt. You don't mince words, do you?"

She found herself coloring. "I sense that you're a man who doesn't trust easily, especially not women. There are dark places in your heart. You've suffered hurt."

He stared at her, eyes widening, looking shaken. Why had she spoken her thoughts, her insights out loud? He was obviously sensitive on the subject, a man with secrets he wanted to keep hidden.

"What about you? Have you ever been seriously involved with anyone?" He waited for her answer, his eyes impaling hers.

# CHAPTER TWELVE

"There was someone, but it didn't last."

"You wanted it to last?"

She would rather not discuss this, yet it was her fault the conversation had taken such an earnest tone. "Let's just say it didn't work out. I take it nothing like that has happened to you?"

"I suppose I never allowed myself to get that close to anyone."

"You're a careful man. I used to be like that."

"You're thinking *cold*, aren't you? I sense the disapproval."

"No, I didn't mean that at all. I think you just don't trust easily."

"Let's say I'm cautious." His eyes at that moment reminded her of honed steel; his expression gave nothing away.

"I guess that's wise." Her mood had turned solemn.

"The relationship you had, it made you wary?"

"It made me mistrust myself and some of my instincts about people."

"Did he hurt you deliberately?" The tone of their conversation was becoming tense.

She told herself Hank had no right to ask such personal questions, and yet she felt compelled to answer him. She took a deep breath and exhaled shakily. When she thought about Mike, it was always with regret. She hadn't even told her mother about why they broke up; yet she was going to tell Hank Anderson.

"He was my first real love." She swallowed hard, unable to

look into his inquisitive face. "I thought he could walk on water, which just goes to show how inexperienced I was."

"What happened?" There was an odd tightness in his voice.

She glanced at him to determine if he was expressing disapproval, but it didn't seem that way. "I found out that he was still married. It never even occurred to me that he might be. When we were together, he told me how much he loved me. He said he wanted to marry me. He told me that they were divorced. But it turned out that she never signed the papers."

"He lied to you?"

She shook her head. "No, he never intentionally lied. He's a good, decent man. In fact, his wife cheated on him. He was a faithful husband and a good father."

"What happened when you found out the truth?" Hank's voice was low and restrained.

"I was devastated. I broke it off with him immediately."

"How did he react?"

She managed a small, sad smile. "He was hurt. But his ex came back and is living in their house. There was no way I could or would continue the relationship."

"Have you been involved with anyone since?"

She shook her head. "I've thrown myself into my work. It's just as well."

"Are you teaching at the university too?"

"Just one course for this semester. That's about all I can handle with the demands at the high school."

He was so close to her she felt his breath against her cheek. It made her feel very warm, very aware of him in the physical sense.

"You take on quite a lot, maybe too much."

Kim's eyes registered a harried expression, an almost haunted look. Hank wondered about the things that troubled her. Of course, it was possible that she was overly ambitious and driven. He knew people like that. His father was one of them. The truth was, Hank didn't think he was very different from Todd Anderson. He'd worked very hard all his life, although he didn't need to do so. Was it to prove something to himself? To feel a sense of worthiness? Maybe. When his father had expressed disappointment that Hank was going into a low-paying, poorly respected occupation like teaching instead of working in business, Hank had grown angry.

"Teaching kids is the most important job there is."

They'd never discussed the subject again.

Kim brought him back to the present moment. "There's something I've been meaning to ask you. Why do you feel such contempt for Will Norgood?"

Hank stiffened. "Norgood is not a good choice for a mentor. You need a different kind of person. Norgood's a poor role model for any teacher."

He saw her eyes ignite like the flames of a gas jet. "I believe Will is a good choice. He's helped me tremendously."

His own temper erupted. "Let's see. As I recall he blackmailed Morgana. You admire him for that? In my book, he's got no character. A gentleman doesn't kiss and tell. Terrific influence he provides!"

Kim bit down on her lower lip. "It was really her fault. What she did was very wrong. I don't want to get into that issue again. But Will is a friend and he does know a lot about teaching."

"Like how to humiliate and demean students via sarcasm?"

"He only does it to the disruptive ones."

"Do you really think he demonstrates appropriate ethical behavior for a teacher? I thought you had higher standards. I seem to have been wrong."

He knew as soon as the words came blurting out that he'd

gone too far. He saw the hurt expression in her eyes and regretted losing his temper. God knew, he hadn't meant to sound so harsh and judgmental. Why was he so angry when she defended Norgood?

Kim turned on her heels and hurried from the room. A moment later, he heard the front door slam. With a deep sigh, he determined that he would go after her and make amends.

The man was infuriating. His way or no way! She'd go back to the guest cottage, pack her things, and call a cab. Whatever it cost, she'd leave tonight and go back to her own apartment. She'd told Hank too much about herself; let him know her too well. When would she learn? It had been stupid to stay at Hank's home, to allow herself to become vulnerable to another man, particularly this one.

She could hear him coming after her, calling her name, and increased her pace. The shortcut would be across the pool area. She decided to take exactly that path, except her vision was so blurred by tears and her pace so hurried, she ended up falling into the deep end of the pool. There she sank like a stone.

Emotionally spent, Kim gave in to a sense of panic. Choking down water, she feared she would drown. Then there were strong arms encompassing her, holding her tightly and drawing her to the surface where she coughed and then gasped for air. Hank lifted Kim and ferried her to the side of the pool; his mouth breathed air into her lungs.

"Are you all right?"

She nodded, still coughing. Finally, when her breathing was restored to normal, Hank helped her to stand, but her feet were like sponges. He kept his arms around her, firmly maintaining support.

"I'm lousy at making apologies. I was wrong, way out of line in what I said. Really I didn't even mean it."

"You meant what you said." Her voice was little more than a hoarse whisper.

"Forgive me. But if you can't, I'll understand." Although his manner remained impassive, his apology sounded genuine.

She gave a small nod of her head. When she tried to speak, Kim began coughing again.

"Hell, this is my fault too." He lifted her into his arms and carried her the rest of the way to the cottage, holding her gently as if she were delicate and fragile. Somewhere along the way, the anger completely drained out of her.

# CHAPTER THIRTEEN

Hank kept things casual the next morning, much to Kim's relief. By tacit agreement, they didn't talk about any serious matters. They spent a leisurely Sunday morning reading the newspapers that had been delivered and basking in the morning sunlight streaming through the large living room windows of the house. Kim watched Hank read in a concentrated manner and smiled to herself. Hank always seemed to give his all to whatever he was doing at a given time. He had great vitality and enthusiasm. She was beginning to appreciate those attributes in him.

"There's a nice local restaurant that serves a good Sunday brunch. Why don't we go there?"

"Sounds lovely."

She was positive that beneath the rigid outward control existed a man of kind nature. He'd wanted her last night; she was sure of it. His integrity had stopped him from acting on those feelings, but her awareness told her that there was something more as well. It was clear he was not going to confide in her. It was just as well.

Kim checked her watch. "I need to phone my mother. I do it every Sunday morning."

"Why don't you use the phone in the kitchen? It'll give you some privacy."

"I have my cell phone."

"No need."

"I'm calling Florida. It's a long-distance call. I'd rather not stick you with the charges."

"The phone plan in this house covers the entire U.S. and Canada. So make yourself comfortable and feel free to talk as long as you like."

Kim appreciated Hank's generous nature. The phone was picked up by her mother after the first ring. Kim thought Ma must have been waiting near the telephone expectantly. It was good to hear her mother's voice again. She wanted to tell Ma about Hank Anderson, but this did not seem like the right time or place.

"I hope you're not working too hard, dear."

"I'm fine, really good." No point in mentioning her car problems either.

"Are you remembering to take your vitamins? Are you eating properly?"

Kim sighed deeply. Her mother always worried too much. Kim supposed it didn't matter how old she became; to her mother, she would always be a child in need of advice and protection. "I'm taking very good care of myself."

Relieved, her mother launched into stories about friends and neighbors that reminded Kim of how far away they were from each other.

"How's Ginny doing?"

"Poor darling, her lungs are acting up again. The doctor says it's the asthma. When will you come down to Florida for a visit? We'd all love to see you."

"I'll be down during the Christmas vacation. I won't have time until then. Tell Ginny I love her too. I'm looking forward to seeing you and Ginny and Mary. And I'll have a check to send you soon."

"Not if you need the money for yourself."

She could almost visualize her mother's warm eyes, the gentle, loving expression on her face.

"I'm managing just fine, Ma. Besides, it's only right that I contribute."

"I'm sure I'll find a job down here soon, at least part time. When the house sells, I'll be better off. Can you check with the realtor for me? I hate imposing on you, but I really do need your help."

"Sure, not a problem. I'll find out how things are going." Kim couldn't bring herself to go back to the house, recalling her childhood there that had been so unhappy. There were ghosts there, figurative and literal. But she would help her mother sell the house. She'd contact the realtor and pay a visit to the office.

"I don't suppose you're seeing that policeman anymore?"

"No, Ma, I can't. You know how I feel about being involved with someone who isn't free."

"But from what you said, Karen, it's not really his fault."

"That's true, and I don't blame him. But I can't be part of making a bad situation worse."

Kim heard a noise behind her and turned to see Hank standing there. She could tell by the expression on his face that he'd overheard at least part of the conversation with her mother. His expression was guarded. She wondered what he was thinking.

"I've got to go now, Ma. A friend is waiting for me. I'll call you next Sunday morning."

Hank remained while she concluded the conversation. "I wasn't trying to rush you," he said. "I just wanted to let you know I need something at the cottage, so I'm going back there for it." His manner was oddly formal.

What was he thinking? No question that he was a hard man to read. He had his secrets, but she also had hers.

Brunch was pleasant. The food was excellent and the establishment's decor was one of understated elegance, the service unobtrusive. Privately, she had to admit that it was not so much the place or the food but the company that really mattered. Kim was very much aware of being with the most charismatic man in the restaurant. There were a number of well-dressed, distinguished men present, but not one of them compared to Hank Anderson in height or build.

"I've always favored a buffet," Hank said. "Gives a person a chance to pick and choose."

"And quite possibly overeat."

He gave her an appraising look that brought the color to her cheeks. "You don't have to worry about that. In fact, you could stand to gain a few pounds."

"And where would you suggest I gain them?"

This time it was his turn to look embarrassed and that brought a slight smile to her lips.

"You're terrific just as you are."

Kim observed a family sitting together, a mother, father, and two boys. One of the boys reminded her of Sammy Granger; maybe it was the short sandy hair, but there was something about the boy, even though he was certainly younger.

Kim took a forkful of poached egg and chewed thoughtfully. "Did Sammy Granger have any fights or arguments with other students in school?"

Hank dropped his own fork on the floor and then retrieved it. "You kind of surprised me. Where did that come from?"

"I'm not certain. It's just that since he attended the high school and died under mysterious circumstances, I've been thinking about him. I met his sister in the library. She's a lovely girl. I think she and her grandmother need closure. I thought you might know something that could be helpful."

Hank folded his hands. "Afraid not. A policewoman questioned me about him not long ago. There wasn't much I could tell her either. The boy was a good student at one time, but he'd been going through some personal problems, kind of a rough patch. He'd become rebellious and hostile."

"So he was a discipline problem?"

Hank shrugged and refolded his cloth napkin. "Nothing major. In fact, his attitude improved toward the end of last year. I thought he was getting it together."

"But he was friends with Nick James, wasn't he?"

Hank stared at her. "Maybe. Why all the questions about the boy?"

She contemplatively turned her head from side to side. "I just found myself thinking about him again. I've also met his grandmother, and she's really a nice woman. I feel sorry for the family."

At that moment, there was a commotion at the front of the restaurant and they both looked up.

"Why can't I collect money here? Hey, man, I know those people. That's my English teacher, Ms. Reynolds, and there's the principal of my high school. They'll tell you I'm okay. Hello, Mr. Anderson. I didn't know you liked Miss Reynolds."

Kim felt herself flush for the second time in the last few minutes. Facing them was Emory Dunne sitting in his wheelchair, staring at them with unblinking eyes through black-framed eyeglasses. The younger boy with him also watched with interest.

"Please, leave now," the proprietor said to Emory. "You're disturbing my clientele." He quickly thrust a dollar bill into Emory's hand and pushed some quarters into the canister the younger boy held out.

"Okay, I'm going. I know when I'm not welcome." Emory deliberately smashed into some empty chairs and made his way out, followed by the smaller boy Kim suspected was his brother.

"You can bet that everyone at school will hear about this," Hank said in a tight voice.

"I can tough it out if you can," she assured him. "Funny, I didn't think Emory was the kind of boy who'd go around collecting for charity."

"He's not. Emory's favorite charity is Emory. Every time he's short on cash, he takes a canister and goes around from place to place collecting."

She shook her head. "What a character."

"That he is. No hope of reforming him I'm afraid."

Emory's antics would have been humorous if she didn't know the boy's prognosis. Somehow, Emory's unexpected appearance cast a pall over the rest of the meal. Maybe it was just reality intruding. She had hoped her relationship with Hank, however minimal, might have been postponed until Monday morning, but now it could not be ignored.

It was a windy afternoon but very suitable for walking. Hank took her on a tour of the more artsy area on his side of town with its old-fashioned, quaint shops. She decided to buy him a small gift as a thank you. While Hank put additional money in the meter, Kim stepped into a crafts store and found a ceramic paperweight in the shape of a red apple; immediately, she paid for it and had it gift-wrapped. The perfect thing for his desk. The choice had been intuitive, the decision spontaneous and impulsive. Kim was feeling good about it, about trusting her instincts.

"I bought something for you," she told him happily. She slipped the gift into his hand.

"I don't know if I should accept it."

"You have to."

He thrust it into his pocket without looking as they walked back out to the street. He appeared suspiciously uncomfortable.

"Aren't you going to open it?"

"Later."

She supposed it was childish, but she felt a crushing sense of disappointment.

Hank was very quiet during the rest of the afternoon. Whenever she spoke to him, he responded but soon became preoccupied again. Kim sensed that something was wrong.

Once they were back at the house, Hank mentioned some work he had to do and retired into the study. She realized that he was withdrawing from her but still had no idea why. His changed mood was too perplexing to dwell upon. She soon became occupied with her own schoolwork and did the best she could to put him out of her mind. Understanding Hank Anderson was as difficult as a postgraduate seminar.

In the late afternoon, she saw Hank swimming laps in the pool. No point in joining him. If he wanted her company, he'd have asked for it. Kim took a walk around the grounds by herself and ended up near the tennis court. Hank eventually found her there.

"You play tennis?" he asked.

"No, but I'd like to learn. Do you play?"

"I did at one time. My father got me involved. He had this court built. Tennis is his favorite sport."

She couldn't help wondering what Hank's father was like; did he love his son? Was he affectionate?

"Tell you what, suppose I get a racket and some balls for each of us. I'll teach you how to volley."

Hank was a very patient instructor and she did learn a lot about tennis in a relatively short time. But there was a different game going on as well; and regarding the rules of that game, she could learn nothing.

Even when Hank's body moved behind her and he lifted her arm to demonstrate a stroke or technique, there was a studied remoteness to his gestures. His manner was cool and impersonal, as if he were working with a student.

As they walked back from the tennis court, she took his arm.

"You've been so distant this afternoon. Is something wrong?"

"I've been thinking about our situation. In a way, seeing Emory Dunne at the restaurant put some matters in perspective. I realize that I can't close out the real world and make it go away, no matter how much I'd like to do it."

She blinked in confusion. "Are you worried about gossip? About your reputation?"

"Not exactly that." His eyes were darkened to the color of slate. "We've agreed we don't know each other very well. That was brought home to me this morning when I heard you talking to your mother."

"You shouldn't have been listening. That was a private conversation." Immediately, Kim was on the defensive.

"I didn't listen deliberately. But it did make me question certain things. For example, you never mentioned whether or not you'd ever been married—or if you had children."

She was perplexed. Didn't he realize she'd never been married? Yet he thought she might have a child that she hadn't bothered to mention. That must have been the conclusion he drew after overhearing the conversation with her mother. Did he actually think she had a child tucked away somewhere? Worse still was the implication he thought she'd concealed information from him; she, who had told him so much about herself, and much of it painful.

She began to tremble with indignation. He was the one lacking in trust. How much had he told her about himself? Very little. He'd told her virtually nothing about the woman he'd loved, the woman who'd caused him to suffer so badly he was left fearing emotional intimacy. Yet he expected her to completely bare her soul to him.

"Ginny is someone I care about. However, at the moment, I do not wish to discuss her with you, just as you do not wish to discuss the woman you loved and lost with me."

He squared his jaw. "It's hardly the same thing."

"Really? I don't happen to see it that way. Of course, since I know nothing about your situation, I concede you might be right."

They had reached an impasse and she knew it. Hank was just as upset with her as she was with him. It was time to go her own way. She excused herself and told him she intended to spend the evening alone.

Kim settled into the guest house for the duration. She regretted not having a good book to read. Reading always comforted her. Nothing better than reading fiction, escaping into another world. It gave one perspective. As the evening wore on, she turned to the television for comfort, but could not concentrate on a single program. Eventually, she shut off the set and tried to get some sleep. Her thinking would not shut off as easily as the TV. She spent most of the night reflecting on Hank Anderson's absurd behavior. Then her thoughts turned to Mike Gardner. Another impossible situation! She had no intention of crying, but somehow the tears flowed anyway. Men were jerks in general. She'd never felt more alone or miserable in her life.

At six o'clock in the morning, Hank knocked at the front door of the cottage. She climbed wearily out of bed and padded to the door in her bare feet.

"I thought I better warn you I like to leave for school around six-thirty."

She stared at him in surprise. "Teachers don't have to sign in until seven-thirty."

"True, but as much as possible, the principal should be at school early to set a good example."

"I'll be ready," she said, then closed the door in his face.

She'd packed the evening before, and her clothes for the day were laid out in advance so there was no problem getting ready.

As for breakfast, she had no appetite.

They drove to school in tense silence. It suddenly seemed as if they had nothing to say to each other, no words to communicate. She found herself feeling just as wretched and angry as the previous night. After what seemed an interminable time, he drove into the school parking lot.

"I'll get a lift to the service station to pick up my car after school, so you needn't concern yourself about me anymore," she said, getting out of the car.

"If you change your mind or happen to need assistance, let me know."

"I won't."

He looked as if he wanted to say more but then stopped himself. It was small comfort that he appeared to feel as badly as she did.

"I'll be all right," she said. "I can take care of myself. I've had plenty of practice." She walked away from him, head held high, but her heart was lead.

# CHAPTER FOURTEEN

Kim asked Shandra to drop her off at the Lake Shore service station after school. She would neither ask nor accept more favors of Hank Anderson; that was over and done with.

"Want me to hang around until you take possession of the car?" Shandra looked at her with a concerned expression.

Kim shook her head. "They've had plenty of time to get the car ready. It'll be all right."

Shandra twisted a lock of hair and readjusted her eyeglasses. "Hope you know what you're doing." With a shrug, she drove off.

The car was out front and looked ready. Kim took a deep breath and let it out slowly, relieved to see her vehicle. *Independent again.* The thought pleased her, made her feel whole.

She located Jeff Miller at the front counter going over a bill with another customer. She waited as patiently as she could manage, anxious to be on her way.

When her turn came, Jeff recognized Kim immediately. "Car's in good shape now. You should notice the difference right away. We took care of everything that needed doing. Gotta tell you though, somebody really did a number on it. You ought to report it to the police."

"Thank you. I think you're right. I'll do that."

Then she asked for the bill. Jeff's grime-encrusted hands held it out to her. She reached into her purse for her credit card and then blinked hard as she studied the bill.

"You haven't listed the charges, only what's been done."

The expression on the young mechanic's face was one of embarrassment. He ran his hands through unkempt hair. "The bill's been paid."

Her brows raised in confusion. "I'm not certain I understand."

"Mr. Anderson stopped by at noon. He took care of it."

"I intended to pay for the work myself."

Jeff Miller eyed her uneasily. "Maybe you better take that up with him. But you shouldn't be upset. He meant to help you."

"It was the wrong thing for him to do." She kept her voice as even and controlled as possible.

Jeff handed her the car key. "Look, I don't mean to talk out of turn, but there's something you should know. Mr. Anderson's a terrific person. He's gone out of his way to help a lot of people when they needed it. You don't have to ask him for a favor. He's got a generous heart. When I was in school and he was my math teacher, I got in some trouble. My folks were furious. My dad was going to kick my sorry butt out of the house. Mr. Anderson made a home visit, spoke to my old man. Calmed him down. Then he encouraged me to try out for sports. See what I mean? He goes the extra mile for people. And he doesn't ask anything in return." With the last comment, the young mechanic's face colored noticeably.

"Thank you. I think I understand."

Jeff Miller had given her something to consider. What else didn't she know about Hank Anderson? Likely quite a lot. Then again, wasn't that part of the problem? Hank had effectively shut her out of his life. Well, that was for the best, wasn't it? She didn't need any further complications in her life, any more upsetting involvements. He obviously felt the same.

The car ran beautifully; Hank was right in his choice of mechanics. Jeff Miller knew a great deal about fixing cars, but did he know as much about people? It was important that she repay Hank as soon as possible. Her pride demanded it. She drove back to the school. However, she discovered that Hank was not in his office. His secretary, Mrs. Sylvestri, was getting ready to leave for the day.

"Mr. Anderson's working out in the weight room. If there's some important message, you can just leave it on his desk." The secretary eyed her speculatively.

"No, nothing that can't wait." Kim left quickly with a distinct sense of awkwardness. With a sigh, she decided that her talk with Hank would have to be postponed until the following morning. It was probably a good idea for her to think over what she would say to him. Kim conceded that sometimes she was impetuous and that just led to more problems.

She was back at the main office at 6:45 A.M. the next day. Probably it was just as well she hadn't spoken to Hank Anderson earlier; her emotions had been in too much turmoil the previous day. She was much more under control today. Before knocking on the door that had *Vice Principal* stenciled across it in large black letters, she willed herself to be calm and poised.

Hank expressed surprise at seeing her there.

"I need a word in private with you. I thought this might be the best time."

"Was there something you wanted to tell me?" Hank saw the faint blue shadows under her eyes and thought she looked tired, as if she hadn't slept very well. He took a grim satisfaction in that observation since he hadn't slept very much himself.

He was angry with Kim but refused to let her know it. If she saw how bothered he was, the woman would think she had some sort of power over him. No way was he going to let that happen.

The plain truth was he couldn't trust her. She'd refused to be honest and open with him about her past. Then she'd used the strategy of trying to put him on the defensive. He considered that manipulative. Suddenly, he realized Kim was talking and he hadn't heard a word of what she said. She looked at him questioningly.

"I'm sorry. Could you repeat that?"

"Please don't evade my question. Why did you pay my bill?" Her hands were on her hips in a confrontational stance.

"I was checking to see that the car was ready and Jeff handed it to me. It seemed like the right thing to do. I didn't have any kind of sinister designs on you, if that's what you're thinking."

"I know you meant well, but I can't accept. It would seem as if you were dispensing charity."

"I never thought of it that way."

"Then you'll understand why I need to have a copy of the bill so that I can repay you."

He studied her as she stood before him dressed in a neat, conservative brown suit that very nearly matched her large, expressive eyes. The color in her cheeks was high and her eyes sparkled with fire. He thought she was beautiful, but no way was he going to allow himself to be mesmerized by her. If she wanted the bill, he'd give it to her. Hank reached into his top desk drawer, drew it out, and handed it to her. With some satisfaction, he saw her face pale as she surveyed it.

"I'll have to pay you back in gradual installments."

"How were you planning to do it before?"

"By credit card. It's the American way."

He frowned deeply. "You'd be owing quite a bit."

"Yes, I know. Please don't lecture me."

"Someone should."

"I'll pay you back with interest."

He hooked his thumbs into his belt and met her gaze directly.

"I'm not a bank."

She glowered at him. "I didn't think you were."

"Good, then pay only when you can afford it. And I refuse to accept any interest."

"Fine," she responded in a clipped manner.

"There's something else. Something we haven't discussed. As it happens, I feel responsible for the vandalism of your car."

Kim looked surprised. "Why on earth would you ever think such a thing?"

He cleared his throat. "I told you that I'd taken care of your problem with Nick James. Clearly, I was wrong."

"We don't know that it was him, at least not for certain."

"From now on, I'm going to have a security guard on duty every day sweeping the parking lot at regular intervals. When the budget allows, I'll have security cameras installed as well. I never want anything like this to happen again, not to you or anyone else who works at or attends this school."

Kim nodded her agreement. She didn't thank him. Well, what had he expected? That she would fall into his arms? That would certainly be a foolish expectation. He didn't want her gratitude. What did he want? *Her honesty; her passion.* Yet he knew very well he couldn't buy those things. They had to be given freely or not at all.

"All sorts of fascinating, juicy rumors are circulating about you and the boy wonder. Ah, romance." Will Norgood's voice dripped sarcasm. He viewed Kim through pursed lips. "Don't keep me in suspense. Are they true?"

Kim choked on the orange juice she was drinking.

"Sorry, dear one. Didn't mean to upset you."

She coughed, clearing her lungs. "I'm fine. You just surprised me with what you said."

"If you are seeing him, that could be a clever move. Morgana will leave you alone. She sucks up to those in authority and consequently their favorites. That's how she got ahead."

"I'm not dating him."

"Amazing. The student grapevine is usually so accurate. But if Morgana should happen to ask, just give her a cryptic smile and don't answer."

"I hate playing games."

"But winning is such fun." His eyes glittered with malevolent amusement.

"Why is it when we talk, I feel like a conspirator in a political assassination?"

"Because, my dear one, we are the chosen ones, designated to point out what is wrong with establishment thinking." His voice was heavy with mockery.

"Don't poke fun at the establishment," Shandra said. She joined them at the table, placing her salad plate beside Kim's sandwich. Then she turned to Kim. "And don't you listen to Will. He's an anarchist at heart."

"Nonsense, I believe in law and order as much as any teacher." He pretended to be offended but a crooked smile belied the seriousness of his response.

"There is a devil in that man," Shandra said. She pointed an accusing finger at Will, her manner half-joking, half-sincere.

Will held his hands to his chest as if wounded. "She cuts me to the quick. I must find a new love now. Madam librarian, will you be my adored?" Will took Kim's hand in his.

At that moment, she felt a pair of blue eyes bore into her. Kim looked up to see Hank Anderson staring at her. His expression was stern and commanding, startling in its intensity. Their eyes connected as he seated himself on the other side of the room.

Will released her hand. "Methinks I've drawn the wrath of a jealous suitor and deadly adversary. Shandra, I am a coward.

Please take me back."

"Fickle, isn't he?" Shandra laughed. "And ridiculous."

"My goddess, life is of itself absurd. So says the philosopher. Therefore, we must learn to laugh at it or be forever reduced to tears."

"I'll just write down those words of wisdom to live by," Shandra said. She began cleaning her eyeglasses with a tissue.

Kim cast a quick glance at Hank, only to find his gaze still fixed on her. She forced herself to look away.

The following day, Kim received a note in her school mailbox from Hank's secretary requesting that she come to his office during her prep period. She considered ignoring the note but realized it was unlikely to relate to anything personal.

Mrs. Sylvestri led her into his office as soon as she arrived. Hank took the initiative and invited her to take a seat as soon as his secretary left the room, closing the door behind her.

"I'll get right to the point since our time is limited." Hank came around his desk and spoke to her directly, his voice soft with concern. "I know there's been some gossip about us. Is it a problem for you?"

"Nothing I can't handle. Was there anything else?" She felt uneasy now, aware that if he chose to touch her, she would likely dissolve in his arms. What a foolish, ridiculous thought! Where had such a thing even come from? She licked her dry lips with her tongue and waited for him to speak.

The intercom buzzed and he reached for it, his eyes never leaving hers.

"I better go," she murmured.

"Wait," he said.

But Kim left quickly, feeling too uncomfortable to remain.

★ ★ ★ ★ ★

Anita Cummings returned to school after an absence of several days. The girl's eyes were red-rimmed and puffy as if she'd been weeping recently. Her hair hung limp and oily, her clothing wrinkled and dirty. Kim was concerned. She called on Anita twice during the lesson. On neither occasion was the girl responsive. Anita seemed lost and frightened.

When the bell rang, Kim asked Anita to stay behind. It was clear to her that the girl needed help.

"Sorry, can't stay, Ms. Reynolds. I'll be late for history." Anita's eyes fixed on Nick James as if looking for approval.

"If you should want to talk about anything, I'm here after school for extra help."

Nick glowered at Kim. "Anita doesn't need your help, so don't interfere in her life. I'm taking care of her." He took Anita possessively by the arm and shoved her forcefully out the door. A moment later, he returned.

"You can't even help yourself, lady."

"What are you talking about?" Kim asked. But one look into those menacing obsidian eyes and she knew.

"I heard you had some trouble with your car, like it was wrecked."

"No one could know that unless they were responsible." Kim stared back at the youth, refusing to back away, although all her instincts warned her that he was toxic.

Nick James smirked. "Yeah, well, I got my sources of information." He pulled out his iPod and sauntered into the hall as if he owned the school.

Kim was upset the rest of the afternoon. She had to do something about that boy for her own sake and also for Anita. It worried her that Nick of all people had such total control over Anita. Kim hoped that Anita would come and talk to her, but it didn't seem likely. Finally, she decided to drop a note to the guidance department asking that Anita's counselor have a talk with her.

The next day, Kim followed up with a visit to the guidance office during her prep period. Kim was able to discover from a busy secretary that a Mr. Ogden was Anita's counselor. She made it known that she only needed to see Mr. Ogden for a few minutes.

"Is it really important?" the secretary asked, giving her a dubious look.

"Extremely important."

Deep sigh. "All right. I'll see what I can do."

The guidance counselor finally granted her an audience. The overworked secretary showed her into the cozy office with an air of impatience and disappeared as Mr. Ogden waved Kim to a chair. Kim glanced around the cubicle while Ogden spoke with a parent on the telephone.

Kim's first impression was of a short, strident man of middle years trying to conceal a bald spot by combing hair over it. Neat and conservative, he wore thick eyeglasses with dark-colored frames and was dressed in a Harris tweed jacket, white shirt, black slacks, and beige tie. She waited politely for him to finish with his phone call. When he finally got around to her, his expression was not particularly friendly.

"You wanted to talk to me about Anita Cummings?" Mr. Ogden turned to her as he hung up the telephone receiver.

"Yes, I do. I'm very concerned about her."

"As it turns out, Anita came to me of her own accord this morning. She and I had a lengthy conversation. I completely concur that she has a serious problem. I've encouraged her to see Dr. Bell. We can't just sweep this matter under the rug. I may be a male counselor but I try to be completely fair-minded. Men can be abusive pigs."

"I think once Anita realizes she has to free herself from Nick James's influence and domination, she'll start to get some sense of self-worth. I thought that you being her counselor, you'd be able to help her come to terms with it."

Mr. Ogden stared at Kim blankly. "Nick James? The problem she discussed with me has nothing whatever to do with him."

"I don't understand."

"Apparently not." Mr. Ogden twisted a gold wedding band on his finger.

"What did she talk about? What did she say?"

"I'm afraid that must remain confidential for the time being. It will be up to Dr. Bell to determine and decide when to make the matter public. Of course, Anita may wish to talk with you directly. However, I cannot break her confidence." Mr. Ogden spoke rapidly in a monotone. He looked down at his watch. "And now I have another appointment. You'll have to excuse me."

Kim left the guidance office more puzzled than before. She would very much have liked to tell Hank about Anita, but what would he think if she went running to him? Especially now. He would probably conclude that she was looking for an excuse to see him. And maybe he'd be right. Maybe she was the one who needed counseling.

# CHAPTER FIFTEEN

That afternoon, Kim made a difficult decision. She didn't much like or trust police in general, not after the way she and Ma had been treated by them after Carl murdered those people. It seemed as if the police felt that what Carl had done was in some way their fault. Kim hated even thinking about it.

But Mike and Bert were different. She knew they could be trusted. Still, she couldn't very well see Mike now, not after what had happened. She was certain he would press her to continue their relationship. While Evelyn was living in his home and would not sign the divorce papers so that they could be filed for a final decree, there was no way Kim would consider getting involved with Mike again. That left Kim with only one option—contacting Bert St. Croix. It was the only thing she could do. She needed help and advice quickly. Instinctively, she understood that Bert could be trusted. Bert wrestled with her own demons and to some extent had overcome them. Kim respected Bert for that.

As Kim surveyed the architecture of the municipal building, she thought the dark brown oblong resembled nothing so much as a dismal prison—or a school. But then, the municipal building did house the court and police headquarters and she supposed they were not meant to stimulate aesthetic appreciation.

She asked for Detective St. Croix at the front desk and was sent through to the drab room shared by the plainclothes detectives. Kim was relieved to find Bert alone attending to paperwork behind a battered desk.

"Hi, girlfriend, what can I do for you? I hear you've been real busy lately."

Kim appreciated Bert's friendly manner. Obviously, she wasn't taking sides. "Honestly, I haven't phoned you because I thought you might feel funny hanging out with me."

"Since you and Mike aren't together anymore?"

Kim nodded her head.

"Yeah, I know all about that. Mike told me. I met Evelyn, just once. Real piece of work. Ain't none of my business, but if he were my man and I wanted to keep him, I wouldn't let that bitch stand in my way."

Kim smiled. "You're probably right."

"Stake your claim, girl." Bert smacked her hand on the desktop for emphasis.

"I'll think about it."

"You do more than think, you hear?" Bert tossed her braids. "Mike's a good man, and like the old song says, they're hard to find."

"I know."

"But you're not going to take my advice, are you?" Bert gave her a knowing look.

"Probably not. But that doesn't mean I don't respect your opinion."

"How's the new job going?"

Kim shrugged. "Not great. I have a student who's been giving me trouble. He vandalized my car. I didn't see him do it, but my instincts tell me he's responsible. I'm not making an issue about it because the school principal is trying to handle the matter. However, I also discovered that this boy is in an abusive relationship with another student, a young girl who's vulnerable. I'm concerned."

"You want me to do something about that?" Bert's expression was fierce.

"Well, not exactly about either of those matters. I think they can and probably should be handled at the school. I really came to see you on another matter. At the open house during Back to School Night, I happened to meet Mrs. Granger, Sam's grandmother."

"Right, the grandmother of the murdered boy."

"Exactly. She mentioned that her grandson had been friendly with Nick James. That's the same boy, the one I mentioned to you. Nick's come to class smelling of pot. I don't know if he deals drugs as well as uses them. But I have this definite feeling that he was involved in Sam Granger's death in some way."

Bert came around the desk and stood in front of her, an imposingly tall figure. "If someone else talked about hunches without any real facts or evidence, I might blow it off. But I know you. Like Mike, your instincts usually hit the mark. Give me all the information you got on this kid."

Kim was surprised. "You haven't already talked to him?"

"I spoke to Mrs. Granger, but she didn't mention anything about the James kid. Now I got to wonder why."

"Maybe she was afraid. He's really mean. He's got a friend who's always with him too. They can be intimidating."

Bert was writing in her small notebook. "Name of the friend?"

"Billy Kramer." Kim provided Bert with all the information she had.

Finally, Bert looked up from her note-taking. "You did good. Sounds like the first solid lead we've had on this case. I'll be in touch." Bert gave Kim an approving nod and then smiled.

Shandra and Will were arguing, not their usual hard-edged bantering. Their voices were loud and angry. Kim was walking by Shandra's classroom when she heard them. The bell had rung and the halls were clear of students.

"What's going on?"

Shandra ran her hand irritably through her short, dark hair while Will sniffed the air distastefully. Neither one of them answered or even looked in her direction. She was puzzled by their behavior.

"Whatever it is, don't lose your tempers. Keep your sense of perspective. After all, you are friends."

Neither one of them seemed pleased by her self-appointed role as conciliator. Shandra tapped her foot against the floor. Will folded his hands across his chest. Neither would meet her gaze.

"Why don't we go down for lunch? I came by to see if you were ready." She forced herself to sound cheerful.

Shandra stepped out from the doorway of her classroom, closed and locked the door. "All right, I'm ready." She turned to Kim. "You'll be just as annoyed as I am when you hear what Will said. At least I think so." Shandra placed her arms on her generous hips and took a stance of intractability.

"Some people are totally unreasonable," he said archly.

"Some people are as venomous as cobras."

They hadn't taken a step. Kim sensed an impasse.

"Maybe I can act as peacemaker," Kim offered uncertainly.

"All I said was that I believe the current rumors going around about our acting principal are right on the money," Will observed.

"Excuse me, what rumors are those?" Kim's stomach lurched with an immediate sense of alarm.

"Come now, you must have heard. You have Anita Cummings in class, don't you?"

Kim turned to Shandra. "What's going on?"

Shandra spoke haltingly. "Kim, it's all over the school. Anita Cummings went to Dr. Bell and accused Hank Anderson of making sexual advances toward her."

"What?" Kim's mouth hung open in shock. "That's truly absurd. I don't believe it, not for a moment."

"What don't you believe? That Anita made the accusation or that Anderson is guilty?" Will's voice was smooth as a knife blade and just as sharp.

"Both. There has to be some misunderstanding," Kim said in a firm tone of voice.

"Kim and I agree," Shandra said. "This is a phony charge."

"We shall see," Will said with a lofty inclination of his head.

"You're always ready to believe the worst about people." Shandra pointed her finger in an accusatory gesture.

"Only those who deserve it."

"Is that so?" Shandra was in Will's face.

Her accusation appeared to anger him. "I'm not hungry. Why don't you ladies have lunch without me today?" With that he stalked off down the corridor.

"I don't understand Will's attitude toward Hank," Kim said.

"It doesn't take a rocket scientist to comprehend how jealous he is of Hank. Always has been. More so now since he thinks you're interested in Hank."

"But Will and I are just friends," Kim protested. "Besides, I am not involved with Hank Anderson. He's tried to help me. That's as far as it goes. I'm not ready to be involved with anyone at the moment."

Shandra shrugged. "That might be true for you but it's not for Will." Shandra glanced at her watch. "Think about it. Meanwhile, time's passing. Come on. We better go eat."

Kim could hardly manage to swallow any lunch. She kept thinking about Hank. It was absurd; he was much too honorable to ever seduce a student. Anita had to be lying, but why would the girl do such a thing? She said as much to Shandra.

"I agree. The whole thing's stupid. Still, the charge is so serious that it'll be brought before the school board. Sometimes it doesn't matter whether something is true or not. A person's career can be ruined and his reputation destroyed on the strength of a false allegation."

Kim recognized the truth of Shandra's comments. "It's just so unfair."

"Guilty until proven innocent. That's how most folks think."

Kim looked around the faculty room. Hank was not present. In fact, the room was virtually devoid of supervisors today.

"I just can't conceive of anyone believing Anita's story."

Shandra sipped thoughtfully on a cup of coffee. "I hate to say it, but although the rumors about you and Hank have died down, in a sense, that paved the way for acceptance of this. The thinking would be that there's a certain pattern here of inappropriate conduct. Some kind of unwritten rule being broken, you know, like a bird must never foul its nest." Shandra raised her hand as if to ward off protest. "I'm not saying Hank's guilty of anything. I'm just explaining why people might readily accept that kind of accusation regarding him."

Kim was stricken; she felt at least partly responsible for Hank's trouble. "People were talking about Hank and me?"

"That kid, Emory Dunne, spread the word around of how he saw you and Hank out on a date."

"It wasn't a date. He was helping me out when my car was vandalized."

Shandra shrugged. "Look, whatever. I'm certainly not passing judgment. But you know how people are, especially in a small community like a school. Gossip travels like wildfire. And people always assume the worst."

"I cannot accept this."

"What can you do about it?" Shandra gave her a pensive look.

That was the significant question. What could she do? If she felt a certain sense of blame for Hank's difficulties, it seemed only right that she do something to help him. Kim told herself that interfering on his behalf was only just. Doing so was not because she had feelings for the man. No, she'd already decided such emotions would be premature and impulsive on her part. She must put any such thoughts out of her mind completely. She refused to even consider a relationship with Hank. Besides, why analyze reasons? Hank had helped her more than once. She simply wanted to repay his kindness. She owed it to him at the very least.

The first thing she decided to do was talk to Anita Cummings. She had to get to the bottom of the matter. There was too much that made no sense. She must find out the truth. It was the only way she could possibly help Hank Anderson out of this ugly situation.

With impatience, she waited for her most difficult class of the day to begin. But neither Anita nor Nick James made an appearance. Nick's friend Billy was also absent. In fact, few students were present. Kim commented on it as she took attendance.

"Must be senior cut day," Emory said with devilish glee, although his expression never varied.

Kim taught the rest of the day in a preoccupied manner. She was working mechanically, by rote, her mind fixed on the problem of helping Hank. There ought to be some simple way of communicating with Anita. She could find out the girl's home address and visit her. Kim felt that her rapport with Anita was good, although that had been before the girl had come so completely under the domination of Nick James. Still, Kim couldn't help feeling that if she got to speak to Anita alone, she would find out what was really wrong, hopefully help Anita solve her problem, and get the girl to drop her ridiculous accusation against Hank. Was she being naive and simplistic?

Maybe, but she hoped not.

Immediately after school, Kim paid another visit to Mr. Ogden. She wasn't going to take a chance on him slipping out of school before they could talk. As Kim saw it, the matter was urgent and time was of the essence.

The guidance secretary was not so harried at this time of the day. She announced Kim's presence with alacrity. Mr. Ogden eyed her askance, clearly not pleased to see her.

"If you've come to discuss Anita Cummings with me again, I feel I should remind you anything she and I discussed is held in the strictest confidence. The trust I share with these children is no different than a doctor or a clergyman."

"And yet the entire school seems to know about Anita's problems." Kim tried not to sound accusing.

Mr. Ogden grimaced. "That was hardly any of my doing."

"Could you please give me Anita's phone number and home address."

"Why do you want them?" The voice sharpened.

"I'd rather speak directly with Anita."

"I'm afraid that is not possible. I prefer you not hound the girl."

Kim found the man's patronizing tone offensive. "I can assure you, I have good reasons for wanting to speak to Anita. For one thing, she's hardly been in class lately."

"I'll handle that situation. You're to keep out of it."

Kim felt frustrated and angry. How was she to help Hank if she couldn't even speak to Anita? There had to be a way.

"If I can't phone Anita or go see her, maybe you could contact her for me."

"That is inappropriate."

"This is extremely important."

"So you said before." Ogden drummed his fingers on his desk. "My first responsibility is to the child."

"I'm not asking you to violate your sense of ethics." Kim wrote out her home phone number on a sheet of paper. "Please, just call Anita now and urge her to contact me. This is my home phone. She can ask to have the phone charges reversed. I'll accept them. Here's my cell phone number as well. She can contact me at either number. Please explain that I want to help her."

Mr. Ogden accepted the paper grudgingly. "Since you are a new teacher here, just a word of caution."

"Everyone seems to have advice for me." She gave him a rueful smile.

"Perhaps you should listen. Someone who sticks her neck out too far is in danger of having it chopped off."

"I'm well aware of my precarious position."

"I also happen to be Betsy Peters's guidance counselor."

"Oh," was all she could manage to say.

"I had quite a time placating the girl's parents. She's planning to go Ivy League. I suppose you didn't realize that?"

"She's no scholar."

Mr. Ogden narrowed his eyes. "With her father's money and influence, she doesn't have to be one. If I were you, I'd think twice about giving that girl another failing grade. I'm in charge of supervising the counseling, just as I should have been right along. I have a key role in this department. You should listen to me. Don't cause trouble for yourself or others."

Kim left without further comment. It seemed as if being threatened was becoming routine for her in this job. She decided to leave school early that day. It was impossible to concentrate on doing lesson plans; she wasn't able to remotely consider schoolwork right now. And besides, if Anita did phone her at home, she wouldn't want to miss the call. She paused only to stop in the main office located next to guidance to check her mailbox, which proved to be totally empty, in itself something of a relief.

Turning to leave, she collided with someone. She glanced up to see Hank looking down at her. The momentary contact with him caused an immediate reaction. She felt weak and gulped air.

"Sorry," he said. His hands lingered on her arms, making them tingle. "You okay? Did I knock the breath out of you?"

"You take my breath away." She hadn't intended to say it in just that way. Heat rose to her face.

"Can you come into my office for a minute? I want to talk to you." His expression was grave.

She nodded her head, not trusting herself to speak.

Hank turned to his secretary. "Please hold my calls."

As he closed the door behind them, she felt his breath against her cheek. They were perhaps a heartbeat apart.

Then Hank moved away and cleared his throat. His eyes were cast down. "I suppose you heard what happened?"

She nodded her head.

"Do you believe the accusation?"

"Of course not!"

Hank exhaled deeply. "I thought you might accept it as true."

"We've had our differences but I do know the kind of person you are. And no one else who really knows you would believe anything so ridiculous."

"People prefer to believe the worst." The pain he felt was evident.

"Not everyone." She reached her hand out to him and noted it was trembling slightly. She wanted to offer words that would sooth and comfort, but they did not manage to leave her lips.

He stuffed his hands into his trouser pockets and looked out toward his office window.

"The thing is, there's talk there might be a hearing. It's also been mentioned that you might be called as a witness to demonstrate my inappropriate behavior with staff. I might be accused of hitting on you or even be accused of sexual harassment." His eyes wouldn't meet her own. "I felt I ought to warn you in advance."

"That so idiotic! I'll just tell them the truth. Don't worry on my account. I'll do what I can to help you."

He gave her a grateful smile. She thought not for the first time what an attractive man he was.

Suddenly, the intercom buzzed and jarred them both. He muttered a curse under his breath and answered it.

"Mrs. Sylvestri, I asked you to hold all calls." He listened for a moment. "All right." Hank turned to her with a reluctant sigh.

"Dr. Bell is in the outer office waiting to talk to me."

"I'd better go then," she said.

He gave her hand a quick squeeze. "I'll walk you out."

Dr. Bell was pacing the outer office. He glanced from Hank to her. There was a speculative look in his eye. Then he turned back to Hank.

"I came by to inform you that there will be a meeting of the school board tomorrow evening."

"You want me to come?"

The diminutive school superintendent shook his head. "Actually, I'm insisting you don't go. I want to see what develops. The meeting will be telecast on the local cable access station. Why don't you watch it and we'll discuss what occurs the next day?" Dr. Bell's tone of voice was cool, as if he were distancing himself from Hank.

"How can I defend myself if I'm not there?"

"My boy, I've had a lot more experience than you handling irate parents and board members. Your presence would only add fuel to the fire. Trust me. I'm on your side."

Kim could only hope that Dr. Bell was sincere, but she wasn't at all certain of that. She left immediately because she realized that her appearance beside Hank was doing him no good. If Dr. Bell viewed Hank as a womanizer, her presence certainly wouldn't help his situation.

In the parking lot, she glanced at herself in the rearview mirror before starting the engine of her car. Her cheeks were flushed with color and her hair was messy. As a matter of fact, she looked like a woman who could have been involved in a passionate embrace. Obviously, Dr. Bell had been aware of her appearance. Meaning to help Hank, she'd only managed to make him appear guiltier. Tears formed in her eyes as she drove away. Kim knew only two things for certain: Hank Anderson was in a great deal of trouble, and she was likely the only person on the planet who might be able to help him.

# CHAPTER SIXTEEN

Anita Cummings did not phone Kim that evening, nor did she show up for class the next day. Kim was desolate. She hadn't told Hank what she intended to do; he wouldn't expect or want her to get further involved, of that she was certain. However, in a real sense, she was very much involved.

One thing she'd learned from this awful mess was that a good teacher paid attention to details. For instance, if she had the year to start over again, she would have every student fill out an index card with parent names, home addresses, phone numbers, and maybe even work numbers. Then there wouldn't be such a problem getting hold of Anita.

A thought struck her. The students had to fill out cards with all that information for the school nurse at the beginning of the year. It occurred to Kim that she could just go down to the nurse's office and request to see Anita's card. As she acted on the idea, she suddenly felt much better. Luckily, the nurse's secretary was still at her desk. Fifteen minutes later Kim was hurrying to the faculty room with the precious phone number written on a slip of paper. In the empty room, she used her cell phone to make the local call. The girl who answered the phone sounded disappointed Kim was not a boy called Butch; however, the girl also informed her that Anita was around somewhere, and Kim was able to persuade the girl to call Anita to the phone.

Kim waited patiently, trying to determine the best approach to use. If she blew it, there wasn't going to be a second chance.

Anita had to be handled carefully; the situation was volatile, like a bomb that could detonate at any moment. Above all, she should hurl no accusations. That would be the fastest way to shut down any avenue of communication.

Anita's hello was uncertain.

"This is Ms. Reynolds, Anita, how are you feeling?"

"Okay, I guess." The voice was hesitant, fearful.

"Did Mr. Ogden give you my message?"

"He called yesterday."

"I'd like to visit you."

*"Here?"* The idea seemed to upset Anita.

"I thought it might be good for us to get together. Maybe I could help you catch up on your work. You haven't been coming to school and you're falling behind."

"Don't come here." The voice was nervous but emphatic.

"I want to help you. I'm worried about you."

"Talking on the phone's good enough."

"It's not the same thing. We really do have to speak in person."

"What about?" Anita sounded guarded, cautious. This wasn't going well.

"I think we should discuss your problem. I know you have one and I believe I can help you with it. So why don't I just come over right now?"

"No, you can't! Nick is sure to find out and he won't like it." Now her fear was unmistakable.

What did Nick James have to do with this? Kim had a gut instinct. She wanted to ask Anita outright but knew it would be unwise.

"Anita, we have to talk, and it has to be today. Where should I meet you?"

"All right. I could come by the school. Will you still be there?"

"I'll be waiting for you in my classroom."

"Will anyone else be around? I don't want any of the other

kids to see me." There was no question that Anita was afraid.

"Strictly confidential," Kim said, trying to sound as reassuring as possible.

The phone clicked. There was nothing else to do but go back to her classroom and wait.

The time passed very slowly. She stood looking through the window. Outside the leaves were turning a profusion of colors: red, orange, yellow, many of them already falling. Usually, this was her favorite time of year. Unfortunately, this autumn her life had been too turbulent to allow her to properly enjoy the serenity and beauty of nature.

Anita arrived at four-thirty looking even worse than the last time Kim had seen her. Kim noticed at once the purple bruises on Anita's face. Would Nick James have hit her? Obviously he could and would hurt the girl. Careful, Kim warned herself, best not to ask too many questions up front, particularly ones that Anita would not care to answer.

"Why don't you have a seat? I'm so glad you came." Kim hoped her manner was properly solicitous.

Anita sat down opposite her, head down, eyes fixed on the floor. Kim thought the girl looked like a criminal waiting for sentencing.

When Anita chose to remain taciturn, Kim carried the conversation, talking slowly and carefully. "You really don't look very well."

"I'm sick to my stomach."

"What's wrong?"

Hunted eyes regarded her for the first time. "Think maybe I'm pregnant."

Kim inhaled sharply. Had this something to do with the reason Anita decided to accuse Hank? No, there was much more going on here. She was determined to ferret out the truth.

"Who knows about this?"

"No one else. Only Nick."

"And he's the father."

Anita began to tremble. "I didn't say that, did I?"

Kim kept her voice steady and unemotional. "Nick is your boyfriend. Naturally, I would make that assumption."

"Well, you're wrong. It's Mr. Anderson. He did it to me." The girl sounded close to hysteria.

Kim's own heart was beating rapidly. "I wasn't aware that Mr. Anderson had taken a personal interest in you. Of course, if you intend to prove what you say is true, you'll have to accuse Mr. Anderson publicly face to face. You know many men who are accused of fathering children do demand a paternity test."

At least Anita had the decency to flush a bright scarlet, Kim observed with some satisfaction. She didn't wait for a response from the girl.

"Anita, what did you tell Mr. Ogden?"

The girl hunched down in her chair. "Mr. Ogden says I don't have to tell you anything."

"That's perfectly true, you don't." Kim decided to try a different tactic. "But whatever you told Dr. Bell will become public knowledge. Did you know there's a school board meeting tonight?"

The expression of fear was raw and undisguised. "Are they gonna talk about me?"

"Probably. They could ask Mr. Anderson to resign based on your accusation. Do you understand what you said could cost Mr. Anderson his job and his reputation? Do you really want that?"

Anita looked miserable but did not answer.

"If what you said is the truth, then you did the right thing, but if you lied, you're hurting a very good man for no reason."

"Nick says Mr. Anderson's a rotten bastard."

"Did Nick give you a reason?"

"Mr. Anderson punished him."

"Because Nick slashed my tires and destroyed my car."

"Did he?" Her eyes widened.

Anita began to rip at her fingernails. "He doesn't mean any harm. His father's real nasty and it makes Nick angry."

"Is that the excuse he used for hitting you?"

Anita's hand went to the side of her thin, narrow face. "He said he didn't mean it. It was only 'cause I didn't want to tell Dr. Bell those things about Mr. Anderson. So Nick, he got angry."

"Do you really think that gives Nick the right to hit you? And should you be telling lies about Mr. Anderson?"

Anita refused to look at her. "I didn't like doing it."

"Telling lies to please Nick won't make him treat you any better, Anita. There's something wrong with Nick. He's abusive and he's going to keep finding reasons to hurt you. The only way out for you is to stop seeing him and to stop telling lies to please him."

Anita burst into tears. Kim wanted to touch the girl, to reach out and hold her, but she knew that was a mistake. Teachers weren't allowed to physically touch students, even if it was only to offer comfort.

"What am I going to do? When I told Nick about maybe being pregnant, he was so furious with me. The next time I saw him, he told me how I was to tell my guidance counselor that it was Mr. Anderson who made me pregnant. He said that was the way he'd get even with him and you. I can't take it all back now, they'll punish me. And Nick swore he'd tell everyone I was a slut who slept around if I didn't do what he said."

"Anyone who knows you won't believe it." Kim tried to sound reassuring.

Anita bit on her ragged fingernails. "It's worse than that. I'm afraid he'll kill me."

Kim rose to her feet. "Nick isn't coming near you again, not if you tell the truth. We'll see to it."

"I'm real scared."

"I know a very good policewoman. She'll protect you."

Anita shook her head. "No cops. Please."

"I'll be with you. We'll go to the school board meeting tonight and you can speak during the time that's open to the public. It'll be all right. You admit the truth and things will get better. Meantime, I'm taking you out for supper. What would you like? Burgers? Pizza?"

"I can hardly eat."

"A guilty conscience will do that to you. You'll feel better after you've told the truth. Let's order tea and ginger ale along with supper. It'll soothe your stomach."

Kim did not tell Anita that she'd never been to a school board meeting herself. She was surprised to discover how few people actually attended. She recognized Dr. Bell sitting up front with a group of individuals who comprised the board. They sat on the stage in the school auditorium. Most of the business before the board was incredibly dull. It dealt this evening with allocations of funds for a new roof. She might have dozed off if she hadn't been so wired. Anita was apparently feeling the same way. She bit at a fingernail already ripped raw.

When the public portion began, a woman who identified herself as a concerned parent took the podium. She began a discussion of how there were rumors about Mr. Anderson, that the acting high school principal was a womanizer and that he was preying sexually on teenage girls.

"I was very concerned when my daughter told me about this. I could hardly believe it. However, other parents have heard the same stories. I'm asking the board to clarify if these allegations are true, and if they are, I move for a dismissal of Mr. Anderson from his job and that criminal charges be filed."

Dr. Bell looked directly at Anita. Kim took a deep breath and turned to the girl.

"You have to tell them the truth right now before this goes any further. If you don't, you'll never know another moment of peace as long as you live."

"Will you stand up there with me?"

"I wish I could, but you have to do this on your own. You *can* do it."

For a moment, Anita sat as if torn. Then she stood up, walked to the lectern, and asked to speak. She told the truth in a soft, frightened voice, but she was heard and understood.

"I told Dr. Bell that Mr. Anderson had sex with me. It wasn't true. I made it all up. I lied. I'm sorry for what I did."

There was stunned silence for several seconds after she finished speaking, then Dr. Bell rose hurriedly.

"I move that we conclude our meeting for tonight so we may consider what has been said here. I promise to look into the matter further."

It was unanimously agreed upon and the board meeting quickly ended. Dr. Bell took Anita aside and spoke to her quietly for some time. It was clear to Kim that he believed Anita had in fact lied.

Relieved, Kim drove Anita back to her group home. There wasn't a great deal to say, and she allowed Anita to fiddle with the car radio and play whatever music she liked.

Anita sat for a while in Kim's car before going into the house where she resided. "I'll never go back to school," the girl said.

"I think you're wrong. Hold your head up. You've done the right thing. You made a mistake, but you had the courage to rectify it. I'm very proud of you and you should be proud of yourself. The most important thing in this world is being able to respect yourself. You've earned that right."

There were tears in Anita's eyes, as there were in Kim's.

"I didn't tell them about Nick. I couldn't. You think I'm a coward?"

"I think you were very brave tonight."

Anita nodded her head in solemn agreement. "It was the hardest thing I ever had to do, getting up like that in front of all those people and admitting the truth."

"You're going to be all right. Have you taken a pregnancy test yet?"

Anita looked downward and shook her head.

"You tell me when you want to go, and I'll take you to see a doctor. It should be soon though."

"I'm not ready for that yet."

"Promise me you won't put it off much longer."

"Okay, I won't."

Anita got out of the car. Kim waited in front of the dark building just long enough to make certain Anita got safely inside; then she drove away lost in thought.

She'd never felt more exhausted, but suddenly it seemed terribly important that Hank know what had happened. After a single wrong turn, she found her way to the winding road that led to his home.

Somehow it didn't surprise her that there were still lights on in the guest cottage, although it was past eleven o'clock. Hank answered the door before she even knocked.

"Mental telepathy?"

"No, I heard you drive up. Come on in."

She followed him shyly. "I hope I'm not disturbing you."

He was dressed casually in a yellow knit shirt that displayed his wide, muscular chest to perfection. His cut-off jeans were worthy of a surfer. In fact, he had the casual look of a California beachcomber rather than a serious educator.

"I wasn't expecting you, but I'm glad you came. As a matter of fact, I've been watching TV. The local cable access station was broadcasting the school board meeting, and I just happened to catch a glimpse of the audience. Funny, but I saw someone who looked exactly like you sitting next to Anita Cummings, or was that your clone?"

"No, I was there."

He regarded her warmly.

"I wasn't certain you knew what happened tonight. I just wanted to stop by and tell you the good news to put your mind at ease as quickly as possible. But I see you already know."

"Nothing like the wonders of modern technology," he said dryly.

"I assume you're relieved."

"Let's just say what happened tonight was not what I expected."

He gave her a wide, dazzling smile that jolted her. The perfect porcelain white teeth, the firm lips were devastating to her weary, susceptible body.

"Mind telling me how you managed to do it?"

"I spoke to Anita. Got her to see that telling the truth was the only way she'd be able to live with herself."

"That was quite an achievement. Maybe you should consider law rather than education. You're a very persuasive advocate."

"I am?"

"You are."

"Actually, Anita's basically a good, decent kid. She just needed someone to help her, some gentle guidance. Well, I guess I better go," she said, aware that her voice was unsteady.

He moved to block her way. "Don't leave. Stay the night."

She looked up at him. She could barely speak. "I don't think that would be wise."

His hands rose. "No strings, no demands. I just want you to

get a good night's rest and I don't want you to take that long drive tonight by yourself when you're tired."

She studied his powerful physique and strong masculine features. A woman could get very accustomed to being taken care of by such a man.

"If I stay, I doubt either one of us will get much sleep."

"All right, then at least don't come in tomorrow. I'll arrange for a sub to cover your classes."

"I don't want any special treatment. I'll be in school. It's Friday. I can get through anything on a Friday."

He pulled her into his arms and kissed her ever so gently, brushing his lips against hers.

"Goodnight," she said in a voice that was little more than a breathless whisper.

The drive home was accomplished nearly on automatic pilot. There were hardly any cars on the road this late in the evening. She was relaxed now, finally letting down from the high stress of the long day. She didn't want to analyze her feelings for Hank. It was much easier not to think at all. She was tired and vulnerable. Not a good time for deep thinking.

# CHAPTER SEVENTEEN

Kim dragged through Friday propping herself up with coffee, but energy did not reach her tired eyes behind which a throbbing headache formed by mid-afternoon. It didn't surprise her that Anita wasn't in class again. The girl had expressed bone-deep embarrassment at the thought of returning to Lake Shore Regional anytime soon. Anita would need intensive counseling. Kim made a mental note to discuss that with Hank. She had no intention of talking with Mr. Ogden again, having found him pompous and unpleasant.

What did surprise her was the audacity of Nick James, who showed up for class fifteen minutes into the class period with great commotion. His look was hostile; she'd seen a friendlier expression on a pit bull.

Kim braced herself. She was reading and explaining a short story to the class and tried to ignore Nick at first. But Nick, it seemed, had no intention of allowing that to happen. Kim could see his mind clicking away as he looked restlessly from one student to the next. She realized he was ready to explode.

Suddenly, Nick moved toward Emory Dunne and gave him a hard shove. "Outta my way, cripple, you're in my spot!"

Emory responded with a loud expletive. Kim adroitly moved between the two antagonists.

"Mr. James, it appears that you once again intend to disrupt this class. Unless you can behave properly, please leave at once."

Nick's eyelids lowered. "I can do what I want."

"Not in my classroom." This was a confrontation she could not avoid.

He came at her in an intimidating manner. "You're the one who's got to leave. You made Anita change her story. Anita told me. You got her to help that bastard Anderson. You're gonna be sorry for that. You're gonna pay!" Nick raised his hand and made a fist as if to strike her.

Kim shrank away. But before Nick could touch her, he suddenly toppled over with a surprised cry of pain as Emory smashed his mechanized wheelchair at full force into the back of Nick's legs.

"I think Nick had a little accident," Emory said. As usual, there was no expression on his face, but Kim detected a certain smug satisfaction in his voice.

Nick lay on the floor groaning. "You broke my legs, you asshole!"

"Hey, dude, I hope so. You had it coming," Emory said.

The other students gathered around and stared at Nick while he alternately cursed and moaned. Kim, as calmly as she could manage, sent Billy Kramer for the school nurse, Mrs. Clemins.

Hank Anderson appeared in the doorway what seemed like moments later. Kim felt an immediate sense of relief, as if a great burden had suddenly been lifted from her shoulders.

"I'm so glad you dropped by, Mr. Anderson."

"The pleasure is all mine. Mrs. Clemins's secretary informed me there was an accident in your classroom. I came to see if I could lend assistance."

"Do something, man! The cripple attacked me." Nick's coloring was now a mottled purple.

"He was about to punch out Miss Reynolds," Emory said. "He threatened to hurt her. Everybody heard him. He tried to cause trouble and wouldn't leave when she asked him."

"Is that so?" The hint of a grim smile crossed Hank's lips.

"Well, Nick, it's like this: assaulting a teacher, even an attempted assault on a teacher, is punishable by expulsion. But don't worry, I'll see to it that you're placed in an alternative school. In fact, I know just the facility. You'll fit in perfectly."

Mrs. Clemins arrived then. On his walkie-talkie, Hank called for a hall aide and together they lifted Nick into the wheelchair the nurse had brought with her.

"This young man will be just fine in a few days," the cheerful nurse said as she examined him. "His legs are merely bruised. Nothing's been broken."

"They're fractured," Nick insisted. He groaned again for emphasis.

"Nonsense, you're not seriously hurt," she chirped.

"Yes, I am. I'm gonna sue all of you."

"The boy has a very low pain threshold," the nurse confided with a smile. "We'll just see to it that he's x-rayed at the hospital. That should dispel his fears."

Nick was removed from the classroom in a rapid, professional manner by the hall aide who also was part of the security detail, a man nearly as tall and muscular as Hank.

"We'll leave you to teach your class, Ms. Reynolds," Hank said.

Billy Kramer shook his head in disgust. "Man, Nick's a real disappointment. No guts. A wuss."

Like most bullies, it was clear that Nick James was only brave if he was picking on someone he considered weaker; Kim was glad his peers had the opportunity to see his downfall.

After the bell rang, Kim turned to Emory. "Thank you." Her voice was quiet with restraint, but the gratitude was real.

"Hey, I kind of owed you. I mean if it wasn't for me blabbing it around about seeing you and Mr. Anderson in the restaurant, no one would have known. I'm awful sorry about that."

On his way out, Emory knocked over a few chairs just on

general principle. Kim shook her head; Emory was not going to change. She watched as he rode his wheelchair down the corridor singing off key about getting by with a little help from his friends.

Saturday morning Kim slept late. She was feeling more relaxed and at peace than she had since before starting her teaching job at the high school. For a change, her dreams were pleasant. She was being made love to by a very sexy man. Her eyes began to flicker open as she sighed, lost in delight. She felt a feathered kiss at the nape of her neck. Kim sat bolt upright in bed, startled.

"You look delicious, like a juicy peach, ripe and ready to be eaten. I'd like to climb in that bed with you and . . ."

"Mike! What are you doing here?"

"You mean in your apartment or in your bed?"

"Both." She was wide awake now. "Let's start with the apartment. How did you get in? The door was locked."

"Yeah, about that, I was meaning to fix that for you. Not much of a lock there. Anyone can loid it. You need a dead bolt."

"Thanks, I'll look into it myself," she said dryly.

"I came to invite you to breakfast. I hoped you hadn't already eaten. Thought I'd surprise you."

"You did that all right."

He gave her an appreciative smile, and Kim realized she was in a thin nightgown and it was virtually transparent. His eyes roamed to her breasts; she felt her nipples harden and grow erect against the soft material in reaction to his marauding gaze. Kim pulled the blanket around her.

"Please wait outside while I change."

"Such modesty. Blushing becomes you, but you do recall, don't you, I've seen you au natural more than once?"

She certainly hadn't forgotten; in fact, she hadn't forgotten anything. "I was under the impression you agreed that our relationship would now be one of friendship."

He threw her a look of amusement. "You know that isn't true."

"You've got me very confused." She met his gaze steadily. "Has your wife signed and mailed the divorce papers?"

Mike shook his head.

"And is she still living in your house?"

He had the decency to look embarrassed. "She has no place else to go."

"So she says. I'm assuming you offered her money?"

"I did." He met her gaze.

"I'm sorry, Mike. I don't see how we can be together, at least not right now. Not until your marital situation is settled."

"You want me to leave?"

She nodded her head, not trusting herself to speak.

"Just remember that I love you. Don't write me off."

When she heard the door close, she allowed herself to shed a few tears. She lay there, unable to move.

Twenty minutes later, the phone rang and she went to answer it.

"I'd like to give you a proper thank you for what you did for me. I want to ask you to brunch this morning. Before you automatically refuse, I'd like to point out that it's in the way of a very small thank you for what you did for me this week." Hank Anderson cleared his throat, sounding surprisingly unsure of himself.

Kim was thoughtful. "I accept your gratitude. But you've been helping me right along, so brunch really isn't necessary."

"How about if I said that I would really enjoy your company?"

She smiled to herself. "I'll be ready when you arrive."

Kim dressed quickly and casually in faded jeans, striped silk shirt, and a light jacket, brushed her hair until it shone, and then worked with it until her dark auburn hair was plaited into one thick braid that hung over her shoulder. Her only makeup was a touch of lip gloss.

Hank arrived just as she finished.

"Where are Jessica and Su? I'd like to say hello."

"They generally go shopping on Saturday mornings. They've asked me to come with them several times, but I prefer to shop on my own."

"I like your neighbors," he said.

"And they like you. In fact, Jessica left a note that concerns you the other day. I'm afraid I'd forgotten all about it until now." She nodded her head toward the small dining table in the alcove.

Hank found the note, lifted and scanned it. He smiled and then read out loud.

"Kim—I doubt you'll want us around when that stud muffin comes visiting. But please remember to ask if he has any friends, preferably ones that look like him with tight buns and broad shoulders."

"She wants to meet one of your friends."

"So I notice. Don't have any," he said with a wry smile.

"I think the new football coach is unattached."

"Have you been making inquiries?" He raised a golden brow.

"Shandra might have brought it up."

"So bring your neighbor to a game. I'll make the introductions."

"That would please her."

"Got to warn you. They probably have nothing in common."

"Like you and I?"

He moved toward her. "Let's not get into that." He stood tall and straight, his warmth alluring.

"Where did you want to eat?"

"I'll let you make the suggestions. I don't know the restaurants around here all that well."

"Neither do I, at least not the better places."

Hank took her hand and stroked the thumb with an unconsciously sensual motion. "Then I guess you're forcing me to take charge. What about you pack a bag with a few things and I take you somewhere special that's a distance from here?"

"Why do I need to pack anything?" She eyed him with suspicion.

"Because you might want to stay overnight with me."

"I don't think we should get that involved. That was your decision, and I believe it was the right one. Frankly, I don't want to be hurt again."

"Neither do I. On the other hand, being alive means sometimes needing to take risks. So why don't we give ourselves a chance?" The velvet voice was persuasive. "I'm duly chastened. Our relationship will not go beyond the bounds you dictate."

"You make me sound like a fascist," she said.

"How about benevolent despot?"

"Mr. Anderson, you are something of a complex paradox, which I find difficult to comprehend. You run hot, and you run cold. I do not wish to be burned or frozen. Therefore, I'm going to proceed with caution around you."

"And you make me sound like a natural disaster." His voice was deep, but not without a pleasant inflection.

"Let's just say I consider you dangerous and I know enough to watch my step."

"Okay, will you feel better if I promise to keep it light?" His well-modulated voice was mellifluous, smooth like honey.

"Absolutely, just friends. A person can never have too many friends—or so I've been told."

"Let's go then." He took her hand.

Hank drove to Perth Amboy. They parked near the waterfront area and walked along the boardwalk observing small boats docked in the marina and people fishing off the pier.

"It's lovely," she said. "Really charming."

"Part of a reclamation project." He took her to a small park overlooking the Atlantic and she admired the view.

"Look at those gulls flying overhead. They seem so free."

"Don't you feel free?" he asked.

"I don't think of my life in those terms. Do you?"

"I suppose not," he agreed. He took her hand in his larger one and held it tightly as they walked along. "This was always the nicest part of the city. In colonial times, Perth Amboy was a more important port than New York. People engaging in the triangle trade built elegant Georgian houses up on Water Street overlooking the harbor. There's still a lot of beautiful old architecture there if you'd like to take a look."

They did exactly that. It was strange how much she enjoyed just being with him. Privately, she acknowledged it wouldn't really matter where she was as long as her time was spent with him. Unlike Mike, Hank Anderson was unmarried. However, he was still the principal of her school. She warned herself that she didn't want to be romantically involved with either one of them, at least not now. But she had to admit the truth to herself: they were both very attractive men. A woman would have to be dead not to find them appealing.

"I'm beginning to realize that you know a lot about history. Your knowledge obviously isn't limited to math and science."

He gave her that broad, boyish grin that she admired. "I'm not exactly a Renaissance man, but I do enjoy knowing a little bit, a smattering, about everything. I like to read. After all, I'm an educator, right?"

They walked back to the waterfront and Hank took her to an unusual restaurant.

"It used to be an armory. They did some modernizing and turned it into a great eatery. It's gone through a few owners, but it's still in business I'm happy to say."

Kim was impressed by the circular layout and the enormous spiral staircase. There was warmth and beauty here. They got a window table that had a spectacular view and she sat back and enjoyed the sunny Saturday morning.

"So what do you think?"

"It's wonderful here."

He took her hand and kissed it, sending a tremor through her.

"I believe we agreed to keep our relationship platonic." Her voice sounded unnaturally husky, like well-warmed brandy.

"I promised, but I never said for how long." Still, he released her hand.

Then his eyes snared hers, and when their food came, she ate but hardly tasted a thing.

After lunch, Hank decided to take Kim for a drive; it was the only way he was going to keep his hands off her.

"I think we'll take a walk in the Pine Barrens. Have you been there before?"

"I have, but not recently."

He looked into those deep dark eyes and was lost for a moment. Quickly, he turned his attention to the road.

"We're close to the Garden State Parkway, so the trip will be easy."

He kept the conversation as casual as he could manage. The drive itself was relaxing. He told her about the history of the Pine Barrens before they began walking. He had the feeling that she already knew all about the Pine Barrens but was too polite to tell him.

"The Barrens are vast and amazingly unspoiled, considering the small size of the state and the fact we're denser than any other state in regard to population."

"Do you come here often?"

"No, it's too far usually. But I like the sense of being alone and able to think when I do get out here."

"There are no clocks in the forest."

"Quotation?"

"Shakespeare. *As You Like It.* It's my favorite Shakespearean comedy. We Bardolators quote the master wherever appropriate."

He liked it when she wasn't quite so serious about things. "The only thing I've got memorized are football plays."

She looked at him with sudden concern. "I just realized. Are you missing a football game on my account?"

"It's tonight, so no, I haven't missed it."

"Everyone will expect you to be there."

"That's true. I never miss a game. Maybe you'll come with me tonight?"

She studied him intently. "It'll start tongues wagging all over again if we're seen in public together. I don't think it's such a great idea."

"After all that's happened, I don't think we should worry about that. Promise me you'll at least think about it."

She gave him a wan smile. "Now you're forcing me to confess the truth: I don't know anything about football."

"But you're a fast learner. And I'm an excellent teacher."

They walked through an area where the ground was burned and only dwarf trees grew. Far above, birds shrieked as if in warning.

"Likely arson or someone careless with a lit cigarette," he said with a wave of his hand. "Thousands of acres have been lost that way. When there's a dry spell, the forest becomes a tinder box."

They roamed the sandy trails and talked easily. He inhaled the sweet, fragrant scent of her, which contrasted with the earthy smell of their surroundings.

"Those aren't pine trees," she said and pointed upward.

"White cedars. Before the Revolution, there were giant cedars here that swayed in the wind like the masts of sailing ships. Unfortunately, they're gone now."

She bent over to examine the water in a slow-moving stream while he admired the grace of her form and the shape of her derriere.

"What gives the water that orange color?"

"Iron ore. There were once iron furnaces in the pines—iron plantations, actually. The ironmasters made the cannonballs that Washington used to win the Revolution. We could go for a tour of the ironworks at Batsto if you like."

She shook her head. "Maybe another time. I'm enjoying just exploring the area on our own." She pointed to a painted turtle that had bright orange and black markings around the edge of its shell and sat contentedly sunning itself on a large rock in the stream.

"All sorts of interesting flora and fauna."

He eyed her appreciatively. "Yeah, sure is."

She flushed and began to talk again in a rapid flow. "Lovely here really, rather like the English moors, though the darkness is just a tad eerie."

"Lots of scary legends and stories about this place, probably for that reason."

"We literary types love legends, so tell me more." Her voice was animated with interest and enthusiasm. She put her arm through his.

"Well, there are stories about pirates and smugglers who hid themselves and their gold in swamp." He guided her around oozing marshland.

"Messy," she observed.

"There are cranberry bogs out here, blueberries too. Then

there's the holly and laurel."

"I'm going to bring back some pine cones if you don't mind."
She stopped to collect a few. "Tell me more about the legends."

He bent down beside her, helping to select a few cones. For a
moment their hands joined and they paused to look at one
another. Kim lowered her dark lashes.

"The Pineys—people who live in the Barrens—used to believe
that a devil lives here."

"The Jersey Devil."

He eyed her askance. "You know all about this, don't you?
You're just humoring me."

Her laugh was throaty. "I like the way you tell it. So please
continue."

"The theory is that the Jersey Devil was just some poor,
deformed child who grew up wild and unwanted. He might
have been so horrible to look at people confused him for a
devil. Other stories have it that he was really just a sand hill
crane confused with a supernatural creature because of its
strangely human cry."

"I wonder. Did anyone actually see it?"

"There are descriptions. Some say the devil has the head of a
dog, the body of a kangaroo, the feet of a horse, the wings of a
bat. Oh, and a forked tail."

She laughed again. "All pretty absurd, don't you think?"

"I don't know. To quote your bard, there are more things in
heaven and earth than are ever dreamed of in our psychology."
He lowered his head, but couldn't keep the smile from twitch-
ing at his lips.

"Well, I'd be the last one to disagree with that," she said. "All
right, where is this monster? Should we look for him?"

"People say: don't look for the Jersey Devil or he'll find you.
Mostly, they look for him not far from Leeds Point. Supposedly,
he was a thirteenth child born to a Quaker woman, Mother

Leeds, in 1735. Since then, he's been seen variously in the company of a headless pirate and a beautiful, blond-haired girl dressed in a white, flowing gown."

"How romantic. Do you believe ghosts haunt the Barrens?"

"I don't consider myself a romantic. But before European settlers ever came to southern New Jersey, the Lenape Indians spoke in fear of a ghost spirit that roamed the Barrens. Are you getting frightened? Maybe I should hold you close for comfort."

"No, I'm just fine thanks. Do you have any more legends?" She licked her lips and he nearly groaned, finding that slight gesture provocative.

He shrugged. "Think I've about run out for the moment."

"Then we'll have to invent our own," Kim said with a smile.

"People often create the things they fear, don't you think?"

"Do you believe in ghosts?" she asked, suddenly looking serious.

"No, I look for natural explanations and reasons."

"I know there are ghosts," she said, and he realized she wasn't joking with him. "I've seen them, spoken to them."

There was a rustle in the treetop nearest them. Startled, Kim pressed herself against him. Hank told himself he was not going to take advantage of the situation, but he was only human, after all. He held her tightly in his arms for just a moment before releasing her.

"Just a squirrel," he said. "I'll protect you from devils, ghosts, and rampaging woodchucks."

"But who'll protect me from you? Let's start back," she said. "I'm afraid of getting lost."

"I've got a great sense of direction," he said.

"I don't. I wish they made a GPS system for the soul. Maybe then I could avoid making wrong turns."

# CHAPTER EIGHTEEN

"Why did you bring me here?"

"I thought you'd like to stay over tonight."

She was angry and her eyes glittered like stars.

"All right, I suppose I could have just as easily driven you back to your apartment but I wanted us to spend more time together."

She viewed him warily. "You took advantage of the fact that I fell asleep while you were driving and did what you wished."

"Not exactly what I wished." He met her accusation with a hot look. "Relax, I'm not going to try to seduce you. In fact, you'll have to ask me."

"I will?" She narrowed her eyes suspiciously.

"That's right. After the insult you've given me, you'll have to beg. And then I'd have to think it over." His teasing made her smile.

"We'll see who begs for what."

He seemed to be searching for a safe subject. "How about a cold drink followed by a tennis lesson?"

"I'll settle for the cold drink," she said. "Where do you get so much energy? We must have tramped through the forest for miles and miles."

He got out of the Corvette, came around the passenger side, and opened the door for her. It was an unnecessary, old-fashioned courtesy but endearing just the same.

"Cold drink it is."

They watched the sunset from the patio, sharing the beauty of it.

Kim sighed. "I love this sight," she said.

"I'd rather look at you."

"Wow, where did that come from?"

"You shined the way you handled the situation with Nick James. You were calm and courageous. I've just begun to recognize and admire your inner beauty as much as your outward appearance."

Kim felt her cheeks burn with embarrassment. "I don't deserve such extravagant praise. And I'm rather plain in the looks department."

"I think you underestimate yourself." Hank squeezed her hand. "I know you have some doubts about getting involved with me. If you want to move slow, that's all right with me too, but I want you in my life. You don't have to say anything right now."

"I should be getting back to my place."

"How about relaxing in the hot tub?"

She looked in the direction of it wistfully. "I didn't bring my bathing suit."

"You don't need one."

She gave him a dubious look. "Forget it."

He scooped her up into his arms amid much protest.

"What are you doing?"

"You'll see."

The next thing Kim knew, Hank settled her beside the hot tub and unceremoniously yanked off her sneakers and socks. Then he pushed her feet into the gloriously warm water.

"I could turn it up for you."

"This is perfect." She sat on the edge of the tub, legs immersed calf deep in the shimmering aqua water. "Heaven."

Hank excused himself, disappeared for a few minutes, and then returned in bathing trunks carrying two large, fluffy towels. He splashed into the water and heaved a great sigh of pleasure. Then he was holding her feet in his hands and massaging them. He pressed her toes against the broad expanse of his chest. The feel of his silky hair sent little excited chills down her spine. She'd never considered feet an erogenous zone until now.

"Feel good?"

"Great, thanks."

"Why don't we order that pizza right now? I don't know about you, but I'm starving to death." He threw her a towel and wrapped the other one around his waist.

By the time the pizza arrived, Kim had poured out some Cokes for them and asked herself for the tenth time what she was doing here. Hank had gone off to change into dry clothes. She had the opportunity to think about what was happening. Could she trust herself not to respond to him? Could she trust him? Would he ever open himself to her? Maybe in time. But did she even want that?

"I'm dressed for the game tonight," Hank said, joining her in the kitchen.

In his Lake Shore Regional sweats, he didn't look much older than the students. His thick neck and strong, muscular build gave Hank Anderson the look of a serious athlete. She watched him bite into his first slice of pizza with a healthy appetite.

"About tonight, I think maybe you should take me back to my apartment. I'm really rather tired."

"I never took you for a coward."

"I'm not."

His eyes met hers. "I want you with me. I'm not ashamed for

people to know that we're dating each other. They're going to have to find out eventually because I don't intend to stop seeing you."

Her heart began to beat a little faster.

"You really want me to go?"

"I do."

"Okay, let me call Jessica. I just want to let her know about the game tonight in case she'd like to come."

Hank looked surprised. "I doubt she would."

"You never know."

Hank was about to leave the kitchen but she signaled that he should stay. They had argued once over a phone call; she decided it would not happen again.

Su answered the phone. They spoke for a few minutes and then Kim asked for Jessica. Su told her that Jess had gone out for the evening with a new fellow she'd recently met. Kim thanked her, cut the connection, and then checked on her calls. She'd shut her cell phone off earlier and wasn't expecting any calls, but it was always a good idea to check. She was glad she had when she discovered there had been a phone message of interest.

"I got a call earlier from Anita Cummings," she told Hank.

"Call her back immediately," he urged.

All sorts of terrible thoughts raced through Kim's mind. What if Nick had beaten up Anita? What if the girl had tried to commit suicide? Kim was relieved when the telephone was finally answered. Anita's voice sounded stronger, healthier.

"I just wanted to thank you for helping me get myself together," Anita said.

"Has Nick bothered you?"

"No. I don't think he will either. Mr. Anderson's been terrific. He talked to people. Nick knows the police will come if he calls to threaten me or tries to do anything to me. I'm not scared anymore. I feel a lot better. There's something else too." Anita paused but then went on to tell Kim the rest of the reason she'd phoned.

Kim mostly listened sympathetically and reassured the girl by saying she would keep in touch.

Hank sat waiting patiently, listening to her end of the conversation. When Kim hung up the phone, she turned to him with some sense of relief.

"Anita wanted me to know it was a false alarm. She's not pregnant after all."

"That's good news. She's still a child herself. She certainly isn't prepared to be a mother."

"Anita really needs help so she doesn't fall prey to another Nick James," Kim said, worrying her lower lip.

"We agree about that. I've got her scheduled to attend a different school where she'll be receiving first-rate counseling."

Kim was pleased; Hank really did care about the girl's welfare. "That was thoughtful. She was too ashamed to come back to Lake Shore."

"Just as well. A fresh start will be good for her."

"At least now she won't be dropping out."

During the football game, quite a few people recognized Hank and came over to exchange some words or shake hands. Hank introduced Kim to a number of unfamiliar faces, mostly local residents and parents. Kim, generally reserved and shy with strangers, would have hung back, but Hank wouldn't permit it.

Dr. Bell joined them at halftime. "Good to see you," the older man said, slapping Hank on the back in a genial manner.

"I like to watch our boys play. You know that."

"We had the best teams when you coached."

Dr. Bell removed his eyeglasses, at the same time acknowledging her presence. "Ms. Reynolds, you like football?"

"I think I'm going to learn."

"So you two are seeing each other officially?"

"Ms. Reynolds and I are friends. Any objection?"

There was a slight hesitation. "I suppose not."

"Good, glad to hear it."

"Enjoy each other's company and the game. So far we're winning." The school superintendent indicated the scoreboard. "But this will be a close one."

Hank agreed with him, and they discussed the strengths and weaknesses of both teams before the superintendent rejoined his own party. After that, Hank excused himself for a few minutes and spoke with the football coach. He returned to her just as the third quarter began.

The evening had grown chilly, and she began to shiver. Hank went back to the car, brought back a blanket, and placed it around both of them. Patiently, he explained everything that was happening to her on the playing field as the game continued. By the fourth quarter, the two teams were tied. From there, the excitement mounted. In the final minutes, Lake Shore's punter kicked a field goal, scored, and the game was over.

"Great game," he told her on the drive back to the house. "Glad we got to see it. Hope you weren't too bored."

"Not at all." But she was very cold.

As soon as they were back at the house, Hank noticed her shivering and insisted on fixing them hot chocolate.

"I could do that," she protested.

"Nope, I have a special, secret recipe given to me by Peruvian monks."

She eyed him skeptically. "Peruvian monks?"

His eyes glinted. "I might have made that part up for your benefit. You did say you like legends and stories."

"And here I thought you were so literal-minded and linear in your thinking."

"Just goes to show," he said and pulled her along with him. "I'm getting a fire started. It'll be the first of the season, but the fireplace is all set. So just sit down on the sofa and get comfortable."

She did exactly that, seated herself in the family room in front of the fireplace, getting toasty warm until Hank returned with two big mugs of hot chocolate that boasted marshmallows floating on top of the froth. She blew on the beverage until it cooled and then drank it greedily.

"This is delicious. How did you make it?"

"It wouldn't be a secret recipe if I told you. However, I could be seduced into giving it to you."

"I wouldn't dream of degrading you."

He threw back his head and laughed. He'd been standing near her; now he seated himself at her feet and began removing her sneakers and socks. His hands rubbed rhythmically against heels and toes.

"You must have a foot fetish."

"I'm working my way up in life. Care to help a guy out?" He pulled her down beside him on the carpet. "Now I believe you were about to seduce me." His words teased but his eyes were serious.

"I don't think so."

"Hate my guts?"

"Not exactly."

# Chapter Nineteen

With surprise, Kim heard the front door opening.

"Hank, are you here?" a strong voice called out.

The distinguished man who walked into the room had silver hair and a sophisticated demeanor. Todd Anderson for his sixty-some-odd years still carried himself with the vitality of a young man. He extended his hand to Hank.

"Good to see you, son."

"What are you doing here?"

"I live here, as I recall. And what about you? I could ask the same. Last I saw, you were dug in at the cottage."

Hank changed the subject. "Where's the bride?"

"Val's taking a walk around the grounds while I bring our things inside."

"She's never been here before, has she?"

"I thought she might like to see the place, even though she's a city girl at heart."

There were footsteps behind them and they both turned.

"And who is this lovely young woman?"

Kim smiled at Hank's father. She doubted very much she looked anything except tired at the moment, but it was kind of Hank's father to compliment her.

"Dad, I'd like to introduce you to my friend and co-worker, Kim Reynolds."

"*Friend?*" His father emphasized the word with a curious smile.

Kim stepped forward and shook his hand politely. "It's very nice to meet you. I've wondered about Hank's family."

"Ask me anything," he said with a warm grin.

"I might just do that."

They were soon joined by his father's new wife. She was a striking redhead of about forty, Kim approximated. The woman's figure was attractive with a tendency toward the voluptuous. She had a ready smile for each of them.

"I don't think you've ever met my son before."

"Hello," Hank said politely. "We've spoken several times on the telephone but never actually met."

"That's because you couldn't make it to the wedding. I see the son is as handsome as the father," Val said. She leaned forward and gave him a peck on the cheek.

"Just get back from the honeymoon, Dad?"

"A few days ago."

"Hawaii was fabulous," Val said. "Wonderful place to get married. So romantic. Everyone should travel there for a honeymoon."

"I'll keep that in mind," Hank said dryly.

"Let's go out to breakfast in the morning," his father said. "We can talk better over pancakes."

"Whatever made you come out so late?" Hank knew his father very well. There wasn't a whimsical bone in the man's body.

"It was Val's idea. I've talked so much about you and this place, she just decided on the spur of the moment to come and see it. My bride is impetuous." Todd turned to Kim. "Will you be staying over? We'd love company at breakfast."

Kim turned to Hank, flushed with embarrassment. He seemed to understand how uncomfortable she was feeling.

"I was just about to drive Kim back to her apartment. Kim, you have a choice: stay over at the cottage tonight, or I'll drive you home and pick you up tomorrow morning so we can join my dad and Val for breakfast."

"I hate to inconvenience you, Hank, but I'd prefer to go back to my own place. As to picking me up tomorrow, that won't be necessary. I'll drive back here in the morning. I'm an early riser anyway."

"Just so long as we have your company for breakfast tomorrow," Todd said in an affable manner. "I like being surrounded by attractive women." He smiled at his wife.

Kim and Hank talked very little on the drive back to her apartment. Yet the silence was comfortable.

She went to sleep that night with a smile on her face. Everything would have been fine except for the strange dreams she had.

First, Sammy Granger was reaching out to her. "Remember me," he said. "I need your help."

Sammy dissolved into the mist. Then there was a large black vulture standing over a dead body in the woods. The atmosphere was hazy, but she felt a sense of fear and dread. Kim woke up in a sweat at three in the morning, and was unable to return to sleep. Had the dream meant something? God, she hoped not! And why had it come to her after such a pleasant day spent with Hank Anderson?

"I'd like to cook you a welcome-home breakfast," Hank said to his father.

"Your cooking doesn't thrill me. Besides, I've been telling Val all about Delbert's and the Belgian waffles they serve with huge strawberries and thick whipped cream."

"The strawberries may be out of season."

"Then they'll have something equally as good." His father was in an expansive mood, full of energy and vitality; clearly, this new marriage was making him happy.

"Come on, son. Let's get moving. I'm starving."

There was no arguing with Todd Anderson when his mind was set on something. The only argument he'd ever won with his father was over his career, and that had taken a lot of doing. Dad was a stubborn, strong-willed man, almost comparable to a force of nature.

Delbert's did have a wonderful brunch, and Val was a charming woman who took an immediate liking to Kim. The uneasiness he'd felt at his father's unexpected arrival began to gradually wear off.

Kim was having a good morning. In a way, it was a great relief to be with company. She wasn't sure what she'd have said to or done with Hank if they had remained alone the previous evening.

Todd Anderson asked questions about her, which she had no difficulty answering since they weren't terribly personal. But when Hank went out to feed the meter and Val excused herself to visit the ladies' room, Todd leaned forward in a more intimate manner.

"Now that we're alone, I want to ask if you and my son are in a serious relationship."

She felt warmth rise to her face. "We're just getting to know each other. I don't know that either of us should be involved. I do know that he once cared very deeply for a woman, but she didn't respond in kind and he was badly hurt."

Mr. Anderson frowned, lines forming like a mosaic pattern on his face. "I'm not aware of any serious emotional attachments in my son's life. Hank's always kept to himself. Not that he and I have had the closest relationship. When he was young, I was busy building up the business. He faults me for that. I suppose he needed me then and I failed him. It was never the same after we lost his mother."

"Was her death very hard on Hank? I'm assuming that it was."

Mr. Anderson gave her a bewildered look. "Didn't Hank tell you that his mother and I are divorced? It was a very bitter thing. She left when he was seven years old. He loved her devotedly, but she really wasn't worthy. She took off with her lover without a thought to her own child. Just left him and me without a backward glance. She was always self-centered, but what she did to him was downright cruel." There was genuine outrage in his voice. "She never tried to get in touch with Hank. All he's gotten from her over the years is a few Christmas cards. I hear she has a whole new family now. The thing is, Hank was heartbroken and he blamed me."

"I don't see why."

"Children can't be objective where parents are concerned. Hank didn't see his mother's flaws. She was rarely with him. There were always servants to take care of the menial part of child care. My wife would kiss her son, praise him lavishly, and then breeze away."

"Maybe as an adult Hank's had an opportunity to reevaluate his childhood memories."

Mr. Anderson gripped the table as if he were in real pain. "No, he'll always consider it my fault that she left. I suppose I wasn't around enough to give her the kind of attention she expected. In the note she left, Julia claimed I neglected her. In her loneliness, she'd taken up with another man. There was an element of truth in that. Anyway, my son and I became alienated. He cut himself off emotionally from me. Still, I've tried to maintain some semblance of a relationship with him."

Kim pressed his hand warmly. "Thank you for telling me all of this. I appreciate your candor. I know it couldn't have been easy. But it does help me understand Hank better."

His eyes brightened. "You really care about him, don't you?"

"I think he's a very special man."

"I would say my son is luckier than he deserves."

"What's this?" Val said. "I let the man out of my sight for a few minutes and he takes up with another woman, and a younger one at that." Her tone was tongue-in-cheek, but there was a touch of actual concern in her voice.

"Now, darling, you have nothing to be jealous about. Kim and I were just discussing a subject of mutual concern."

Val seemed to quickly get a sense of the situation and smiled in comprehension. She said nothing else because they were rejoined by Hank.

"I believe dessert and champagne are in order. We have a great deal to celebrate."

Hank studied his father and thought he'd never seen the man more cheerful. They took a walk around the center of town after finishing their meal. Val remarked on the quaint shops.

"Main Street has undergone a facelift."

"Well, I think it's quite charming," Val said. "An unexpected bit of Americana."

Hank noticed her expensive jewelry and designer suit. She obviously came from money and was comfortable in a material world. She seemed perfect for his father.

"So how long do you plan to stay?"

Todd Anderson threw his head back and laughed. He had a deep, resonant voice like his son. "Hank, you always did get right to the point. Don't worry. We won't be in your way. We're just staying one more night."

"I didn't mean it that way," he said sheepishly. "I just wondered."

"I came to a decision a little while ago. Since Val and I both work in Manhattan and we intend to travel together extensively, there's no point in me holding on to the house. I'm writing the deed over to you. Then if you want to stay in the cottage or prefer to move back to the main house, you can have your choice. I only ask to be made welcome when we occasionally visit. Is that all right with you?"

Hank was astonished by his father's declaration. "You don't need to do that."

"I know. I thought about making a provision in my will, but I don't intend to die for a very long time. In fact, I don't think about dying at all—there's no future in it." He smiled with self-amusement. "The estate is yours as well as mine, and I want you to feel that it belongs to you legally. Now don't argue with me when I'm feeling magnanimous. Lord knows, it doesn't happen all that often."

"Your father's right," Val said, taking her husband's hand. "The place really should be yours. We have a fine condo in the east eighties. It's large and perfect for our needs. Of course, the estate is lovely and rustic. We would like to visit from time to time."

"If that's what you want," Hank said finally.

He didn't get a chance to be alone with Kim until noon. At that time, his father announced that he and Val were tired and would take a siesta. Hank invited Kim to take a walk with him. They ended up by the pool.

"Your father told me some things today. I wanted to ask you about them."

Hank sat down on a bench. "What did he say to you?"

"He told me about your mother."

Hank stood up abruptly. "He shouldn't have said anything."

She came and stood in front of him, a worried look on her face. "I'm glad he did. I wish you'd told me yourself though."

"My father and I don't get along very well. I sometimes suspect he does things like this just to irritate me."

"I sense that he loves you very much."

"You're entitled to your own opinion." He was unaccountably annoyed with her.

"Hank, was your mother the woman who hurt you so much you never felt like loving anyone again?"

When he didn't answer right away, she put her hand over his. "Please," she said imploringly.

He nodded abruptly. Her hand squeezed his.

"I don't want your sympathy. That's partly why I didn't discuss the matter with you. It all happened a very long time ago. Ancient history. It doesn't matter anymore."

"I think it does. *The child is father to the man.* There's a student at Lake Shore. Her name is Evie Gardner. Her mother took off and left her husband and children in much the same manner your mother did. It's been awful for her and she's bitter. But you can't let what other people do destroy your chance at a happy life. There's something I want to tell you. Remember when you asked me who Ginny was? You thought I had a child tucked away, didn't you?"

He turned to look at her directly. "I was out of line on that. I had no right to ask you about it, to assume such a thing, or act judgmental. I know I was wrong."

"You were wrong in a lot of ways. And it is a personal matter. But I want to tell you about Ginny—actually, I insist. I never meant for it to be a secret. I just became angry with you. You'd been such a clam about yourself and expected to know everything about me. I was insulted by your line of thinking. But there's no secrets necessary between friends." She wouldn't let go of his hand and led him firmly back to sit beside her on the bench.

"You don't have to tell me anything. It doesn't matter. I mean that."

"It does matter. There shouldn't be doubts or suspicions between us. There ought to be trust. So I'll tell you about Ginny.

My mother has a cousin, Mary, who she moved in with down in Florida. Mary's also a widow. Mary's older sister, Helen, died recently. Ginny was Helen's daughter. She's mentally and physically challenged. Actually, I believe multiply handicapped is the correct terminology. Helen took care of Ginny at home. My mother and Mary have now taken over that responsibility. Ginny is a sweetheart, but she does need special care and it's expensive. I contribute whatever I'm able. Ginny is family and I love her. Ma felt terrible about asking me, but right now she's in a transition period herself, between jobs, and the house hasn't sold here as yet."

Hank was so surprised he hardly knew what to say. Kim was waiting for some sort of reaction from him. Her eyes were fixed on his.

"Thank you for telling me."

"That's all right. I really want you to know. I want us to have an open, honest communication. I think it's important. I grew up in a family where there were always secrets and lies. It was awful. It made me want to be truthful in my relationships with other people. I suppose as a librarian and teacher, I'm always searching, looking for truth."

Hank didn't answer, but he understood.

On Monday morning, Kim began her school day in the usual way, but something seemed wrong. She wasn't certain what it was except that her sensitivity was giving off warning signals. At lunchtime, she felt restless and didn't want to eat. Instead, she felt compelled to take a walk.

Around the school, the grounds were wooded. The trees were beautiful with the colored leaves falling. Yet Kim felt an acute sense of wrongness. She'd slept poorly again the previous night. More bad dreams had plagued her and she'd woken in the middle of the night perspiring and breathing hard. All bad omens from her perspective.

She began walking away from the school buildings, urged on by a compulsion she didn't understand. Something was definitely off, but what was it? She shivered, although the day itself was not cold in the slightest. Kim wasn't certain what she was searching for. All she recognized was that it was there waiting to be found, something dark and sinister drawing her. As a child, she'd feared that there were monsters hiding beneath the bed and lurking in the closet, waiting to devour her. She remembered with vivid clarity. She recalled running terrified to her mother. Ma always swore it was just her imagination. Then Ma would put on the lights in her bedroom to prove there was nothing to fear.

Kim was an adult now, and yet she still felt fear.

She was compelled to continue her walk, aware that she was searching for something vague she could not define, something dark, ugly, sinister. Then, dear God, she saw it, and all her fears were confirmed.

# CHAPTER TWENTY

Rufus Ogden heard about Kim Reynolds finding the body almost immediately after she reported the death. He took pride in the fact that very little went on in the school that he didn't know about. That was as it should be, he reasoned.

Kim Reynolds was a stupid woman, meddling in matters that did not concern her. She was nothing but a nuisance and a troublemaker. If he were in charge, she would already have been forced to resign. He would discuss that little matter with Morgana Douglas.

By rights, he ought to have been named head of guidance when the position first became available. It should not have been offered to that young upstart Anderson. It was he, Rufus Ogden, who should have been named acting principal as well. After all, he'd been teaching in the school system over thirty years. He still yearned for the job, but knew it was unrealistic to live in hopes of replacing Anderson. It might have happened if that stupid child, Anita Cummings, had stood behind her accusation and not confessed that she'd lied, but that was over and done with. He sat back in his desk chair and let out a deep sigh.

The increase in salary would have been a real benefit, what with his wife's cancer surgeries. And soon now he'd be forced to retire. It hurt that he'd been passed over so many times. He deserved better! They always chose the tall men as leaders. Superintendent Bell was a short man himself. Yet he insisted on advancing men of six feet tall and over to positions of authority. The stupidity of it! Alexander the Great and Napoleon Bonaparte had both been short men, and look what they'd accomplished.

Rufus Ogden knew he deserved better than he'd gotten. Well, there were other ways of obtaining extra money. It was fortunate he'd been clever enough to figure them out. An intelligent, determined man could always find ways and means to deal with adversity. He smiled grimly with self-satisfaction.

Kim's hand shook as she tried to drink a cup of coffee. She wanted to pretend to herself that she was composed, but it just wasn't working. She made an effort to live the life of a normal human being and somehow it never seemed to work. She closed off the part of her mind that supported her psychic ability. And yet, it refused to be totally suppressed. How wonderful it would be to live an ordinary life free from disturbing, dark visions!

Will sat down beside her in the teacher's cafeteria. "I just heard the news," he said. "This is about the most shocking thing that's happened in the high school's history. Now do dish all the ghastly details."

"Kim, what are you doing in here? We have lunch duty starting," Shandra said.

"What? I'm sorry. I completely forgot."

"Haven't you heard the distressing news?" Will smiled, flashing his yellowed teeth.

"What are you talking about?" Shandra's tone of voice betrayed her impatience.

"Why, our lovely young thing has uncovered a murder most vile, right under our very noses as it turns out. She found one of our students dead out in the woods." Will's well-modulated voice rose and fell in mock admiration.

"That's unbelievable!"

"The truth often is," Will said.

Shandra sat down and joined them. She didn't so much sit as plop down in the chair. "Well, you certainly don't lead a dull life," she said as she turned to Kim.

"I suppose not," Kim agreed. "But excitement like this is not what I prefer."

Hank Anderson walked into the cafeteria, looking around. When he saw Kim, he came directly toward her. "Are you feeling any better?"

"How would she be expected to feel?" Will countered. "Finding a dead body is traumatic. To think one of these young devils is actually a murderer!"

Kim shuddered. "We don't know that."

Will reached over and patted her hand. "Poor darling. Such innocence. Isn't she sweet, Anderson? But you and I, we know better, don't we? We know what evil these youngsters are capable of doing. Think *Lord of the Flies.*"

Hank ignored Will. "Kim, I phoned the police. They should be here shortly. They'll want to talk with us. So stay right here for now. And don't worry, I've got your duty period covered. I also found people to cover your classes for the rest of the day. You just come to my office when the police arrive."

Kim didn't speak. She merely nodded her head miserably. Would they send Mike? She hoped not. Maybe Bert would come. She was still investigating Sammy Granger's death. Kim had a strong suspicion the two deaths were connected. She would have to tell the police so.

After Hank left the cafeteria, Will said to no one in particular, "We are living in interesting times."

"If you want to call them that," Shandra said.

The passing bell rang and they both got up to leave.

"Kim, if you feel like talking, you can catch me at home this evening," Shandra said to her with a sympathetic smile.

"Thanks, I'll keep that in mind."

Mike Gardner looked out the window and saw storm clouds start to gather. His attention was drawn by Captain Nash, who was walking briskly into the squad room followed by Mayor Ryan. The beefy-faced politician was making the rounds. He affably gave each man present a hearty handshake and a smile. He even knew some of their names. What some people wouldn't learn for the sake of winning an election! Ryan knew he wasn't exactly popular with the township police force. He and the chief were continually at war. Ryan, a mortician by trade, approached Gardner and firmly shook his hand. The mayor's hand felt cold and clammy; Gardner withdrew his own digits as quickly as was polite. Comparisons to the feel of a corpse ran through his mind.

"Mike's our resident homicide specialist," Nash said.

"I knew that. And where's that African American policewoman you work with?"

"Bert's grabbing some lunch. I'll tell her you were asking for her."

"You just do that, Mike!"

"Did Mitch give you the info on the new case?" Nash asked.

"What case is that?" Ryan asked.

"A student was killed over by the high school," Gardner said.

"What? Our high school? How is that possible? Why, I was just over there the other week for career day. Lovely youngsters. Bright children."

"I have one of my own kids going to school there. So I'm very concerned myself," Gardner said.

"Well, keep me informed," the mayor said as he walked away.

Gardner planned to visit the high school as soon as Bert returned. There wasn't any point spoiling her lunch. The dead student could wait, wouldn't be going anywhere. Besides, he'd already arranged for forensics to be on the scene. He took a deep breath and then exhaled slowly. He was both anxious to talk to Kim and somehow dreading it. He hadn't been surprised when he learned that Kim was the person who found the vic. Nope, not surprised at all. If there was trouble in her vicinity, she'd find it—or it would find her.

Gardner knew the minute he laid eyes on Kim that she wasn't happy to see him, at least not under these circumstances. But she looked over at Bert and smiled. Gardner realized it was wrong, but he felt a pang of resentment. Did Kim really think the connection between them could be severed that easily? They'd been intimate, tied together emotionally, physically, and psychically. They were linked in a very special way. He knew it, and she had to be just as aware of it as he was. That wasn't ever going to change, no matter how she might try to deny their connection.

"So what's the deal here?" Bert said, breaking the silence. "You go and find another dead kid? That's just plain weird."

Kim bit her lower lip. "Believe me, I know that better than anyone. And he was one of my students."

"Well, you won't have trouble controlling your classes anymore. Kids are gonna say, that Ms. Reynolds, if you don't listen to her, she'll whack you. She's one tough teacher. Now why doesn't that make you smile? You don't have much of a sense of humor, do you?" Bert said.

"Cop humor," Gardner said with a shrug. "Not everyone gets it."

"Guess not," Bert agreed.

"I'm not much in the mood for banter."

"Got murder on the mind?" Bert asked.

Kim nodded her head in a subdued manner.

Gardner thought how hot she looked, even though she was

trying to hide her beauty under a dowdy teacher suit. Didn't she know the disguise wouldn't work? At least not with him.

"So tell us what happened. Take us through it," he said.

"I just had this feeling that something was wrong. It was a strong intuition. I found myself going toward the woods. And that's where I found him."

"You said you knew the student?" Gardner asked.

Kim nodded her head. "He was in one of my English classes. Point of fact, he'd been nothing but trouble. Hank, Mr. Anderson, was getting rid of him."

Gardner exchanged a look with Bert St. Croix. He realized they were both thinking the same thing. He hoped Kim wasn't picking up on it. But when he studied her, Gardner recognized how distraught she was. Best to keep her talking.

"So did Mr. Anderson say how he planned to *get rid* of the kid?"

"Hank planned to send Nick James to an alternate school, a special school for disruptive and emotionally disturbed students."

"The vic was a serious troublemaker?"

"Big time."

"Lots of enemies?"

Kim gave a slight nod of her head.

Bert tapped her pen against the desktop. "You told me that Sam Granger and Nick were friends. You see a connection here?"

"I feel there's one."

"You think the same perp might have killed both of them?" Bert asked.

Kim looked up at Bert. "I don't know. I wouldn't have been surprised to find out that Nick killed Sam. But now I don't know what to think."

"Kim, give us some names: friends, enemies, anything you can think of that might help us," Gardner said.

"All right." She was pensive for a few moments. "Nick's best friend was a boy named Billy Kramer. He wasn't as bright as Nick, but they hung out together. Emory Dunne might know something as well. He's disabled, but he was in most of Nick's classes. Anita Cummings was also in Nick's classes. She was his girlfriend for a time. They had something of an abusive relationship. They broke up recently."

Gardner recognized instinctively that Kim wasn't telling him everything she knew. They hadn't nicknamed him the psychologist at the cop shop for no reason. He saw into people, knew when they were lying and when they were telling the truth. Kim was clearly protecting other people. He remembered when she distrusted cops in general and him in particular. He thought that had changed, but old habits died hard.

"What about teachers? Any of them have a motive for whacking the kid?"

"What?" Kim looked genuinely surprised. "The boy wasn't liked at all. He was a nasty bully. But I can't imagine that to be enough of a reason for killing him. And teachers deal with difficult students all the time. That doesn't mean they'd solve the problem by murdering them."

Kim appeared indignant and Gardner decided not to pursue the matter.

"Okay," he said. "I think we have enough from you for the time being. Would you send Mr. Anderson in? Then you can go." It felt really strange talking to her in such an impersonal manner, but he supposed it had to be that way, at least for now.

Bert turned to him the minute Kim left the office. "So what do you think?"

Gardner shrugged. "If Kim were anyone else, I'd be suspicious of her. But I know it's not in her to kill people. She just has this unique ability to connect with the dead."

"I don't see Kim as a suspect either."

"You think this student's murder and the other one are somehow related?"

"I didn't get anywhere with Sammy Granger's murder. I had to put it on hold for a while because of other assignments I was given. It's so frustrating! I might have prevented this killing if I'd been able to figure things out." Bert looked dejected.

He pulled gently on one of her braids. "Hey, sometimes there's just nothing to go on. I know how diligent you are. Since it's still an open file, we can work both cases in tandem."

Bert smiled at him, pleased with the reassurance. She was a handsome woman with high cheekbones and a generous mouth. He thought she ought to smile more often.

Hank Anderson entered the office. Gardner sized up the acting high school principal. No doubt he would impress people. Gardner and Bert St. Croix were both six feet tall, but Anderson topped them by a good several inches. He was a big, blond guy, good-looking, charismatic. And the Viking did not look stupid.

"So Mr. Anderson, we understand from Ms. Reynolds that the dead boy was a troublemaker." Being blunt from the start was always best with guys like this.

"Did she elaborate?" This character was sharp, all right. He wasn't giving anything away.

"I believe she thought you ought to be the one to tell us about the kid, since you're the boss around here."

There was a moment's hesitation. Gardner knew that Anderson was thinking about what he should be saying. No one really liked talking to cops. No one trusted them.

"Nick James was always in one kind of trouble or another. I was in charge of discipline, so I saw quite a bit of him. Recently he threatened Miss Reynolds and vandalized her car. That's when I finally arranged for him to go to an alternative school."

Gardner was alarmed. Kim was much more involved in this than she'd given him reason to believe. This wasn't sounding so good. Still, Kim clearly had nothing to do with Sam Granger's death except for finding the boy's body.

"What other teachers had problems with Nick James?"

The acting principal was thoughtful. "Anyone who taught Nick had problems with him. You might talk to Rufus Ogden, his guidance counselor. Mr. Ogden knows a lot about Nick. Then there's William Norgood. He's an English teacher who had some run-ins with Nick previously. Also our English chairperson, Morgana Douglas. She dealt with him on more than one occasion. He seemed to dislike English teachers in particular. I can't say why exactly. Maybe it was because he had difficulty reading. Anything else?"

"Not for now, Mr. Anderson. We appreciate your cooperation, and we'll be in touch with you regarding interviewing some of the teachers and students who knew Nick James."

"That's fine." Anderson extended his hand and Gardner shook it. Strong handshake. Not surprising.

When they were finally outside the high school, Gardner turned to Bert. "So what's your take on this?"

"I think something really evil is going on there. Bad juju, as the island people say."

"I have to agree with you," Gardner said. "I'm really sorry now I helped Kim get the job."

Bert studied him, sunlight shadowing her high cheekbones. "Like they say, no good deed goes unpunished."

They walked into the woods ready to collect impressions of the murder scene.

# CHAPTER TWENTY-ONE

Bert St. Croix returned to the high school with Mike Gardner the following morning. Bert turned to Gardner. "So I guess we're partnering on this," she commented as they walked into the building.

"Looks that way. Kim thinks the two deaths are connected. I have to agree."

"Your girlfriend has a real instinct for sleuthing. She's part bloodhound. Should have been a cop instead of a librarian."

Gardner frowned at her. "Kim's not my girlfriend anymore. She's made that plain enough."

"Mike, all you have to do is kick that skinny-assed bitch out of your house. You're too soft-hearted. It's a definite flaw in your character, man."

"Look who's talking? Your heart's as tender as it gets."

"Well, don't tell anyone. I like my reputation as a hard ass."

"Evelyn will eventually sign those divorce papers and I'll make certain that they're filed. It's just a matter of time. Nothing but a temporary glitch."

"I hope you're right." Bert frowned.

"Yeah, well, I was dumb to ever trust Evelyn. That mistake is costing me. The thing is, I'm afraid Kim will have moved on by the time this is over."

"Don't know about that. I think this new job is keeping her real busy."

Gardner narrowed his eyes. "Yeah, like I said, I didn't do any real favor getting it for her."

"You meant well. No one's got a crystal ball."

"Not one that works anyway. You ever get to talk with Nick James in connection with the Granger homicide?"

"I did. But I couldn't get much from him. He'd been arrested before but only for small-time crap. He might have been the perp, except now I'm not so sure. We could be looking for a single perp."

"What about Billy Kramer?" Gardner's eyes sharpened.

"We need to talk to that kid. I spoke to him one time and didn't get much there either. But I've done some more checking. Want to guess what Billy boy's mom does for a living?"

"Okay, let me take a stab at it. Wouldn't be a nurse, would she?"

"Damn, how do you manage that?"

Gardner shrugged. "I read over your file notes on the Granger case yesterday."

"Okay. Then you know that Marge Kramer works in the O.R. and the drug that was injected into Sammy Granger is available in the operating room of most hospitals."

"Well, I guess we're ready for him."

Gardner appropriated the principal's secretary who, Bert had to admit, was efficient. When she ushered the student into the office, the secretary closed the door firmly behind her without comment.

Billy Kramer appeared worse than the last time she'd seen him. His dirty blond hair looked like it hadn't seen a comb in a week. His eyes were shadowed and his angry zits reminded her of mini volcanic eruptions. His chest was concave and he appeared malnourished.

Gardner turned to her, and Bert realized he expected her to carry the interrogation. She liked that about him. No big macho ego on the guy. She took a deep breath and began.

"So Billy, you don't look so good. Taking the death of your friend hard?" She indicated the chair opposite them. He took the hint and sat down.

"It was like a big shock, you know." He folded his hands together in a tight double fist.

"Guess it would be. First your friend Sammy and now Nick James. Real downer. You have any idea who might want them dead?"

"Like I told you before, Sammy didn't have any enemies. He hung out with Nick and me sometimes. I didn't know him all that well. He was Nick's friend."

Bert pursed her lips. "But you and Nick were tight. So who didn't like Nick?"

"Lots of people didn't like Nick. He was a real cool guy, but he kinda rubbed people the wrong way."

"Yeah, that happens. Like, who did he offend? Give us some names."

Billy hesitated. "Well, there was Anita, for instance."

"Anita Cummings?" Bert asked.

Billy nodded his head. "Yeah, her. She was his girl for a while. Nick kind of used her. And Miss Reynolds, she didn't like Nick one bit. She got all snooty with him. But he fixed her."

Bert looked over at Gardner, who was now leaning forward in his chair.

"What did Nick do?" the lieutenant asked. His sharp gray eyes bore into the kid.

Billy sensed the heightened interest and fidgeted. "He kind of trashed her car. The first time, it was just keying the body and slashing her tires. Next time, well, it was sugar in the tank and ripped out wiring."

"And you helped him, didn't you?" Gardner pressed.

Billy's eyes widened. "Me? Hell, no. I mean he just told me about it. I didn't do anything."

Bert could tell that Gardner didn't believe a word of it. She decided to take back control. Gardner couldn't behave impartially with Kim involved. It was screwing with his objectivity.

"So what did Ms. Reynolds do about it?" Bert asked.

Billy looked down. "She told Mr. Anderson. He got on Nick's case, gave him detention and stuff."

"Why didn't Mr. Anderson report what happened to us?" Gardner asked.

"Nobody saw Nick do it. They couldn't prove anything. Nick was slick, you know?"

"Yeah, I know. So what else did Nick do that pissed people off?" Bert asked.

Billy's smile curved. "Well, it was way cool how he got even with Mr. Anderson. Nick got Anita to tell everybody how Mr. Anderson was doing her. He nearly got fired."

Bert exchanged looks with Gardner. If that was true, the school principal had a good motive for murder. Bert decided it was time to bring in the heavy artillery, eyeball the kid for heavy mortar.

"So, Billy, there's just one other matter. The medical examiner found that your pal Sammy was killed by a lethal injection of a drug found in hospitals and used in operating rooms. It's not available to the general public. But your mother's a nurse who works in the O.R. Did she bring it home for you? How did you get it, Billy? You can tell us."

Billy Kramer looked green around the gills. "I need to be excused," he said. "I don't feel so good."

"Sure, in just a minute. Just tell us how you got the drug."

"It wasn't for me. It was for Nick. He used a lot of stuff. I was looking around one day. I went to visit my mother to see what I could find. Nick was pushing me. I asked my mother to give me a tour of where she worked. I saw this stuff lying there with a syringe. Figured it was some kind of drug. Maybe Nick could use it or sell it. Whatever."

"So you just took it?"

"Yeah, I kind of did that." He gave a nervous little laugh. "Figured they wouldn't miss it. Got so much there. You know?"

"And you gave it to Nick? Just to be a pal." Bert was fairly disgusted with the kid, but tried hard not to show it.

"That's right."

"What kind of drugs were you and Nick into?"

"We just smoked a little weed together when we could score it. Neither of us had money for the good stuff. But Nick said that was going to change. He told me he had a way to make some real bucks."

"Planning to rob liquor stores?"

"No, nothing like that. He knew something he could use to get people to give him money."

Bert licked her dry lips. "And that would be?"

Billy shook his head. "Don't know. He wouldn't say. Maybe he didn't trust me enough to tell me."

Gardner leaned forward. "We'll want to talk to you again. Next time, we'll contact your mother. She might want to get you a lawyer."

Billy rose unsteadily to his feet. He shook with sudden fear and anger. "I don't need a lawyer. I didn't do nothing. I didn't kill Nick. And I don't know who did."

"You stole drugs from a hospital. That's a serious crime."

Billy Kramer's right hand shook as he opened the door to leave the office.

"Billy, this isn't just going away. Be prepared," Gardner said.

The boy slammed the door as he left without looking back.

Bert turned to Gardner. "What do you think of Billy's story?"

"Looks like Nick James may have killed his pal Sammy Granger."

"But why?" Bert asked, feeling perplexed. "I mean, why bother? I don't see a motive, do you?"

Gardner turned his gaze toward the blank wall in front of him and focused on it without really seeing it. "Sammy might have given Nick the information he intended to use for blackmail."

"Then I've got to wonder if someone at this school did something that made Nick think he could extort money, and would that person feel it necessary to commit murder to protect said secret. That's a lot of supposing." Bert shook her head, frankly stumped.

"Good question," Gardner said. "Sure wish I could answer it. If I could, we might find ourselves a killer."

"People and their secrets," Bert said, shaking her head. "Guess there's a motive for murder around there somewhere."

"Maybe we better talk to Anderson," Gardner said. "He knows more than he's shared with us."

Bert agreed. For sure, the guy was cagey.

They had to wait a little while before the principal could join them.

"Want your desk back?" Gardner offered.

"No. Stay where you are. This will do fine." Anderson took the seat opposite them that Billy Kramer had recently vacated.

"We understand Nick James was causing a problem in the school for Ms. Reynolds and you dealt with it."

"Yes, he was a nasty individual. I believe I told you all about expelling him from our school. In fact, he shouldn't have been in the vicinity of this school. I don't know why he came back here."

Gardner eyed the principal steadily. "Who says he ever left in the first place? Let me get the timetable right. You expelled the kid on Friday."

"That's correct," Anderson said.

"Harsh words between you and the James boy?"

"Nothing out of the ordinary, given the situation."

"He didn't threaten you?"

Anderson looked surprised. "Not at all."

"The reason I ask is because Billy Kramer told us that Nick got a girl named Anita Cummings to claim you had sex with her. He said you nearly lost your job. I can't imagine you having any warm feelings for the kid."

"That's true. But as you can see, I didn't lose my job. Anita told the truth. It ended there."

"Did it?"

Gardner and Anderson faced each other.

"I hope you don't think I would ever physically attack a student, no matter how difficult he might be. I try to help students, not harm them."

Bert observed the hard set of the principal's square jaw and thought Anderson could be a tough guy when firmness was called for. But she knew from experience that Mike could be damned tough himself.

"Thank you, Mr. Anderson," Gardner said, rising to his feet. He checked his list of names. "Could you have your secretary send for William Norgood, Rufus Ogden, and Morgana Douglas?"

"Certainly. In any particular order?"

"Just as they're available. I realize they all have busy schedules."

After the principal left, Bert turned to Gardner. "You still think he knows more than he's telling us?"

"Probably. Administrators generally try to cover up problems in their school until they become too serious to ignore—like now."

"Think Anderson could have killed the kid in a fit of anger?"

Gardner shrugged. "It's possible. Not ruling anything out when it comes to homicide. We need the M.E. report. Hopefully, we'll know a lot more then. Meantime, we'll just continue to collect information from the staff."

Gardner was pleased to be working with Bert St. Croix. They had established an easy rapport that hadn't been possible when they first worked together. But Bert was happier now, adjusting to being a cop in the burbs.

"Do you want to take the lead?" Gardner asked her.

"No, not with these people. I'll just throw in a question here and there when I feel it's called for."

"Okay, then, I guess we're ready."

Rufus Ogden was the first to appear of the three teachers that Gardner intended to question. He reminded Gardner of a parakeet. The chest of the diminutive man puffed up. His wispy graying hair flew around his face like feathers. After they got over the formalities, Gardner drove to the point.

"We understand you were Nick James's guidance counselor. What can you tell us about the boy?"

"Nothing good, I'm sorry to say." Ogden's mouth puckered as if he'd been sucking on a lemon. "James was in trouble with all of his teachers. He was a bully and a troublemaker."

"Mr. Anderson told us he was arranging for James to go into a special school. Did he talk to you on Friday afternoon about it?"

Ogden shook his head. "No, afraid not. But then in education, the wheels grind slowly. I'm certain he would have gotten around to the matter. Probably today if the boy hadn't died."

"Can you provide us with the boy's school records?"

Ogden cleared his throat. "I don't know if that would be appropriate. All such information is kept confidential."

Bert gave him a hard look. "The kid is dead. Murdered, from

the look of it. We need to learn everything we can. And while you're at it, we want the school records on Sam Granger as well. And we need them A.S.A.P. Got that?"

The small man swallowed hard. "My secretary will bring them to you shortly. May I leave now?"

Gardner nodded, and Ogden quickly vacated the office. Gardner turned to his partner. "I love the way you do that."

"What?" Bert asked innocently. But when he smiled, she did as well.

The second teacher they interviewed was the English department chair, Morgana Douglas.

Gardner studied her thoughtfully. Unlike Ogden, Morgana Douglas imposed herself into a room. A tall woman, she dressed youthfully, although she was clearly in her fifties. Most noteworthy, her shoes were expensive stilettos. Gardner wondered in passing how women managed to walk in those kinds of shoes—not easily, for certain. Her short skirt rode up as she seated herself.

"Did you know Sam Granger?" Gardner asked, changing his line of questioning.

Ms. Douglas looked surprised. "Why, yes, I did know the boy."

"Was he in special education classes?"

"He was. But he wasn't stupid. He was dyslexic. We were dealing with the problem."

"Did you have Sammy as a student at any time?"

"No, I did not. I teach two honors English classes for juniors. The rest of my time is taken up by department business."

"Did you know Nick James?"

The department chair recrossed her long legs. "He posed a serious problem for many of our teachers. I can't say that I felt he was much of a loss, quite frankly."

Bert looked at Morgana Douglas. "Anything you think we

should know?"

The English chair was thoughtful. "You might want to talk with William Norgood and Kim Reynolds. They both had particular problems with the boy. And now if you'll excuse me, I have important department matters to which I must attend."

After the door closed, Bert turned to Gardner. "Kind of a snotty bitch."

"She wasn't giving much away. That's for sure."

Before they could talk to William Norgood, Gardner received a phone call from Nash calling him back to headquarters.

Bert gave him a questioning look.

"It's about another case. It won't take long. You can question this Norgood guy yourself."

Gardner left her, and Bert sent for the teacher.

She didn't warm to the man. Norgood's slightly hunched posture reminded her of a willow tree. She also noted the thinning hairline and narrow lips set in a mild sneer.

"Mr. Norgood, what can you tell me about the deceased student Nick James?"

"Quite a lot, as it happens. He was a Neanderthal. No manners, the attention span of a fruit fly, always distracting other students from their work while refusing to do his. I failed him for the year. He was held back as a sophomore. Did you know that the Puritans were Calvinists? They believed in the doctrine of original sin, that man is born in sin. James was an exemplar for original sin. Born bad. Evil incarnate. Someone did humanity a great service. I believe congratulations are in order."

"You sound hostile, bitter."

Norgood examined his neat fingernails. "Do I? Perhaps I am. I don't think the Nick Jameses of this world should be in a regular classroom setting where they can be disruptive and destroy the opportunity for other students to obtain an education. They contaminate the ozone."

"Did the kid do drugs?" Bert asked.

"I believe he did." Norgood met Bert's gaze with directness.

"Did he also sell drugs to other students?"

"I can't be certain, but I'd say it was a good possibility. It would not surprise me."

"What about Sam Granger? Did you have him as a student?"

"Sam Granger was actually a fairly competent student until he fell in with James and Kramer. James was older than the other two by virtue of being held back twice. By the time they became thick as thieves, quite literally, Sam had deteriorated as well."

"You have any idea who might have killed Nick James?"

The sneer had returned to the English teacher's thin face. "Detective, I haven't a clue. Anyone and everyone would have liked to see that boy dead, including our illustrious school principal. Perhaps there was a conspiracy? Consider Christie's *Murder on the Orient Express*. Life imitating art."

After William Norgood left the office, Bert phoned Gardner. "Wow, that Norgood guy, he's a real charmer! A snake charmer. Actually, a cobra's got less venom. He hated the James kid. He sure doesn't like Anderson either."

"Get anything useful?"

"Not really. You want me to talk to anyone else while I'm here today?"

"I would if I knew who to question or what questions to ask. What's your take on this?"

"I'm not sure either, Mike. Maybe the murder's drug related, maybe not."

"There hasn't been a real drug problem in the high school that I know of."

"That Kramer kid is a user. Stands to reason the vic was too."

"But Sam Granger came up clean, didn't he?" Gardner said.

"Maybe he stopped hanging out with them," Bert said.

"Then why kill him? We're come back to the blackmail angle again. But right now, that's not leading anywhere."

Bert couldn't answer that either. "There is someone else, another student we should probably talk with," Bert said. "Could be he's the missing link."

"Let's do it," Gardner said. "I'll be back in a little while."

"I'll just chill until you get back here. Maybe hang out in the faculty room, soak up some local atmosphere."

"You just do that. Might even have the case solved before I get back."

"Yeah, right." She disconnected.

Bert thought back to her own days as a high school student and how much she'd disliked them. You always had to watch your back at her school. There were rival gangs and she kept a careful vigil, not hanging with any of those kids. She kept her distance and stayed out of trouble. Life was safer that way.

On the surface, things looked good at this school. But were things really so different in the burbs? Maybe not so much.

# Chapter Twenty-Two

Emory Dunne burst on the scene, crashing his way into the principal's office. Gardner's hand reflexively went to his holstered piece.

"You better learn how to control that thing," Bert said, eyes narrowing. "The lieutenant almost shot you."

"Hey, this chair's got a mind of its own." The youth patted his wheelchair as if it were a pony. "Why'd you want to see me? I didn't have anything to do with that creep Nick James."

"But you were in the same classes. You know anyone who would want to kill him?"

Penetrating dark eyes stared at Gardner without blinking. "Better question is who *wouldn't* want to kill Nick."

"When was the last time you saw him?"

"That's an easier question to answer. It was in Miss Reynolds's class. He threatened her because he said she interfered and got Anita to change her story about Mr. Anderson. So I kind of let the chair have its way and smash into him before Nick could punch out Miss Reynolds."

Gardner was alarmed. Why hadn't Kim told him any of this? Had she gone back to distrusting him?

"What did Nick James have to do with Anita making false accusations against your principal?" Bert asked.

Emory Dunne shifted in his chair. His head wobbled and looked impossibly large in comparison to his wasted body. "Anita and Nick had something going. She'd do anything he told her to do. She was like his slave. Miss Reynolds . . . well, I guess she and Mr. Anderson got something going too. So she got Anita to change her story to help out Mr. Anderson. That burned Nick. He was always a nasty S.O.B. But he really didn't have any balls. When he got knocked down, he started screaming like a little girl, claiming his legs were crippled and how he was gonna sue the school. I wouldn't care if he sued me, 'cause I don't have no money and neither does my family. But the school nurse came and she said he was okay. She took him out in a chair like mine, except she had to push it, 'cause it don't have a motor like this one." He patted his chair again. "Anyway, that was the last I saw of Nick James. And good riddance!"

Gardner was troubled by Emory Dunne's story. "What makes you think Ms. Reynolds and Mr. Anderson have a relationship beyond regular school interaction?"

The youth shrugged. "I saw them together having breakfast on a Sunday morning. I might have told some kids at school and the word got around. So I guess it's okay for the cops to know too. I mean if it was a secret, it's not anymore. Right?"

Gardner felt sick at heart, as if he'd been stabbed. So Kim had moved on, just as he'd feared. Well, what could he have expected? Still, she'd said she loved him. She knew he loved her. Why couldn't she wait? Why get involved with someone else so soon?

After Emory Dunne shoved his wheelchair back through the door, Bert looked over at Gardner. "You don't know for certain that Kim is really seeing this Anderson guy. The kid could be full of it."

Gardner stared out the window watching the leaves blow in the wind. "I don't think he was lying about that. Anyway, Kim has every right to see whoever she wants. If I don't like it, which I don't, it's my problem, not hers. Let's talk to that school nurse."

"Doubt she knows anything useful."

"You never know." Not about anyone. Not even the people you love.

Mrs. Clemins, a gray-haired woman who wore bifocals, had a voice as pleasant as her smile.

"What happened on Friday after you removed Nick James from Ms. Reynolds's classroom?" Gardner asked.

"Let's see." Mrs. Clemins blinked her blue-veined eyelids. "I took him down to my office. He was carrying on something awful. Imagine that, such a big strapping boy behaving like a crybaby! Well, I got him settled and checked his legs. They were a bit swollen and bruised, but nothing seemed to be broken or even fractured."

"You told him that?"

"I did, but he persisted in saying that he was crippled for life and that he was going to sue Mr. Anderson and the school. So I told him that I would arrange for him to go to the emergency room by ambulance. But first I needed to contact his parents. I wanted their permission. I asked if they were both at work. My secretary has all the information. Of course, it's easier sometimes just to ask the student. And information does change. Well, Nick became quite upset. He told me he did not want me to call his parents. I explained in that case, I would put ice packs on both his legs and I was certain any swelling would go away in time. And that's exactly what I did: put ice packs on his legs, twenty minutes on, twenty minutes off. I also managed to calm him down."

"Then what happened?" Gardner asked.

"Oh, well, Mr. Anderson came in later. He told Nick that he couldn't come back to this school again, that he'd made all the necessary arrangements for his new placement. Nick became agitated all over again. He stood up and threatened Mr. Anderson."

"Threatened him how?"

"The boy said something I didn't quite understand. Nick insisted that he would be back in school. He said he'd make everyone sorry they messed with him. I think then he said something about getting paid, or maybe it was about payback. I'm not exactly certain." In Mrs. Clemins's sing-song voice pattern, repeated threats hardly sounded worse than nursery rhymes.

"Did James elaborate any further about how he was going to make the teachers sorry?" Gardner pressed.

Mrs. Clemins shook her frizzy head. "Sorry. He was upset and not all that coherent. He left my office then, and I didn't see him again."

"Did he leave on his own or did Mr. Anderson have to help him?"

The school nurse was thoughtful. "Let me see. Mr. Anderson left first by himself. As I mentioned, the boy became agitated all over again during their conversation. He was angry and muttering something under his breath. Then he stomped out of my office. He might have limped a bit, but he was able to walk on his own."

"No idea where he went after that?"

She shook her head and the frizz moved like swirling dust motes. "I'm sorry. I really have no idea."

"Do you think he was going to see Mr. Anderson, to continue their conversation?"

"I don't know." Her brows knit together, and Gardner realized she was genuinely perplexed.

He thanked the nurse and allowed her to leave. He was certain she'd told them all she knew, which wasn't very much.

"I get the feeling there's something going on here that we're not getting. The question is, what?" Bert pulled at her braided ebony hair.

"Looks like we need to question some more people." Gardner sighed. "Maybe we're just not asking the right questions."

"Guess we'll know more when we get the forensic reports."

Gardner wrinkled his brow. "Let's hope so. Two deaths of high school students in a couple of months. We're going to need to dig deeper."

The truth was he had a bad feeling about this. And when he thought about the distance that had developed between himself and Kim, he felt even worse.

"Ready to go?" Hank asked her.

Kim looked at him and nodded her head. She'd never wanted to leave a place more. "It's been a long day. Are Lieutenant Gardner and Detective St. Croix still here?"

"They left a little while ago."

Kim breathed a sigh of relief.

"But I think they'll be back and want to question us again sometime in the future."

"I hope not."

The teacher's lunchroom was deserted now. Hank took her hand and held it. "You feeling okay?"

"I'm fine."

"It had to come as quite a shock, finding a dead body."

Kim lowered her gaze. "Actually, I have found a few."

"Coincidence?"

"Not exactly. I suppose there's something you should know about me. I don't advertise it, but I have this sensitivity, a certain sixth sense, an awareness. I sometimes have strange visions, see things in dreams or just know when something is wrong, like when a crime has been committed, when violence has occurred. I know I'm not explaining it very well at all. I don't tell many people about this. I don't want them to think I'm a few slices short of a loaf. But I think you have a right to know."

Hank turned his head to one side in a gesture of appraisal. "Are you trying to tell me that you're psychic?" His golden brows rose in an expression of disbelief.

"I don't know if that's it exactly. In most ways, I'm pretty much normal. At least, I would like to think I am. It's a side of my nature that I basically try to ignore. But sometimes, I find I just can't."

"And that's why you discovered Nick's body in the woods?"

"I sort of had a vision, an awareness of him lying there."

Hank ran his hands through his hair. "I have to tell you I find what you're telling me very disturbing."

"I probably shouldn't have told you at all. But I do believe in being honest."

"I think your finding him was just an accident."

When she attempted to interrupt him, Hank put up his hand to halt her. "No, I just don't believe in paranormal happenings. But I can see you do. Let's agree to disagree and let it go at that."

"We can just call it intuition," she said.

When Kim rose unsteadily to her feet, Hank took her arm. "I'll walk you to your car. If you need to take a day off, let me know. Frankly, I didn't expect you to come in today."

"I'll be here tomorrow too," she said. She wasn't going to take the coward's way out. She'd contracted to do a job and had every intention of being at work teaching her classes.

Back at police headquarters, Bert and Gardner sat down together and discussed the information they'd collected at the high school.

Bert shook her head in frustration. "We're no closer to discovering who killed Sam Granger than we were before. Ditto

Nick James."

"It'll happen," Gardner said. His voice rang with confidence.

"Maybe."

"Ye of little faith."

"Right." Sometimes Gardner was just a little too full of himself.

"Meantime, we've got the unpleasant duty of informing the parents of Nick James that their son is dead."

"I tried phoning them yesterday but no one answered. The phone just kept on ringing."

Gardner glanced at his watch. "You're off duty. I'll drive over to their house this evening and let them know."

Bert tapped her long, slender fingers against Gardner's battered desktop. "Forget it. I'm doing the dirty deed myself. Go home to your family."

Gardner managed a wry smile. "My house is like a war zone these days. I'd rather deal with the grief-stricken."

"That bad?"

Gardner cocked an eyebrow. "Worse."

"You can handle it. I'll take the James gang. Hopefully, no relations to Jesse. You take care of the Gardners."

He saluted her. "Okay, boss."

"Hey, we're partners, right?"

Hank Anderson followed Kim back to her apartment and waited patiently while she changed into casual clothes.

"You don't have to do this," she said. "Really, I'm fine."

"Well, I'm not," he said. "I'd like your company this evening. Let's have dinner together and go for a walk somewhere."

After a difficult day, she would usually prefer to be alone, but how could she possibly refuse him? And the truth was, she didn't feel like being alone right now.

An hour later, they were walking along a deserted stretch of beach where the sand felt like a soft carpet beneath her feet and the only sounds were of the rhythmic sea, the cry of gulls, and the wind mourning a sky that seemed ready to weep on them at any moment.

Kim tied a kerchief firmly around her head and zipped her windbreaker to the top. The one thing she did love about where she'd grown up was being able to walk near the ocean. She'd been missing that, she realized.

"I like your father and Valerie. I think they really are in love. It's also clear that your father loves you."

"If you don't mind, I'd rather not talk about him." Hank appeared to emotionally distance himself from her, and she didn't like it.

"You're very sensitive about certain subjects."

He tilted his head to one side and stared at her. "So are you."

"You're right. We're both very private people. I wish it could be different." She felt a certain yearning, a wistful need to reinvent herself yet again. She was still so far from the person she wanted to be.

Hank looked over at her and frowned. "What exactly do you expect from me? I've already donated blood this year."

She was surprised. "I'm not asking anything of you."

"Those police detectives make me uneasy." He took her hand and held it tightly as they walked down the deserted beach.

"All we have to do is answer their questions honestly. I don't see a problem."

"Really? I do. They think the James boy was killed by someone from the school. It's my responsibility as school administrator to provide a safe environment for students and teachers. Obviously, I've failed at that."

Kim bit down on her lower lip, lost in thought. "You think they're blaming you for what happened? No, that's absurd. I know them both very well, as it happens. They don't play the blame game. They're not judgmental people."

"Think so? When they questioned me, the room reeked of disapproval."

Kim shook her head, and the wind pulled free her bandanna. Her hair blew into her face.

"Sorry. I think you feel guilty for some reason and are projecting your feelings on them." She stopped walking and turned to face Hank directly. "Look, someone once said to me never criticize yourself when others can do it so much better. I believe you handled the situation with Nick James very well on Friday. In fact, I don't think I ever properly thanked you."

Hank smiled for the first time. "There is a way you could thank me."

"Oh, and what could that possibly be?" she teased.

"Now who's playing coy games?"

She turned away from him and fixed her eyes on the hypnotic regularity of the waves hitting the shore. "I never play games with other people's feelings."

He turned her gently but firmly so that she faced him. "What if I told you that I don't believe in love? I think it's all sham, illusion. What if I told you I don't think I know how to love? I'm not capable of it."

"Maybe you're just afraid of emotional commitment. I think people can learn to love. I think you already know how, because once you learn how to love, you never really forget."

"I'm more attracted to you than I've been to any woman I've ever known. But maybe I'm scared to let myself feel certain things for you. Letting another person matter to you can lead to all kinds of pain and misery."

She put her head against his shoulder. "We're just beginning to know each other. In fact, I hardly know myself as yet. Why can't we just be friends? Good friends? I don't think either one of us is ready for more than that."

His eyes glowed with feeling. "Let's say I could prove my friendship to you better with action than words."

His mouth covered hers with a hot, moist kiss.

Kim expelled a long breath as she pulled free of him. "I think we have to keep it slow and easy. I don't know about you, but my life is pretty confused and complicated right now."

"Okay," he agreed. But Hank looked seriously disappointed.

# CHAPTER TWENTY-THREE

Nobody greeted Gardner when he called out he was home. He found Evelyn in the living room painting her toenails.

Jeanie was watching her mother with keen interest. "Mommy, could you paint my nails too? That would be so cool."

"Honey, you're a little young for that," Gardner said.

Two pairs of hazel eyes stared back at him with displeasure. He decided to go out to the kitchen. He found Evie putting some touches on a meatloaf.

"That looks good enough to eat."

Evie gave him a hug. "It better be good. I tried this new recipe I found in a magazine."

"I like what you always do. Why change it?"

"Well, I generally mix the meat with ketchup and mustard. But this recipe says to add oatmeal, ginger, cilantro, and basil. I just put crushed tomatoes on top. It's supposed to be very healthy."

Gardner gave her a dubious look. "If you say so. I'm hungry as a wolf. Whatever you serve will be fine with me. Guess you heard I was at your school today?"

Evie popped the meatloaf back in the oven and pricked the baking potatoes before closing the oven door. "Yeah, I heard. I didn't want to ask too many questions. I didn't tell anyone that the cop nosing around was my dad."

"Ashamed of your old man?"

Evie licked her lips. "Not exactly. But it's kind of like being a

240

minister's kid. People have a certain expectation of what you should be like. And I don't want to get picked on or mocked on by anyone. I mean I'm only a freshman. My close friends know, but other kids don't. I'd just as soon keep it that way."

"Understood."

Evie continued to bustle around the kitchen.

"Is your mother helping around here?"

"Nope." Evie's eyes evaded him.

"Is that your choice or hers?"

"Let's just say it's mutual."

Gardner placed his hands on his daughter's slender shoulders in an effort to stop her movement. "Honey, maybe you ought to make an effort to connect."

"What for? She's just going to take off again. Jeanie's too dumb to realize her mother's a heartbreaker. Well, I know better." Evie's eyes, a deep gray so like his own, were bright with unshed tears. "You ought to kick her out, Dad. She's brought us nothing but misery."

"I can't do that."

"Then you're enabling her, and that's wrong." Evie's chin rose as her lower lip trembled. "I hate grown-ups. You're all so dumb."

Gardner decided to change the subject. This was becoming too emotionally charged. "Did you know about Kim dating Mr. Anderson?"

Evie turned away from him, folding her hands over her chest. "I guess. There's been some rumors going around school. But I think Kim still cares for you."

Gardner sat down heavily at the kitchen table. "Thing is, he's a good-looking man and single. She's vulnerable."

"Kick Mom out. Make her give you the divorce. You can still work things out with Kim."

"You're the second person to tell me that." He smiled at his daughter. "Your mother and I will come to a reckoning soon. I promise. Honor bright."

"Can't be too soon for me," Evie said, her mouth tight.

Bert St. Croix wrinkled her nose in disgust. It wasn't hard to understand why Nick James turned out to be such a creep. Didn't children learn by example?

"You telling me my kid's dead?" Rheumy eyes stared at her with a vague look. "What happened?"

Bert back-stepped, overcome by the fumes of the man's breath. Christ, he smelled like a distillery. "Is your wife at home?"

"Her? No, she's working at the supermarket. Where's my kid now?"

"With the medical examiner's office. He'll be released pending an autopsy."

"Autopsy? What the hell for? I don't want no one cutting open my kid!" The burly man staggered toward her, lost his balance, and gripped the banister in the front hall of his shabby house.

Bert glanced around. "Is there anyone else at home?"

"No, they all leave us when they turn eighteen. Even Nicky was planning on going. He said as soon as he got the money together, he wasn't gonna stick around this dump anymore. Calling this place a dump, can you imagine? The kid had no respect. What the hell, I don't care if he's dead."

Bert gave a nod toward the motorcycle parked in the gravel driveway. "That's a nice hog you've got out front. Is it yours?"

"No, it belongs to Nick. He got it 'bout a year ago."

"Did he pay for it himself?"

The boy's father snorted. " 'Course he did. Think I'm stupid enough to buy something like that for him? I wouldn't even trust him with my old pickup truck."

"Where did he work?"

Mr. James threw her a bleary-eyed glance. "Here and there."

Bert tried not to let her irritation show. She was working on her temper these days, trying to improve her professional manner. "Where's here and there exactly?"

James shrugged. "How the hell should I know? Kid picked up work where he could, mostly off the books."

"Did the school call you about him?"

"He got into trouble now and then. What real boy doesn't raise hell once in a while?"

She persisted. "What kind of trouble? Do you know?"

"Don't remember exactly. But I smacked him up the side of his head. He knew not to do it no more in school. That man teacher who complained about him? He was nothin' but a fag. Know what I mean? He even held my boy back."

Now came the difficult questions. Bert braced herself, not certain how James would react. It was clear to her he could be violent. She was trying hard to avoid those kinds of confrontations. She already had a reputation around the department for being aggressive and volatile. She wasn't kidding herself. The only reason they'd kept her on was because she was a woman of color. That took care of two minorities at once. Both the mayor and the chief were sensitive about being accused of racial discrimination. She was their token. But there were plenty of other people who wouldn't mind having her job. Bert took a deep breath and exhaled slowly.

"Mr. James, to your knowledge, did your son take illegal substances?"

"Drugs?" James squinted at her. "Damn, he was a normal, curious kid. We both drank a little, smoked cigarettes, maybe he tried a little weed. But he wasn't no drug fiend." James was breathing hard now.

Bert knew she had to ask the last important question carefully. "To your knowledge, did he buy or sell drugs?"

"Get out of here! Police or not, you won't insult my boy." The man's face turned as red as a rare roast.

Bert left without another word, convinced that Nick James's father knew more than he was telling her. Somehow, she wasn't at all surprised.

Wednesday morning, Kim Reynolds found herself being asked all sorts of questions by fellow teachers. Students she didn't know stared at her in the halls. Some pointed rudely. She chose to ignore them for the most part. The first few class periods she spent working in the library, mostly cataloging and organizing materials for the teachers to use. The library was an oasis of peace and stability for her.

But she couldn't ignore Will or Shandra at lunch that day, since they sat down on either side of her as if she were the meat in a sandwich.

"Kim Reynolds, why so pensive? Surely to talk is not offensive. All right, I can see you do not like my poem. Next time, free verse and no quotations." Will smiled, pleased with his wit.

"Sorry, I'm not good company today," she said.

"The entire school community is buzzing about the death of Nick James, what with the police interviews yesterday."

"What did they ask you?" Kim looked at Will, who pulled at his shirt collar, and thought he suddenly appeared tense.

"Me? Why nothing in comparison to what they must have asked you. Were you grilled like a burger? Well done or medium rare?"

Shandra gave him a shove. "Will, this is not something to joke about."

"Please! Everyone's positively gleeful to hear of that dreadful Neanderthal's demise. Let's not be hypocrites, Shandra. You know very well that Kim was not the only one threatened by that creature. You yourself hurled him out of your math class more than once as I recall. We all loathed him. Nick James demonstrated conclusively that *Lord of the Flies* was not mere fable."

Shandra acknowledged Will's remarks with a quick nod of her head. "All right, I don't disagree. I hated him myself. He was one of the worst students, behavior-wise, I ever had to deal with."

"There, was it so hard being candid?" Will patted Shandra's hand.

Kim looked across the room and caught Morgana Douglas glaring at her. What had she done to irritate the supervisor now? Kim studied the woman's expression. There was something knowing in the look. Kim shivered. She had the distinct impression that her supervisor wished nothing but ill for her. Kim sensed that something was about to happen to her, and it wasn't going to be good. Morgana Douglas obviously would have a part in it. She shuddered inwardly.

"Why are you so distracted, my dear?" Will asked.

"What?" Kim shook her head. There was no point speculating further on such a vague matter, and certainly not with Will.

"Of course there's something wrong," Shandra said, wiping her eyeglasses with a damp tissue. "I mean, isn't it obvious? Kim found Nick James's dead body in the woods. It had to be awful," Shandra said sympathetically.

"It was," Kim agreed. She concentrated on eating her sandwich, talked very little for the rest of the lunch break, and was relieved when the passing bell rang.

That afternoon, Betsy Peters showed up in her poetry class early. This was the first time in weeks that the student actually came to class. There was no question that she was failing the elective. Therefore, there was no point in discussing the matter further with Betsy. But the girl completely surprised Kim when she held out an official-looking piece of paper.

"What's this?" Kim asked.

"I'm dropping your course. Here's the form."

Kim shook her head. "I'm sorry, but you aren't allowed to drop a course this far into the semester."

"I don't need this course to graduate. In fact, I'm getting an early admission to college. So you can't fail me because it's like I never took your stupid class in the first place."

"Betsy, I really don't want to fail you. But you can't just make up your own rules to suit yourself."

"Who says?" The girl tossed her head of blond curly hair, sniffing the air in a superior manner.

"I'll have to talk to the administration about this."

Betsy rolled her eyes as if condescending to talk with an inferior being. "My father buys and sells people like you all the time. If I'd wanted an A for your crappy course, I could have it."

"Not from me," Kim said, standing her ground. She refused to be intimidated by the teenager.

"Yeah, well you don't matter. Your supervisor's dropped me from this course. Mrs. Douglas is your boss. She'll tell you what you can and can't do." With that, Betsy Peters tossed the piece of paper at Kim and stormed out of the classroom.

Kim looked after her, feeling perplexed and remembering Morgana's expression earlier in the day.

Bert's eyes were bright with excitement as she approached his desk. Gardner looked at her questioningly. "M.E.'s report." She placed it on the wooden desktop. "Blunt force trauma."

Gardner did a quick scan of the report. "Someone smashed James a number of times from behind. Guess we're looking for some big rocks?"

"Could be," Bert agreed.

"So it probably wasn't premeditated." Gardner rubbed his chin.

"We've got lab reports, pathology and toxicology too."

"That ought to be interesting," he said.

"My thoughts as well."

They poured over the information. Bert looked to Gardner for his analysis.

"Cutting out the crap, looks like our vic had a serious addiction problem."

"He smoked crack," Bert said, eyes still glued to the report. "Lungs were already affected, nose and throat as well. Looks like he was floating at the time he was killed. I'm surprised nobody at the high school picked up on it."

"They saw the volatile behavior and the irritability. Probably it just fit in with his usual personality."

"Think we ought to have another talk with Billy Kramer?"

"Right," Gardner agreed, "and take a close look at him at the same time."

"Yeah, crackheads usually hang out together," Bert observed.

"Ms. Douglas, may I have a word with you?" Kim Reynolds stood in the doorway of Morgana's office.

"I am rather busy at the moment. You'll have to make an appointment."

The young woman's lower lip set into a granite pose. "It's very important that you clarify something for me."

Obviously, the pest wasn't going to leave until Morgana spoke to her. Morgana let out a theatrical sigh.

"What is it that you wish to discuss with me?" Of course, she knew but let the obnoxious creature spell it out.

"It's in regard to Betsy Peters. I need to understand how she was able to drop my class."

Morgana had liked the young woman at the time of hiring. A pretty, wholesome face, sensitive eyes, an excellent academic background. She'd assumed Kim Reynolds would be docile and pliant. But such was not the case. The dreadful creature had actually had the audacity to give the daughter of a school board member a failing initial grade. The very nerve to question long-standing procedures! And then to go crying to Will, her bitterest enemy. Kim Reynolds's friendship seemed to give him renewed strength and vigor in his antagonism toward her. She would find a way to force him to resign eventually. She would prevail.

As for Kim Reynolds, she was a troublemaker. They never lasted in the system. It was unfortunate that she'd formed a friendship, a liaison, with Henry Anderson as well. Otherwise, she would have been easy to have fired. But Morgana vowed she'd get rid of the vexing pest—one way or another. Morgana frowned at Kim Reynolds and thought it was truly a shame that instead of finding a student dead, the young woman hadn't been killed herself.

"Ms. Reynolds, you are in no position to question my authority. Don't even think that your relationship with Mr. Anderson will keep you from feeling my wrath if you continue with this. I can and will make you very sorry. And, Ms. Reynolds, incurring my vengeance is not a pleasant thing. Now get out of my office!"

The young woman's face was flushed, but she turned and left, slamming the door behind her. A gloating smile spread across Morgana's lips. She would prevail. She knew where the bodies were buried. No one was going to cross her and survive in her department. Her vendetta against Kim Reynolds had only just begun.

Kim trembled, sick to her stomach. Morgana Douglas nauseated her. What a horrible witch! Did Morgana want to cause her to quit her job? That appeared to be her intention. Well, Kim had no intention of obliging the woman. She needed this position. She could discuss the matter with Hank or Will, but didn't want to go running to either of them for help or support. She'd done that too often already. No, she had to handle this situation herself. Nothing else was acceptable.

Kim was distracted the rest of the day. She thought things would be better for her later when she helped again in the library. Usually, when she spent time working in the library, she felt a lot more relaxed and calm, but this afternoon even here students kept bothering her about finding the body of Nick James.

"Hey, teacher," one scruffy boy asked, "did you really find a dead kid? Was he all covered in blood? Did vultures gnaw on him? Did they like rip out his eyeballs?"

"Are you here to do homework or research?" she asked. "That's the only thing I can or will discuss with you."

Kim found the day extraordinarily long. By the time the final bell rang to dismiss the students, it felt like her own day would never end. She was required to work an extra hour three afternoons a week in the library after school ended, and that time dragged as well.

As she mechanically processed books, it occurred to her that something wasn't quite right in the school. How had Betsy managed to flaunt school rules? She had the impulse to look at Betsy Peters's records. The girl had actually sneered at her today as if she were an ant. Kim refused to accept that. Something was very wrong, and she was determined to find out what it was. She resolved that Morgana's threats of retribution would not deter her.

# CHAPTER TWENTY-FOUR

"I would like to look at the records you have on one of my students."

The guidance secretary glanced at Kim out of the corner of her left eye. "What for?"

"I need some information. Can I give you the student's name and grade and have you lend me the file? I won't remove it from this office."

The secretary shook her head emphatically; her heavily hair-sprayed bouffant didn't budge an iota. "You have to talk with Mr. Ogden about that, and he's gone for the day."

Kim tried hard not to show her impatience. "Look, I only need a few minutes. Why should we have to bother Mr. Ogden?"

"Rules are rules. I don't make them. You have to be authorized."

"Isn't Mr. Anderson the supervisor of counseling services?"

The secretary, whose nameplate read Judith Myers, looked down at the papers on her desk. "Not anymore. When Mr. Anderson became the vice principal, Mr. Ogden took over those responsibilities. So he's the one you need to see. Come back tomorrow."

"Judith, I really need to look at the files on just this one student." Kim hoped personalizing her request might help.

"Like I said, talk to Mr. Ogden tomorrow." Judith Myers announced each word as if she were speaking to someone mentally challenged.

Kim realized she wasn't going to get anywhere with this stubborn woman. She'd have to find another way to get the information she wanted. Should she come back to speak with Mr. Ogden the next day? Her special awareness told her not to do it. She let out a deep sigh as she left the office. Maybe she should just forget about obtaining the information. But every instinct told her not to give up, that it was important for her to discover the truth regarding this matter.

The drive to the high school was a familiar one. Gardner had done several programs for the department at the request of the superintendent, mostly related to drug and alcohol abuse and safe driving practices. That was how he'd gotten to know Dr. Bell. They'd hit it off from the first. Gardner had lived and worked in Webster Township long enough to know just about everyone who was in a position of power or influence. Webster wasn't the best of places, but it wasn't the worst either. Most of the residents living in his part of town were plain, hard-working people, honest and decent, blue-collar workers. They were politically apathetic, unconcerned with improving the town's educational system or doing away with corruption. But that was probably true of most towns, he reasoned.

Even in the daytime, the scenery along the rural route didn't fully hold his attention. Trees and farmland had been stripped away to be replaced by tract homes and townhouse developments. Not that the land had ever been beautiful on his side of town. Even the Native Americans who had been the first settlers in this area had turned their noses up and gone on to other hunting grounds. But at least they'd left the land relatively unspoiled. The state of New Jersey was riddled with pollution problems of water, air, and soil. Heavy industry had raped the land. In the woodlands of Webster Township, dumpers had left chemical wastes that would cost a fortune to clean up.

It was a large township, more than forty square miles in size. The Lake Shore area where the high school was located boasted large homes where the affluent lived. It almost seemed like a different town. There were lots of trees and forest around the school where the leaves had turned color and begun to fall. He loved brisk days like this, felt alive, vital, and energetic. Maybe a good day to solve a murder?

Would he see Kim at the school today, he wondered? He wanted to talk with her again, just be with her. Under the circumstances, that probably wasn't a good idea for either of them. But like Einstein said, common sense was not so common. His feelings for Kim weren't something he could simply ignore. Hell, it was time to get his mojo in motion and earn his paycheck, time to do some detective work and forget about his personal life—if only he could.

"Dude, I swear I don't know nothin' about what happened to Nick." Billy Kramer swiped the sweat from his face with the back of his hand. A colony of angry acne welts criss-crossed his cheeks.

"I'm not a *dude*. I'm a police detective, and I think you've been holding out information." Gardner felt himself becoming impatient with the boy.

"Me? No, honest, I wouldn't do that. I don't want no trouble with cops."

"You and Nick smoked pot together. What about crack?" Bert's nostrils flared.

The youth's eyes looked from side to side, as if he was searching for an escape route.

"Come on, Billy, we know you and Nick were into the drug scene. We think you've been lying to us. In fact, we know it. It'll go easier for you if you cooperate. Tell us everything and maybe there won't be any charges against you."

Billy raised a shaking hand. "I think maybe I need a lawyer."

Gardner nodded. "Sure, you can have an attorney. That's your right under the law. And I can *Mirandize* you. But right now, we're just having a little talk. You help us. We'll help you. Understand?"

Billy the Kid didn't answer. He displayed more smarts than Gardner had given him credit for having. So Gardner decided to prod him a little more.

"Billy, let me lay this out for you. Right now, it doesn't look good for you. Your pal Sam Granger dies from a lethal injection of a drug that you boosted from your mother's work area. Your other pal dies after being attacked in the woods right by the high school. Frankly, kid, you make a terrific suspect. Did you argue over drugs? Was Nick holding out on you?"

"No, nothing like that! I didn't kill anyone!" Billy Kramer jumped to his feet, knocking over the chair he'd been sitting on in the principal's office.

"Pick up that chair and sit back down. We're not through here. You and Nick had a falling-out, didn't you?" Gardner watched the boy's reactions, gauging just how far he could take the interrogation.

"I had nothing to do with either one of them dying. I swear it! All right, I'll tell you what I do know. I think Nick killed Sammy. Nick kept after me to get him some drugs from the hospital where my mom worked. He wanted crack, but figured if I got him something he could sell or barter on the street, it would work out okay. I'm not into the heavy stuff. Nick got addicted real fast. That stuff is poison. Sammy and me, we both smoked joints. But Nick had to be a big-shot and buy crack. Sammy refused it, said he was going to clean up. He had this dream about racing bikes on the speedways. That's why him and Nick got friendly in the first place. Nick bought himself a bike too. Both of them wanted to race."

"Where did Nick get the money for the bike?"

Billy shrugged, suddenly cautious. "How should I know? Guess he must have worked for it."

Gardner tightened his jaw like a pit bull. "What job? Selling drugs?"

"Only pot!" Billy stood up again and eyed the door.

"Sit down! I want more details. Where did these drug deals go down?"

"Newark." Billy's eyes didn't meet his.

"Why Newark? Why not New Brunswick or Camden or Trenton?"

Billy shook his head. "I don't know, man. Nick had a connection there. He boosted a car the last time, and we drove into the city. His old man was on to him about taking the pickup out at night, so Nick decided to steal a car instead. But this last time, the dealer raised the price on him. Nick couldn't buy much. Nick, he wanted the crack real bad, craved the rush. He got mean, irritable. Said he had to make a lot more money. Needed to feed his habit."

"How did Sammy figure into this?"

"I don't know exactly. He said Sammy told him something he could use to score some real cash. But Sammy didn't want him to use it. They had an argument, fell out big time."

"Did it get physical?"

"Yeah, kind of. Sammy's grandmother broke it up. We visited his place. The old lady started screaming, waving a baseball bat around, saying how she'd call the cops if we didn't leave. So we took off."

"What information did Sammy have?"

"I don't know."

"If you're thinking of using it yourself, I'd forget about it. You say you didn't kill Nick. Well, someone did. Maybe it was someone he tried to blackmail."

Billy stood up again, his legs unsteady. "I got to go back to class, man. I told you everything I know."

Gardner stood too. "We are going to need a formal statement from you."

Billy's eyes widened in alarm. "Why?"

"To make it official. It's standard procedure. You can ask your mother to get you a lawyer if you like. In fact, we'll want to talk to her as well. I'll contact you. Meantime, don't take any sudden trips and don't discuss what we said here with anyone else." Gardner glanced at the wall clock. "I guess you better get back to your classroom."

Billy the Kid sprang out of the office like a rabbit. Gardner sat back and thought about what he'd learned. He was fairly certain the boy wasn't the killer. He was pretty sure Nick James had murdered Sam Granger. The motive appeared to be something that Sammy had learned and Nick wanted to use for blackmail to get money for crack. Bert could talk to Mrs. Granger again, except there was no guarantee that she could shed any further light on the situation. She'd already told him that her grandson didn't confide in her. Gardner recalled that the boy had a younger sister, Randi, the one Evie was friendly with. She was more likely to know something.

He turned to Bert and explained that he'd like her to talk to Randi. "I think we've learned everything we can from Billy Kramer, at least for the time being"

"Want me to pull the girl out of her class?"

"No. Talk to Randi Granger privately after school. You'll get better results."

"You really think the kid knows anything?" Bert sounded dubious.

"It's just a hunch. Cop intuition. And I also think she might open up more to you than me."

"No problem." Bert looked at her watch. "Glad I brought my

own car today. I have to do some work on another case back at headquarters."

"Catch you later. We'll share information."

It was time to talk to Kim again. He needed her input. Who was he kidding? He just wanted to see her, whether he had a good reason or not. Gardner walked out into the main office. Mrs. Sylvestri was working at her desk. She raised her salt-and-pepper head at his approach. He asked her for Kim's schedule and marveled at her efficiency in producing it. Wouldn't mind having a secretary like her himself.

He found Kim working in the book stacks at the school library. "Got a minute?"

She turned and looked at him with a wary expression. "Since I'm not working with a class, I don't think anyone will mind if I take a break."

"Let's go outside for a walk. That way we can talk privately."

"That's fine," she agreed.

They walked side by side. He took care not to touch Kim or even brush against her. He didn't want her to think this was anything but professional. But, God, it wasn't easy!

They traveled toward the woods where Kim had found Nick James's body. It was cooler there, with the trees blocking out the sun. There were still leaves on the trees. Gardner liked the sense of privacy.

"So what do you want to talk about?" Kim asked, turning to face him.

"I wanted to give you a heads-up on a couple of things. Just spoke to Billy Kramer, sweated him a little. I'm fairly certain Nick James murdered Sammy Granger. I'm just not certain of the exact motive. Would you have picked up on anything, gotten any vibes? From what Billy said, Sammy knew something that he confided in Nick."

"And that was a mistake I gather."

He loved the way she listened and picked up on things. Her luminous brown eyes intently zeroed in on him.

"Big mistake. Seems friend Nick wanted to do some blackmailing so he'd have drug money. They quarreled about it. Appears Nick decided it would be easier for him if Sammy were out of the picture permanently."

Kim shivered, although the day was not chilly.

"Don't suppose you happen to have overheard anything that could give us a clue?"

Kim was pensive for several moments. "I just can't think of anything. Maybe Emory Dunne might know. My impression was that Emory might have bought drugs, and if Nick was selling at one time, they could have had a common connection."

"Okay, thanks. I'll check that out." He touched her cheek, couldn't seem to help himself. "How are you doing?"

"I'm all right. I have some difficult students, but that's to be expected. I'm managing. Coping."

"You dating Anderson?" He hadn't meant to blurt that out. Damn, he was a better interrogator than that! Whatever happened to subtlety?

"We're just friends." She turned away from him.

"The way you and I were friends?" Gardner knew he shouldn't ask but couldn't stop himself from doing that either.

"No, and that's not really any of your business."

He placed his hands on her shoulders and turned her back toward him. "Wrong. It is my business. You're my business. There's a tie between us that's never going to be broken. I love you, and I believe you still love me. Nothing and no one will ever change that."

He pulled her into his arms and gave her a long, lingering kiss. She didn't resist. Instead, she seemed almost mesmerized.

For an all too brief moment, she clung to him. But finally, she broke free.

"See what I mean?"

"I've got to get back for my next class," Kim said, her voice husky.

"I'll walk you back."

"That's not necessary."

"There's a killer prowling around here somewhere. Maybe ready to kill again. So it is necessary."

Neither one of them spoke after that. He didn't take her arm or hold her hand. There really wasn't any need. They were linked, connected forever. He knew it. She knew it too.

# CHAPTER TWENTY-FIVE

Captain Nash lumbered toward Bert. "Croix, what's going on with this killing out by the high school? I got concerned parents calling nonstop."

"We're working on it, Cap."

"Well, work a little harder." He sniffed at her with his out-of-kilter nose that had been broken at some indeterminate time in the past and made him look like a former boxer.

"I'm on my way to talk to Sammy Granger's sister. She's probably home from school by now. Mike thought it would be best if I had a private conversation with her."

"You think both boys were killed by the same person?" Nash scratched his close-shaven head.

"Not necessarily, but Mike and I believe there's a definite connection. The boys hung around together. Then they had a falling-out. The grandmother doesn't know anything, but the girl just might."

"Well, get on it!" Nash's voice was all hard gravel. "We don't want folks around here accusing us of goofing off on a homicide investigation."

Bert grabbed her bag and headed out the door. Suddenly, it had become important that the case be tied up. Nothing like community pressure.

Randi Granger was talking on a cell phone when Bert arrived at the rundown cottage that housed her and her grandmother.

Bert identified herself, flashing her I.D., and was invited inside.

"If you came to talk to Gran, she's at work, won't get home till late."

"I'm here to talk with you. I think you might be able to help us solve your brother's murder."

"Me?" The girl stared at her round-eyed. "I don't know anything about it."

"Can we sit down? I think you might know something you're not even aware of knowing."

"Sure. That's cool." The girl, slim and petite, was pretty without being striking.

Bert sat down on a straight-backed chair in the shabby living room while Randi sank into a floral-printed sofa. A small brown dog jumped up on Randi's lap and she petted it.

"So I understand your brother was friends with Nick James and Billy Kramer." Bert paused and waited for a response.

Randi pushed her long, straight hair back from her face and wrinkled her freckled nose. "Those two creeps were in his classes. Sammy wasn't always in the retard group. He just kind of went to pieces after our mom died. He started acting out."

"Did he take drugs?"

Randi evaded her eyes.

"Listen, you're not hurting his reputation if you tell me the truth. You want to know what happened to him, don't you?"

Randi nodded her head, tears forming in her eyes. "Yeah, I do. But my brother wasn't any kind of addict. I don't want anyone thinking that. In fact, he cleaned up. And he only smoked some pot for a while, no hard drugs."

"What about Nick and Billy, did they use hard drugs?"

"I'm certain Nick did. I don't know about Billy. I overheard Nick telling my brother that he should try smoking crack. Sammy said no way. Sam said how he'd had a talk with his girlfriend and things were going better between them. He wasn't going to jeopardize that."

Bert leaned forward. There hadn't been any mention of a girlfriend before. Could this be a possible lead? "Randi, who was the girl your brother was seeing?"

Randi shrugged. "Her name's Betsy Peters. She's a senior like Sammy was. They were running hot their freshman and sophomore years. But her parents didn't like my brother. Very snooty people. Her mother's a rich bitch. Didn't think Sammy was good enough for their precious daughter. Anyway, the parents broke them up. But this summer, they started seeing each other again on the sly. Betsy's the one that encouraged Sammy to quit smoking pot. She wanted him to go to college, even if it was just the community school. She said she might be able to help him improve his grades so he could get in." The dog jumped off the girl's lap.

"So Betsy was a good influence on your brother."

Randi tilted her head from side to side. "I guess. But it was for selfish reasons. She's really not that nice. Kind of snotty. Acts like she's better than you. Patronizing. You know the type?"

"Yeah, I do."

Bert decided that having a talk with Betsy Peters might just lead to something. She thanked Randi. "If you think of anything else, even if it doesn't seem important, give me a call." Bert handed her a card with her contact information on it.

Gardner shouldn't have felt out of his element, but he did. Anita Cummings was a ghost of a girl, thin and pale. Bert would have been a better choice to question the kid, but she was working on another lead. They were coordinating via cell phone, and so far that was working out fairly well. Except right now, he wished she were with him. Anita Cummings stared at him with distrust.

"I understand Nick James was your boyfriend."

"Kind of." He noticed a slight twitch in the girl's right eye.

"He talked you into telling Dr. Bell that Mr. Anderson had sexual relations with you."

Anita squirmed in her chair. "Nick, well, he hated Mr. Anderson."

"Oh? Why was that?"

The girl hesitated.

"It's okay to tell me." Of course, he already knew, but Gardner wanted to hear the girl confirm it, to hear it directly from her.

"Nick was always in one kind of trouble or other. Mr. Anderson punished him—well I guess he had to. Anyway, Nick hated him."

It hadn't escaped Gardner's attention that according to the school nurse, Anderson was the last person to see Nick James alive at the school. Anderson was the school enforcer. Nick James had tried to get the principal in trouble before, tried to get him humiliated and fired from his job.

Had Sam Granger known something else about Anderson, something that James could use as a weapon of blackmail? Anything was possible, he supposed. And that's what was making this homicide investigation so difficult. Then again, he thrived on challenge.

"If you don't mind telling me, why did you retract your story?"

Anita studied the weave of the carpet as if it were the most interesting thing in the world. "It was Miss Reynolds. She kind of shamed me into telling the truth, made me see how wrong it was to lie like that. Emory Dunne told me how she's into Mr. Anderson. I guess that's why she did it. But she's a good teacher and a nice person. And I think she really cares about me. So I did what she asked me to do."

Hearing again that there was something between Kim and

Anderson was like a sharp knife blade stuck through his heart. Gardner told himself that personal feelings had to be ignored, repeated it to himself like a mantra.

"How did Nick react?"

Anita sat down cross-legged on the woven carpet. "He got angry at me, real angry. He hit me hard."

"Why didn't you report it as an assault?"

Anita looked up at him. "I thought maybe he would kill me if I did. He threatened me. Then he said he was going to get even with Ms. Reynolds and Mr. Anderson. 'Both of them are dead meat,' he said. Then he slammed out of here."

"Didn't he say anything more specific?"

"No, our advisor came into the room. I guess she heard him shouting."

"Anita, did you still care for him?"

She met his gaze. "I'm glad Nick's dead. He was just plain evil, rotten to the core. Don't know why I couldn't see that before—except I was so flattered he was paying attention to me at first. I was stupid. I'm getting counseling at my new school. I'm making a fresh start. Nick, he really deserved to die. I'm real grateful he's dead."

Anita spoke with surprising vehemence. At that moment, although he never would have suspected it before, Gardner thought the girl might be capable of murder. Whether he liked it or not, Anita Cummings was a viable murder suspect.

Gardner got back into his car and called Herb Fitzpatrick at the police lab. "Discover anything where Nick James was found that could cause blunt force trauma?"

"Funny you should ask. I think we found the murder weapon. There was dried blood on a large rock close by. I ran some tests on it. Definitely matches the boy's blood type."

"Great, what about fingerprints?"

"Just some smudges. Whoever killed the kid realized there

could be prints and did some wiping. We found some tissues scattered around. I don't get the impression the killer planned this out."

"Not like the Granger kid's murder?"

"Clearly not the same M.O."

"Okay, Fitz, thanks. Say hello to the wife for me."

"Yeah, right. Maybe you want to bring your old lady over for dinner sometime now that she's back in town. I seem to remember our two charmers getting along just fine." Since Fitz's wife was a termagant, Gardner knew his friend was being sarcastic.

"Sounds like a real fun evening. Tell you what, why don't I treat you to a beer after work one evening instead?"

"Sounds like a better plan."


Kim was tired. It had been a long, hard day. Talking with Mike had been the most difficult part. She also felt as if she were constantly being stared at and talked about. Maybe she was becoming paranoid. She wanted to call her mother, but recognized that as just plain selfish. Why burden Ma with her problems when her mother had enough of her own? On Saturday, she would drop by the house and check on things so that she could report back to her mother. Going there would also give her a chance to walk on the beach and sort out her emotions. Their piece of the ocean was really just an inlet, but she still found it peaceful and calming.

Kim kicked off her shoes, rolled down her pantyhose, and wiggled her toes. Then she took down her hair, freed it from the tightly coiled chignon she'd worn all day. God, that felt good! She wanted to lie down on the couch and fall asleep. How great it would be if she could just turn off the thinking and somehow manage to quiet her troubled mind.

She closed her eyes, breathing deeply, trying to relax. Patterns of red and green light appeared under her coffined lids. She finally rested.

There was a vision of Nick James lying on a bed of dead brown leaves, except all of a sudden, Nick transformed and it wasn't him anymore she was seeing, but Carl Reyner. Even as she watched in horror, Carl rose from the ground, covered in leaves.

"You're dead!"

He gave her a scornful laugh. "I'm not dead, Karen. You only think I am." Fog swirled around him.

His face was pallid and expressionless.

"Dad, you can't hurt me anymore. You're only a ghost."

"I'm not your father. I never was. Your mother was a liar and a slut. And I can still hurt you."

He reached out to her, and as he did, Carl Reyner turned into a skeleton. She screamed in terror.

Kim awoke disoriented and shaking. It was a dream, only a dream, she realized. It meant nothing at all. She wasn't Karen Reyner anymore. She'd reinvented herself as Kim Reynolds. The past was dead, as dead as Carl Reyner.

Someone was knocking at the door. She rose awkwardly and went to answer it. "Who's there?"

"It's Hank."

She opened the door. "I'm kind of a mess. I fell asleep on the sofa."

He smiled at her. "You look fine. I just wanted to find out if you were okay."

"That was very thoughtful of you. I'm certain you didn't have an easy day either."

"No, I had to talk to a lot of concerned parents who are afraid our high school is now a dangerous place to send their children."

"I'm so sorry."

"It's not your fault."

"Why don't you come in and I'll get you a cold drink. I have pomegranate or orange juice."

"Either one would be fine." He followed her into the small kitchenette. "Police talk to you again today?"

She told him that they had.

"No surprise there. I wonder if they'll ever find the killer."

"I think they will. They're very good at their jobs."

There was another tap at the door.

"It must be one of my upstairs neighbors," Kim said. "Jessica probably saw your Corvette. I think she's got a crush on you."

Hank smiled, a dimple in his cheek winking at her. "I doubt that."

"Don't underestimate your appeal."

A man cleared his throat. Kim turned and saw Mike standing there. She felt her face flush, knowing that he must have overheard what she'd said.

"Hope you don't mind me barging in. I heard voices and figured I could."

"No problem," Kim said. "I was just getting some juice for Mr. Anderson. Can I do the same for you, Lieutenant?"

"Sure, why not? I'm certain I'm every bit as thirsty as Mr. Anderson."

And Kim recognized the double entendre, but didn't wish to pursue it. She simply filled three glasses with O.J., passed one to each of the men and kept one for herself.

"So Lieutenant, what brings you here?"

Mike raised his eyebrows at her formal manner. "I have a question, and I think you're the only one who can answer it, *Ms. Reynolds.*" The hard planes of his face were outlined in the dimming light. Five o'clock shadow made him appear not only masculine, but tough.

If she'd thought his words might hold a double meaning

before, Kim was now certain of it. She couldn't imagine a more awkward, uncomfortable situation.

# CHAPTER TWENTY-SIX

"What question did you want me to answer?" Kim said.

Mike looked over at Hank, his head tilted to one side in a gesture of appraisal.

"Do you want me to leave?" Hank said.

"Not yet. Now that I think about it, I might have a question for you as well."

"Why don't we all sit down then?" Kim said, hoping she sounded like a polite hostess.

Mike pulled over a chair from her dinette. Kim seated herself on the couch, trying to tidy her discarded clothing in the process, while Hank sat on the recliner.

"The school nurse said that she removed Nick James in a wheelchair from your classroom, *Ms. Reynolds.* Was that the last time you saw him alive?"

"It was." She answered the question in a subdued voice.

Mike turned his gaze on Hank, eyes sharp, gun-metal gray. "What about you, Mr. Anderson? When was the last time you saw the boy alive?"

"I spoke to him in the nurse's office."

"What about later, after he left her office?"

"I didn't see him later. I just assumed Mrs. Clemins arranged for him to be picked up."

"You didn't stay and help with the arrangements?"

"Lieutenant, I'm both the assistant principal and the acting principal. I have a lot more than one student to worry about. I have to delegate responsibility." Hank's blue eyes iced over like a glacial winter lake. "Mrs. Clemins is quite capable."

"So you never saw Nick James alive after that?"

"No, I did not."

"Didn't see him walk off toward the woods? Didn't follow him?"

Hank rose to his feet, to his full impressive height, eyes narrowing. "What are you implying?"

"Just asking some questions that need answers."

"You think I would murder a student?"

"I don't know. Would you?"

The two men faced each other. Kim looked from one to the other. She could see them as gunfighters confronting each other at high noon, guns ready.

"From a number of witnesses, I gather Nick James threatened both you and Ms. Reynolds. He hated you, didn't he? Did he know something about you? Something he could blackmail you with? Maybe you panicked and killed him, crushed his skull with a large rock, pounded his head over and over again until he stopped breathing. Is that what happened, Mr. Anderson?"

"That's ridiculous! I'm going to report you for police harassment." Hank's color was high.

Mike shrugged. "You do that, Mr. Anderson. But I'm only doing my job."

The two men stared at each other. Anger wafted through the air ready to ignite like a grenade.

"Maybe you should go," Hank said to Mike.

"Actually, I have a few more questions for Ms. Reynolds, so I think you're the one who ought to be leaving." Mike nodded toward the door, his expression hard as steel.

Hank looked over at Kim. "I'll see you at school tomorrow," he said. "Try not to let anything upset you." He looked meaningfully at Mike and then left with a quick slam of the front door.

"Think I upset your principal?" He smiled, clearly pleased with himself.

She frowned at him. "Now why would he possibly be upset? Just because you practically accused him of being a murderer? No, of course not."

"Now, now, sweetheart, sarcasm does not become you."

"You did that because you're jealous, didn't you?"

"No, I actually think Anderson might have murdered the kid."

Kim placed her juice glass on the small end table. "That is not possible."

"You really think so, do you? And I thought your instincts were better than that."

"Hank Anderson is a decent, honorable man."

"He's in lust with you, wants to get into your pants."

She turned away from him and folded her arms over her chest. "Mike, you're being crude and absurd. Hank never tried to compromise me or take advantage of his position."

"I don't like the guy, and I don't trust him. I know men. He wants you."

Kim turned and faced Mike again. "You're letting emotions color your judgment. Please turn this case over to Bert."

"She's doing her part. We're working together."

Kim heard a phone ring and realized the sound was coming from Mike's jacket pocket.

"Speak of the devil."

"And he'll hear you," Kim said.

"In this case it's a she," Mike said, flipping open his cell phone.

"Gardner." He listened and then sat down. "Yeah, Bert. Right away. I'm at Kim's apartment. Why don't you come by here?

Three heads are better."

"What's going on?" Kim asked as Mike put the cell phone back in his pocket.

"Bert got some interesting info from Sam Granger's sister."

"Shouldn't you be discussing it back at headquarters?"

He removed his jacket with the obvious intention of staying. "You're at that school every day. There might be something you've seen or observed that could help us. I value your input."

She conceded that Mike Gardner could be very persuasive when he wanted to be. As much as she knew it was best for her to avoid him, Mike certainly wasn't making it easy. He was mule stubborn.

Things were less tense between them after Bert arrived. Kim made the same offer of juice; however, Bert refused.

"So exactly what did Randi have to say about her brother?"

"Well, she told me he'd smoked pot with James and Kramer. They were pals but had a falling-out. Apparently, Granger cleaned up. He had a girlfriend at school who was after him to straighten out and dump the druggies."

"You think this girl might know something?"

"Worth a try," Bert said, pulling distractedly on one of her braids.

"Who's the girl?"

"Betsy Peters."

Kim stood up. "Betsy? I have her in the poetry elective—or should I say *had* her. She was very difficult. She somehow managed to drop the course after the allowed time."

Bert paced the small room thoughtfully. "Randi said that Betsy's parents were wealthy, influential people. That's why they disapproved of Sammy."

"According to Betsy, she'll be going to an Ivy League school. My course means nothing."

Mike's eyes swept over Kim with alert interest. "We're look-ing for a reason for James to have killed Granger. I don't think it was because of an ended friendship. I think they quarreled because Granger told James something that James figured he could use for blackmail. Maybe it was something Betsy told her boyfriend."

"Like how her grades were changed to make her look like a better student than she was?" Kim observed.

"Exactly like that," Mike agreed. "What do you think?" He turned to Bert.

His enthusiasm appeared infectious. Bert gave him a gentle smack on the shoulder. "I think maybe we got something."

"My guess is that someone has been changing school records right along to help students get into better schools," Mike said.

"Certain students," Bert corrected.

"Children of affluent people who might also be influential?" Kim asked.

They looked at each other.

"I think we've got a possible motive here. This could connect both murders. I have a hunch that when we go through Nick James's bedroom, we'll find a syringe and some of that drug used to kill Sammy Granger secreted away. I doubt very much he tossed either one. For one thing, he wasn't the sharpest kid, even though he did manage to plan a murder. But I think he was arrogant enough to expect that no one would ever catch on to him." Mike turned back to Kim. "Okay, you're on the inside. Who's responsible for changing grades on the records?"

"I'm not certain," she hesitated. "I asked the guidance secretary to let me see Betsy's records. She flatly refused, and said I had to talk to Mr. Ogden. He's the head of the depart-ment since Hank—Mr. Anderson—became assistant principal a year ago."

Mike's sharp gaze bore into her. "Wait, let me understand

this. Anderson was in charge of the guidance department. Do I have that right?"

Kim frowned at him. "He was the supervisor for math and then he picked up guidance as well."

"I think we're going to have to talk with Anderson again. This time at headquarters."

Kim's eyes widened. "Mike, please wait. I can't believe he'd have anything to do with changing student records."

Mike came close, so close that she could feel his breath tickling the hairs on her neck. "And I'm reminding you that Anderson was the last person to see Nick James alive."

She really didn't want to think about that and shook her head to clear her mind. "Mr. Anderson was the last person that *we* know saw Nick James alive. The murderer was actually the last to see him. I don't believe that was Hank. He has flaws, just like all of us, but he's a decent human being. I don't believe Mr. Anderson would murder a student." They were eyeball to eyeball. Kim hated confrontations, but this seemed so unfair.

"Don't believe it or don't want to believe it?"

"I thought you trusted my instincts," she said, standing firm.

"You planning to help us with this?" Mike was a master of avoiding the answering of questions when he chose.

"I'll get into Betsy's records tomorrow. I should point out to you that it was the English supervisor, Morgana Douglas, who actually allowed Betsy to drop my course. It had nothing to do with the guidance department."

"Go ahead and snoop," Mike said, touching her arm. "Just remember one thing. Someone murdered Nick James, and that person is still lurking around. So be careful—real careful. And don't be embarrassed to call either Bert or me if you need help. Understood?"

"Yes, sir," she said with a small mocking salute.

"Hey, this is no laughing matter." His voice carried a note of stern authority, but then he smiled at her with real affection.

One of the nicest things about Mike Gardner was the way he never stayed angry for very long. She loved his good-natured disposition.

"I think you and I ought to visit that girl and her parents," Gardner said.

"Maybe you should go alone. I'm not known for handling the upper crust all that well."

Gardner smiled at her. "Time to learn from the master," he said.

Bert snorted at him. "Give me a break!"

"Sure, arm or leg?"

"Seriously, this one's on you. I'm off-duty and headed home. April's meeting me for a girl's night out. I'm not going to be an accomplice to you avoiding your family obligations." Her dark eyes jolted him with accusation.

He stiffened. "You think that's what I'm doing?"

"Isn't it obvious?"

He stared at her. "Not to me. I'm just following up on a lead."

"Did the job always come before your family?"

"Bert, don't hurl crap in my face."

She gave him an apologetic nod. "Sorry. Guess I did overstep, but was I wrong?"

"Just blunt, as usual." He let it go. No point getting bugged about her comments. Bert meant well.

They parted company. Gardner put a call in for the Peters' family address and phone number. Then he phoned the house and found out that the wife was at home but not the husband. On the drive over, he thought about what Bert had said. Maybe he had spent too much of his time on the job in the past and not enough with his family. Maybe he should have paid more attention to Evelyn, brought her flowers more often. Maybe that was why he'd lost Evelyn's love, but then again, nothing was ever that simple. Sure, he wasn't perfect, but then neither was Evelyn. He'd intended things to be different with Kim, believed he'd learned from his mistakes. Would he ever get the chance to make a new start?

The Peters family lived well, no doubt about that. The house was impressive and so were the well-manicured grounds. There was a black Mercedes in the driveway, shiny and new. Probably better that Bert wasn't with him, he conceded. She didn't have much use for rich people, especially the ostentatious ones.

A Latina maid opened the door for him. He flashed his I.D. and told her he was expected.

Mrs. Peters, dressed in a purple velour workout suit, hair coiffed, gold and diamond jewelry flashing in her ears and around her neck, met him in a well-appointed family room. She played with her necklace, trying to look casual.

"Mrs. Peters, nice to meet you." He extended his hand but she didn't take it. "Is your daughter around? I have a few questions for both you and her."

She eyed him askance. "Forgive me, but I don't understand why you would want to talk to either of us. We're law-abiding people. We have nothing whatever to do with crime or criminals." She'd been seated on a colonial-style sofa, but now stood up to face him.

"I'm only here to gather some information. I believe your daughter might know something that could help us in our investigation. As a good citizen, you want that, don't you?" It took some more coaxing, but he brought her around.

Finally, she sent the maid to bring her daughter downstairs. They waited in silence so palpable, he could have cut it with a knife.

Betsy Peters looked a lot like her mother. But the girl's eyes were harder and more assessing. He got an impression of shrewdness not usual in a girl her age.

"First, thank you both for cooperating. The Webster Township Police owes you a debt of gratitude." He figured that was enough soft soap, so Gardner went directly for the jugular. "Betsy, it's come to our attention that favors have been done for certain students at the high school. We understand, for instance, that you were able to drop a course when the time was already over to do that."

The girl placed her hands on her hips, her lower lip jutting out. "That English teacher reported me to the police, didn't she? That bitch. I can't believe it!"

"Actually, this is about Sam Granger, not your teacher. We think you might have told him something that he passed along to Nick James. We think Nick used it to blackmail someone at your school, maybe a teacher or administrator."

Mrs. Peters was now just as agitated as her daughter. "Detective, my daughter stopped seeing Sam Granger a long time ago. My husband and I found him totally inappropriate."

Betsy's expression implored him not to give her away. He decided to change his line of questioning.

"Is it possible that some grades might have been changed, or maybe test scores? Maybe both? Not necessarily those of Betsy." He leaned forward, looking directly into the girl's eyes. "What about it, Betsy? Can you help us out here? What do you know?"

Mrs. Peters moved between Gardner and her daughter. "My daughter is still a minor. I refuse to let her talk to you any further. My husband will hear about this when he comes home this evening. And rest assured, so will the chief of police. You are harassing us and it is unacceptable!"

Did he really expect this would be easy? He gave a small sigh.

"Just so we understand each other, Mrs. Peters, this is a homicide investigation. Two boys have been murdered. Your daughter might have some vital information. You can just shield her so much."

"My daughter has no knowledge related to those boys." Her lower lip was set in granite.

Gardner gave a polite nod of his head. "That remains to be seen."

He left without further comment, knowing that these rich people were going to lawyer up fast and be of no help whatever—in fact, just the reverse. Sometimes he found his job damn frustrating.

At nine P. M., the phone rang in Kim's apartment. She reached for it, half-asleep.

"How are you doing?"

"Hank? Hi. I'm fine. Just tired."

"I've been feeling wound up." His voice had an edge to it.

"Because of what Lieutenant Gardner said?"

"Partly. I hope you didn't buy any of that garbage he spewed. Police are always trying to put the screws to someone."

"No, I didn't buy what he was selling," she reassured him. Then a thought occurred to her. Maybe she ought to tell him about Betsy Peters. But if she did, there would be ample time for the records to be altered or possibly disappear entirely. Why was she thinking this way? Of course, she trusted Hank. He was a man of complete integrity. Who knew that better than she? And yet, she held back. She supposed Mike's admonishment lurked in the back of her mind.

"My dad and Val are going to come out for the weekend. I wondered if you'd like to join us. We'll do some fun things. I think you and I could benefit from that. By the way, my father talks very highly of you."

"Good to know," Kim said. But she found herself reluctant to make any commitment for the weekend.

"Well, you think about us getting together and then get back to me. Okay?"

"I'll do that," she said.

After placing the receiver back in its cradle, Kim realized that she'd been careful about what she said to Hank. Had Mike somehow spoiled the chance of a relationship between her and Hank? She couldn't deny that he'd rocked her confidence in Hank's integrity. But Mike didn't know Hank the way she did. Why accept his viewpoint? She couldn't be that naive. She couldn't allow Mike to color her opinion of Hank. She should rely on her own judgment. Trusting men, any man at all, still didn't come easily to her.

She was trying to believe in Hank. She didn't want to doubt him. She had believed in Mike totally—until his ex showed up. She knew it wasn't really his fault that they weren't divorced, and yet she couldn't help feeling somehow disappointed in Mike as if he'd let her down. Still, wasn't it foolish and childish to expect any human being to be perfect? Mike had flaws, just as she did. Hank did as well. One thing for certain: There weren't any easy answers or solutions to her personal problems—just as the murders of Sam Granger and Nick James suggested no easy solutions either.

# CHAPTER TWENTY-SEVEN

Gardner looked around as he made his way to the teacher's cafeteria. The high school was an impressive building, no doubt about that. He'd done his homework and found out that there was a staff of one hundred, which included teachers, administrators and secretaries, but not including all the aides, janitors, and security personnel. Clearly, he was not going to question every one of them. He needed to be selective. As far as he was concerned, he'd already zeroed in on his quarry.

He picked up a cup of black coffee and brought it into the teachers' room, which was relatively deserted. There were several teachers having their morning coffee and correcting papers. He sat down beside one of them. The fortyish man had *teacher* written all over him. He was dressed conservatively in a three-piece suit, brown worsted with a pinstripe tie and beige shirt. Gardner studied the receding hairline and deep frown lines around the mouth.

The "lifer" let out a deep sigh.

"That bad?" Gardner said.

"Worse, actually." He glanced down at Gardner's coffee. "If you're drinking what passes for coffee in this place, I suggest you keep a barf bag handy. I bring my own brew."

"I've had worse," Gardner said, thinking of the coffee Bert called nail polish remover that they served in foam plastic cups down at headquarters.

"Substituting here today?"

"In a manner of speaking," Gardner said.

"I'm Will Norgood, with the English department. If I can help you, let me know."

"Thanks, I appreciate that. You know the student who got killed?"

"I had that misfortune."

"I suppose it came as a shock to everyone here."

"I think relief would be a more apt description." There was a smirk on the teacher's lips. Gardner studied the thin, pale face and the penetrating eyes.

"I gather the student wasn't well liked?"

" 'Nothing in his life became him like the leaving of it.' "

"Shakespeare."

"Ah, another reader of the Bard." There was a faint hint of mockery in William Norgood's voice.

Gardner took a taste of the coffee and grimaced involuntarily.

The teacher smiled knowingly. "You'll find I generally speak the truth."

"Good to know," Gardner said.

"Especially when one is surrounded by so much mendacity." Norgood smiled again, his smoothly cultured voice carrying a multitude of mixed meaning.

"Lieutenant Gardner, there's a call for you in the main office."

Hank Anderson's secretary, Mrs. Sylvestri, had just blown his tentative cover. William Norgood looked at him, mouth open in surprise.

"As I said, one is surrounded by mendacity."

Gardner waited to speak until the secretary left the room. "Sorry, you made a false assumption. I just decided not to correct you."

"Did you think I would confess to murder?"

Gardner shook his head. "No, I wasn't expecting it."

"Good. Although I do know quite a bit about this school. I know every skeleton and where each one is hidden, figuratively and perhaps literally."

"I promise to keep that in mind," Gardner said.

Norgood just might know something about grade-changing in the school. He could prove valuable as an information source—or not. But nothing like having a snitch in time.

Still, Gardner didn't much like people who played games. He decided now was not the time to ask Norgood any more questions. So he dumped the coffee and left the teachers' room. He had every intention of hanging around the school today. He wanted to be there for Kim in case she needed him. Somehow he had a strong intuition that she would.

Kim didn't see Mike until lunchtime, but she knew he was in the building. Will Norgood had informed her of that fact during his prep period.

"The Gestapo are everywhere, my dear girl. Beware!"

"Will you stop being so melodramatic," Shandra said as she laid down her books and papers.

They had both joined Kim in the library where teachers often worked in the backroom, getting their photocopying done and working on lessons. "I spoke with Lieutenant Gardner earlier. He's seeing every teacher who had the misfortune to teach Nick James," Shandra informed them.

"He can't seriously believe one of us would murder that wretch!"

"Who knows?" Shandra said with a shrug.

"Even in death, Nick James is causing trouble," Will observed.

Kim listened but didn't speak. She was too full of conflicting thoughts and emotions.

"I'd bet big bucks that whoever killed Nick James turns out to be another student, one of his nasty friends or enemies. What do you think, Kim?" Shandra asked.

She was saved the necessity of a reply when a student approached her requesting to borrow a CD player for a teacher.

"Sorry, guys, I'm on duty right now." She walked quickly away, putting any thoughts of murder out of her mind, at least for the time being.

Kim was just about to break for lunch when Mike came looking for her in the library.

"How come I keep finding you putting books into the stacks? Don't they have an aide to do the menial stuff?"

"Afraid not. There's just the two of us. I'm trying to create a student library counsel, but kids want to be paid for their efforts. They don't value school service. We just can't compete with the fast-food chains."

"School service looks good on college applications," Mike observed.

"So I've been trying to tell them. Guess I'm not much of a saleslady."

"Tell you what. Why don't I ask Evie to join your library counsel? And maybe she can convince some of her friends to help out as well."

Kim touched his hand. "You are so kind and thoughtful. But leave Evie out of this. She's really angry with me these days. I've disappointed her."

"Because you won't see me anymore?"

"I still seem to see plenty of you. No, she wants me to fight for you. I tried to explain to her why I can't do that, but she doesn't understand."

His clear gray eyes met her own. "Evie and I think alike. Don't lose faith in me, sweetheart. I really do love you."

"If only it were that simple, Mike." Unbidden, tears welled in her eyes.

He squeezed her hand. "It will be. Just trust me. One way or another, Evelyn will be out of my life. Our marriage is over. I'm giving her a chance to get on her feet. When she does, she'll be gone. I'll see to it."

Kim thought that Mike was going to give Evelyn money to divorce him. Kim wasn't convinced that would work, but decided to reserve judgment.

"I have a turkey sandwich for lunch. Want to share?"

"I was thinking you might let me take you out to lunch," Mike said.

"There's not enough time."

"McD's is right down the street. Can I tempt you to be decadent and share some fast food? I could do with a Big Mac attack. What about you?" Mike gave her his special smile, warm and steady as the sun. It was impossible not to be drawn to him.

"Okay, you're making me hungry. I'm free after the next passing bell."


They left together in Mike's car.

"Is this car new?" she asked.

"Very observant. You like the cop shop? It's a new Crown Vic. I think the reason I got it was on account of solving that double homicide in the garden development complex. Of course, you and Bert had a lot to do with it." He squeezed her hand.

"How's Jean coping?"

"Happy that her mother's home." Mike seemed to catch himself. "She'd love to be here with us. Kid has a thing for fast food. She even made up this funny story. Want to hear it?"

"I sure do."

"Okay, just remember, she's only nine years old. Here goes: Burger King married Dairy Queen and they lived happily ever after at the White Castle. Cute, huh?"

"She's got a creative mind."

Mike threw Kim a smile, obviously pleased to have his daughter complimented by her.

They had a quick lunch and were back before the next bell sounded. Then they parted company.

"Keep your cell phone handy," he said, less than eager to let her go. "Call me if anything feels wrong. Don't take any chances. I'll be in the building until you leave today."

"Mike, I don't need a bodyguard. And that's not your job description."

"I respectfully disagree. You need me."

"I'm going back to the guidance office after school today. This time, I'll make a fuss if I'm not allowed to see Betsy Peters's records."

"Let me do that for you. I'll get those records."

"If I'm wrong about this, I don't want you taking the heat," she said. "As soon as I get a look, I promise to contact you."

Neither one of them discussed Hank Anderson. They basically agreed to disagree. Kim knew Mike thought that Hank could have killed Nick James. She felt that Mike was wrong.

That afternoon, she was distracted. Her teaching was off. The ironic part was that her classes were behaving and working with her better than ever before.

At three o'clock, after the students were dismissed for the day, Kim excused herself from library duty and hurried to the guidance office. The same secretary sat at her desk like Cerberus guarding the gates of hell.

"If you've returned to look at student records, you still have to get permission from Mr. Ogden. He's in his office."

"Thank you. I do need to talk to him."

"He's busy right now." The secretary pursed her lips and

looked at Kim as if she were a mosquito the woman would like to swat.

"I'll wait." Kim's heart started to pound. Relax, she told herself. She breathed in and out slowly and deeply, calming herself.

Mr. Ogden strode out of his office and gave her a hard look. "And what can we do for you today?"

"A student of mine, Betsy Peters, was signed out of my poetry class. I believe the authorization was improper. I would like to see her records."

"That is hardly your decision to make. I should not have to remind you, Ms. Reynolds, you are a new teacher here." Mr. Ogden's words came out like barbs. The man was a porcupine with sharp quills.

"I have Mr. Anderson's permission."

"What?"

"Check with him if you don't believe me." Kim hoped she sounded convincing. She rarely lied about anything and conceded she wasn't very good at it. She reasoned that she could well have asked Hank's permission. But Mike had caused her to be uneasy. Mike had shaken her faith in Hank, although she was trying hard not to admit it to herself. She had to see those school records. They might prove nothing or everything.

"Very well," Ogden said with hesitation. "Come into my office. Mrs. Myers, please find Betsy Peters's file for us, and then you can leave for the day."

They both sat down, silently waiting for the secretary to return. Ogden looked at his watch several times. Kim wondered if he were expecting someone else to arrive for an appointment.

Kim heard the phone ring in the outer office. Moments later, the secretary returned.

"Your wife phoned. I put her on hold." The secretary placed a manila folder on Ogden's desk and left. It was all Kim could do to keep herself from snatching the folder.

Ogden reached for the phone. Kim contained her impatience as best she could.

Ogden listened for a few moments. "Yes, dear, I'll be on my way very soon." After Ogden hung up, he turned to Kim. "My wife is ill. I have to take her to a doctor's appointment. You'll have to go."

"I'm very sorry that your wife is sick. But I do need to read that file. I can stay here and read it. I understand the information is confidential and so it will never leave your office."

"Can't be done. We have our rules here. You have to go now. Come back another time."

Kim knew when she was getting a fast shuffle. "I must insist on seeing that file right now." She was polite but firm.

"Miss Reynolds, if you don't leave my office immediately, I will send for security."

She played her trump card. "Mr. Anderson will be quite displeased."

Ogden gave her a knowing look. He clearly wasn't impressed or fooled. "I doubt that very much. Mr. Anderson supports his supervisors. I've known the man a great deal longer than you have. Whatever your personal relationship with him, it won't influence him professionally."

Kim couldn't deny any of what Mr. Ogden had said. She was not a commanding woman. Quiet and reserved by nature, she didn't usually make demands on other people—in fact, it was just the opposite. She stood up to leave, a bit unsteady from the confrontation with Ogden, momentarily gripping his desk. She accidentally knocked over a CD container. When she reached down to pick it up, Kim noticed a small object under the desk. It was a tiny digital audio player. It somehow looked familiar. She picked it up as well.

As soon as Kim touched the metal, a shock went through

her. She was hit by a blast of psychic energy, a vision of rage. Nick James in this office threatening Mr. Ogden.

*"I know all about how you change grades for money, how you've been doing it for years. Well, I need some money and you're going to give it to me. Otherwise, you'll lose your job and go to jail."*

She saw Ogden's reaction: first fear, then fury. The vision faded and disappeared, but it left Kim shaken.

"My God, you killed him! You're the one!" She stared at the diminutive man in amazement and horror.

"What? Are you insane? I haven't killed anyone." Ogden's face turned the color of a blood sun.

She held up the iPod. "This belonged to Nick James. He wouldn't have let it out of his sight. His initials are engraved on it right here." She traced the markings with her fingertip. Ogden had been the last person to see Nick James alive. She was certain of that. It hadn't been Hank. Mike was wrong. Kim had some satisfaction in knowing she'd been correct to support Hank. But in all fairness, she had to admit to having doubted Hank, no matter how much she'd defended him to Mike.

"I think you'd better call your wife and tell her you'll be a little late picking her up. We need to talk to Lieutenant Gardner."

"Not possible." With that, Mr. Ogden removed something from his desk. He came around and grabbed her arm.

Kim let out a gasp. "What are you doing with *that?*"

"Actually, I always keep pain medication on hand for when my wife has emergencies. I inject her with a hypodermic. It works faster than pills. I think you need calming and this will do it."

For such a small man, Ogden was exceptionally strong. Kim tried to twist out of his painful grasp. She was able to pull far enough away so that he failed to jab her with the hypodermic. She let out a scream as he lunged at her again. She struggled with Ogden in a desperate attempt to prevent him from stabbing her.

Mike burst into the office, gun drawn. "Let go of her or you're a dead man. Drop that damn thing!"

Kim breathed a sigh of relief, never more grateful in her life to see anyone.

Ogden, red-faced and perspiring, placed the syringe on the desk and raised his hands. "We had a misunderstanding," he said.

Kim moved to stand beside Mike, none too steady on her feet. She turned toward him. "How did you know?"

"I told you. We're connected. I felt something wasn't going right, and I knew where you were."

"He killed Nick James. Whatever this stuff is," Kim said, pointing to a vial lying beside the hypodermic, "Mr. Ogden used it to dope Nick and then march him out for a walk in the woods."

Mike examined the vial. "The kid was probably so out of it by then, he just sat down on the grass and waited to be bashed over the head, kind of like a deer caught in headlights."

"There's nothing lethal about that drug."

"But you were planning to give Kim an overdose, weren't you?" Mike gave him a knowing look.

"It's a cancer drug. It improves quality of life and gives comfort."

"Yeah, and you were going to use it for the big sleep. We'll just take this with us as evidence. Let's find out if the M.E. found a residue of it in Nick James. Good thing the body hasn't been released yet."

"You'll also need these," Kim said, holding up Nick's iPod and Betsy's school records.

"Turn around, Ogden. You're leaving here in handcuffs," Mike said.

"That really is not necessary, Detective. I'm a peaceful man."

"Right, so I see," Mike said in a dubious tone of voice.

After Mike cuffed Ogden, he efficiently read him his *Miranda* rights. Kim admired the smooth, professional way Mike handled the situation.

"Come with me," he said to her. "We'll deliver Ogden to headquarters. He can lawyer up. Meantime, we'll be able to take your statement."

"Mike, thank you." She smiled at him.

"Just doing my job, ma'am."

But he flashed her a look that was anything but professional.

"I will definitely pay my taxes on time without complaint."

"Good to know," he said with an amused smile.

# CHAPTER TWENTY-EIGHT

"So, my dear, rumor has it that you've been a very busy young woman." Will raised his eyebrows.

"Define busy," Kim said.

"You're going to be evasive, I see." Will sighed theatrically as he signed in for the school day and Kim did the same after he finished.

They had both arrived early. Kim always went to the library first in the morning to help set up for the day. There was generally a great deal that needed doing for both students and teachers.

Hank came out of his office. He'd also arrived early it seemed. Neither his secretary nor the receptionist were in as yet.

"Miss Reynolds, my office, please." His eyes screwed into bullets as he sighted her. What now, she wondered. He went slamming back into his office. Obviously, she was expected to follow.

Kim resented Hank's despotic tone of voice, but she made no comment.

"My, what have we done?" Will said, eyes bright with interest. He *would* find this a source of entertainment.

Kim walked into Hank's office without looking at Will.

"Please close the door," Hank said, "and have a seat."

Kim followed his instructions. "What is it you want to see me about?"

He frowned at her. "I think you know. I had a phone call

yesterday in the early evening from Dr. Bell. He demanded to know what was going on here. Since he knew more than I did, it was embarrassing. Dr. Bell told me that the chief of police phoned him to tell him that Rufus Ogden had been arrested for murdering Nick James. Your name was mentioned. Now why was that, I wonder?"

Kim met his gaze. "It all happened so quickly. I was just trying to get hold of a student's records." She explained how Betsy Peters had dropped poetry. "I didn't want to complain to you about Morgana Douglas's actions. I didn't want to put you in the middle again. But I felt in good conscience I needed more information."

"And that was the only reason you didn't come to me first?" His eyes were searchlights.

She nodded her head, but didn't meet his gaze this time.

"You really disappoint me. I thought you were different, that I could trust you."

She looked up at him in surprise. "You can trust me."

"No, I don't think so. The real reason you didn't tell me what you were doing was because of what that policeman said." He held up his hand as if to call a halt to what she was about to say. "No, do not bother to deny it. He got to you, made you think I might have murdered Nick James. I was the former supervisor of the guidance department. You thought I was the one who Nick was blackmailing, didn't you?"

His accusation hung in the air like a guillotine ready to chop off her head. "I never really thought that. I'm a reference librarian by training. I'm accustomed to researching. I intended to collect facts and information."

"That police detective was looking at you a certain way. He wanted you himself. Was he the man you were involved with before?"

Kim found that she was unable to answer his question.

"That's all right. You don't need to tell me one way or the other. And I don't want to hear lies. Keep your secrets to yourself." The bitterness in his voice resounded through the small office.

"I wasn't going to deny anything. Mike Gardner and I were involved. He asked me to marry him. Then his ex-wife showed up—except, as it turns out, she's not an ex. But in all fairness, he believed she'd signed the divorce papers and received the divorce decree. I did tell you I'd been involved with a man."

"But you didn't tell me that it happened to be Gardner. You kept me out of the loop. Do you know how hard this is for me to accept? I thought we were building a relationship of mutual trust."

"We were. We are! I'm sorry. I do trust you. It's just that I'm a very private sort of person. Old habits die hard."

Hank jutted his square jaw and ran his hand through his sandy hair. "I will admit I'm not so different from you, Kim. But I've been making an effort to change. I'm not convinced you have. I guess we both have to think long and hard about where this relationship is headed, or if there's going to be any kind of relationship outside of work."

She silently agreed with him.

"There's going to be an emergency faculty meeting this afternoon after school in the auditorium. I'll see you there." His voice was crisp and professional again, in command.

Kim left, her face flushed and her heart pounding. The truth was, she hadn't really thought much about Hank Anderson yesterday. She'd been in a difficult situation, playing out an unexpected drama in which she very nearly died. She could have tried to explain that to Hank, but it occurred to her that he'd shown himself less concerned about her well-being than his own image. Was she being harsh thinking that way? Maybe. He probably didn't realize how close she'd come to being killed.

Still, she also hadn't forgotten that it was Mike Gardner who'd been there for her when she most needed help. Actions mattered more than words.

Kim got by during the day essentially going through the motions, her mind preoccupied. The emergency staff meeting was announced over the public address system before the final dismissal bell. A notice had also been placed in each teacher's mailbox, so the meeting came as no surprise.

Kim sat down on a seat near the aisle in the middle of the auditorium. She was soon flanked on either side by Shandra and Will. At the podium stood Dr. Bell, looking almost tiny beside the tall figure of Hank Anderson. They were joined by Bert St. Croix, who wore a neat navy blue pantsuit, and Mike Gardner in a gray sport jacket that matched his eyes, white shirt with patterned tie, and black slacks. Both appeared to have given more thought to their appearance than usual. There was a noisy buzz in the audience as teachers speculated on what they'd so far only heard rumors about.

Dr. Bell cleared his throat and the group settled down. The superintendent of schools shuffled some papers and then fixed his reading glasses. He spoke directly into the microphone.

"We're brought together today by a serious matter in our school community. Apparently for some time now, student grades were altered on transcripts sent to colleges and universities. The scheme might have been going on for years. It is clear that at least one guidance counselor, Rufus Ogden, was responsible. He confessed to altering or deleting grades on student transcripts sent to college admission offices in order to give certain students a better chance of being admitted. We are pursuing a vigorous investigation.

"Mr. Anderson and I are concerned about how this could affect the school's reputation among college admissions officers.

We will notify colleges and of course make the necessary corrections. We'll do whatever we can to restore confidence and integrity. I can't assure you that this problem will be solved immediately, but I can reassure you that it will be handled appropriately."

"Well, this is shocking news," Will whispered to Kim and Shandra. He raised his hand to ask the superintendent a question and was recognized.

"Yes, Mr. Norgood?"

"Did Mr. Ogden name any others who were involved?" He looked pointedly at Hank Anderson, who glowered at him from the stage.

"I think our police spokespeople can answer that better than I can at this point." Dr. Bell introduced Mike and Bert, then turned the proceedings over to Mike, who moved to the podium in a confident manner.

"Mr. Ogden has confessed to killing Nick James. So that's the police department's main concern at this time. As to the motive for the crime, Ogden admits that James was trying to blackmail him, attempting to extort money to buy drugs.

"The chief knows all of this. However, the chief said we can't send in our computer crime unit until the school board completes its own investigation. The chief contacted the prosecutor's office for directions. For now, he's directed the board and Superintendent Bell to do their own investigation. I'll attend the next board of education meeting to coordinate information. Detective St. Croix will also be acting as a liaison. We're the lead detectives on the case. So if necessary, you can contact either one of us if you have any information to contribute or have any questions."

Dr. Bell took back the speaker's spot. "I just want to add that the district will hire an outside company to conduct the investigation. We want no accusations of cover-ups. Everything will be conducted in an open, aboveboard manner. Mr. Anderson, do you have anything to add?"

"No, I think you've about covered it." Hank spoke in a subdued manner.

When the meeting ended, instead of everyone running out to the parking lot as was usual, the teachers milled about in small groups discussing the surprising news.

"I wonder what will happen to Mr. Ogden's wife. She's really ill," Shandra said.

Bert joined Kim, Shandra, and Will. "I got that part covered yesterday," Bert said in a crisp manner. "Mrs. Ogden has a sister and a niece, no children of her own, but the sister is arranging for care. The truth is, the woman's terminal and in considerable pain. Ogden wanted to keep her at home, but she really needs to be in a hospice. The sister is taking care of the arrangements. Right now, Mrs. Ogden is being sedated."

"I'm glad to hear that she's cared for," Kim said.

"I have a few questions to ask you, Ms. Reynolds," Bert said, continuing to sound professional.

Kim excused herself from Shandra and Will, who arched a quizzical eyebrow.

"Nosy guy?" Bert said, indicating Will with a jerk of her head as they got away from the crowd.

"I guess you could say that."

"I don't get a good feeling about him," Bert remarked.

"He's all right. It was kind of you to help with Mr. Ogden's wife," Kim said.

Bert shrugged as if embarrassed. "My own mother died of cancer. It wasn't nice."

"You have a good heart," Kim said.

"Don't spread the word around."

"Whatever you say."

"I wanted to let you know Mike and I are keeping your name

out of this as much as we possibly can. We don't want you to
have any more problems than you already do."

"You're both very considerate."

Bert flashed her pearly teeth. "We are friends, right? Besides,
you managed to solve a homicide for us. So, girlfriend, want to
join April and me for some bike riding this weekend? Also, I
meant to tell you, someone who lives up the street from me is
selling a hog, reasonable price, good condition. Want to take a
look at it?"

"Sounds like a plan."

Mike walked up to them. "We're done here, at least for the
time being," Mike told Bert, and then turned to Kim. "I think
you'll be okay now."

She gave a short nod.

"Call me, anytime day or night, if you want or need me.
Open invite. And as for Evelyn, she'll be out of our lives one
way or another very soon. That's a promise." His voice had a
hard edge that she found troubling.

"You said that before." Time would tell, she supposed.

Kim watched Bert and Mike leave and went back to the
auditorium to pick up her book bag and papers. Shandra and
Will were still there.

"You're such a jerk," Shandra said to Will. "Your tongue is
acid."

Kim was very much aware that Will and Shandra had barely
spoken civilly to each other for quite some time. She felt partly
to blame for their estrangement.

"To paraphrase Descartes, I speak, therefore I am."

"If your tongue were any sharper, we'd all be stabbed to
death." Shandra's forehead creased, expressing her disapproval.

"I'm the one who's wounded. From now on I'll refer to you
as Diana, Goddess of the hunt or the hurt, since you shoot such
deadly arrows."

Will and Shandra faced each other. This really wasn't going well. And Kim was growing tired of their petty disagreements.

"I wish you'd be friends again."

Will gave her a get-real look, but Kim persisted.

"I mean it. Will, you and Shandra shouldn't be arguing."

"I don't bear grudges," Shandra said stiffly.

"Well, I do," Will said. "But as you're both my favorite people, I'll make an exception. Just don't ask me to say anything kind about Henry Anderson or Morgana Douglas."

Shandra shook her head. "Why try? The man is a reprobate, a curmudgeon; he'll never change."

It was difficult not to notice the sardonic tilt of Will's mouth; his lips practically formed a sneer. His eyes were alight with an sardonic gleam. "You don't fancy my wit, dear one?"

"Half-wit is more like it." She snorted.

Will surprised Kim by laughing. He was enjoying this, Kim realized. Glancing at Shandra, whose eyes snapped with vitality, Kim saw that he was not alone.

"You want to know the real reason Will keeps goading Morgana?" Shandra said.

"Yes, oh sagacious one, do tell. I'm most curious," Will said.

"It's because you have to stir the caldron. You wouldn't know what to do if you weren't complaining about someone or something. Don't come moaning to me about your job ever again, Will, because I have no sympathy left for you." She placed an accusing finger on his chest.

Their gaze locked. "Shandra, dear, people don't pay you for what you want to do, they pay you for what they want done. Contrary to Candide, the workplace is not the best of all possible worlds. You malign me unjustly."

"You have a way of twisting things around, William Norgood." Shandra thumped his chest for emphasis.

"And that's why you love me so much." Will surprised Shandra by pulling her into his arms and applying a loud smacking kiss to her lips. Then he released her and quickly walked away.

Kim noted that Shandra's eyeglasses were slightly askew and misted. Kim had a feeling Shandra and Will were destined to be more than friends.

Kim saw that Morgana Douglas was talking with Hank. She decided to grit her teeth and join them.

"We were just talking about you, dear. Were your ears burning? How lovely you look today. Of course, you look attractive every day."

Morgana was gushing, and Kim didn't much appreciate it, but for Hank's sake she was courteous. Besides, she fully understood the reason behind Morgana's about-face in her attitude toward Kim. The investigation would disclose how much involvement Morgana had in grade-changing. Kim could tell the English supervisor was nervous. But Kim realized she simply felt too good to be alive to harbor bad feelings about anyone.

Morgana excused herself, leaving Kim alone with Hank.

"It's going to be an ugly scandal, this grade-changing business. The school system will have a black eye. We've managed to get so many of our top students into Ivy League schools over the years. There are going to be nasty accusations."

Kim moistened her lips. "Sorry, Hank, that really isn't my main concern, not when people have been murdered."

"We can talk about it more this weekend."

She stared into his sky blue eyes. "About that, I seem to have other plans."

"With that policeman? Gardner?"

She shook her head. "Not really your business, but no. Please give my regards to your father and Val."

"Can I tell them you'll be going out with us another time and that they'll see you soon?"

Kim shrugged. "You never know," she said.

She might very well be reinventing herself yet again. She wouldn't be discovering that until it happened. Life was always surprising her. And right now, well, it just felt good to still be alive.

Kim walked purposely down the corridor and left the school building behind. Outside in the fresh, crisp autumn air, she took a deep breath, filling her lungs, and stared up at the vastness of the sky, which never disclosed the source of its mysteries.

# ABOUT THE AUTHOR

Multiple award–winning author **Jacqueline Seewald** has taught creative, expository, and technical writing at the university level as well as high school English. She has also worked as an academic librarian and an educational media specialist. Eight of her books of fiction have previously been published. Her stories, poems, essays, reviews, and articles have appeared in hundreds of diverse publications such as *The Writer, The London Mystery Selection, Blue Murder, Orchard Press Mysteries, Sleuths in Cahoots, Crime and Suspense, Gumshoe Review, Los Angeles Times, Sasee, Tea, Lost Treasure, The Christian Science Monitor, Pedestral, Surreal, After Dark, The Dana Literary Society Journal, Library Journal, The Erickson Tribune,* and *Publishers Weekly.* Her writing also appears in many anthologies worldwide. Her previous Kim Reynolds mystery novels, *The Inferno Collection* and *The Drowning Pool,* were also published by Five Star/Gale.